Izzy, THE RELUCTANT SPY

SANDRA J. HOWELL

WEST RIDGE FARM

PUBLISHING

WEST RIDGE FARM PUBLISHING

Hampden, Massachusetts

Published by West Ridge Farm Publishing
Cover Design: Amy Rooney

Publisher's Note: This novel is a work of fiction. Names, characters, places and incidents are either products of the author's imagination or used fictitiously. All characters are fictional, and any similarity to people living or dead is purely coincidental.

ISBN-13: 978-0-9892282-6-8 (West Ridge Farm Publishing)

Printed in the United States of America

Dedication

*This book is dedicated to women
who open the door to change, growth and promise
at any stage in life.*

*A*s I maneuvered my car into the parking lot of the Build-Em-Up Gym, all I could think about was that spring couldn't come soon enough and who were the crazies who'd drive to a gym in this weather? It was like a blizzard without the snow. Oh, that's right. *I'm* one of the crazies. The voracious wind was bending the young maple trees planted at the edge of the mini-mall, and I wondered if they'd make it till morning. The last freezing blast from a winter that refused to say goodbye proved that it wasn't done with us yet.

Pulling into a parking space as close to the building as possible, I wondered why I was torturing myself at this age. I grabbed my handbag, water, and cellphone, slammed the door, hurried to the entrance, and touched my card to the keypad to let myself in. My breath had formed puffs of mist before I'd made it into the welcoming warmth indoors. I honestly did not enjoy working out that much, but with my obsessive-compulsive personality, I found myself here nearly every morning anyway, five days a week, technically. Pangs of guilt booted me out of the house. Failure to keep healthy at sixty-nine trips around the sun would not bode well for me if I didn't at least *try* to stay fit. I work with a trainer on two days and walk on the treadmill the other three. My friends think I'm pushing myself too much and spend too much time here, but since my daughter pays for it, I feel compelled. Guilt swoops in if I don't. She pays. I go. As a young girl, I was self-conscious of my bushy blonde hair and long, skinny legs, but now that I've lived long enough to be called a senior, I'm done being concerned with how I look, think, or speak. I'm satisfied with the woman I've grown into and the life I have built. I want to enjoy life, so I do what I must to take care of myself, even if I don't feel like it.

I dumped my coat in a cubby, then passed a couple of gutsy members on my way to claim one of the many unoccupied treadmills. To keep inspired, I'd invested quite a bit of money in gym clothes, and today, I was wearing red flower-printed yoga pants, a black long-sleeve t-shirt, and my favorite multicolored sneakers.

After stepping onto it, I tapped the screen, which prompted me to enter my weight. Rather than lie, I accepted the default. Pretty accurate. As the running deck began moving, I tapped the ^ arrow to increase speed then pumped my fists as I walked at a peppy tempo. "Go, Izzy, go," I whispered to cheer myself on.

I'm known as Izzy, short for Isadora. It was special to my mother. She told me she'd heard it on one of her soap operas.

When I was born, she knew that would be my name, which meant, *The Promise.* So, despite being named Isadora, she always called me Izzy, praying I'd eventually live up to its meaning. As a big hugger, from as far back as I remember, with every embrace, she'd whisper, *"You're* promised, *Izzy. Remember that. Why do you think I call you Izzy?"* *"What promise?"* I'd say. It was a secret only *she* knew the answer to, leaving me in suspense, imagining all the possibilities that *The Promise* would reveal. Of course, I believed it meant that *someday*, something big was to be mine. My mother wouldn't lie. *What* was promised? And when would I get it? It was too deep to conceive of. As I grew older, I tried to break the secret code that only she knew. Would I inherit a million dollars, travel the world, meet a prince, or become a scientist and create a magic pill that would heal all of humanity? Throughout her life, I asked repeatedly about it, and when it would happen, but she never explained what, why, or when, and instead, said, *"You'll know when you know."*

Being *Izzy* became a nuisance and burden with Mother's words seared into my brain, keeping me alert for *The Promise.* I became a risk-taker, and the unfulfilled promise played havoc in my life choices, sometimes, intelligent, other times, not. I never did crack the code and grew so tired of the pressure that I contemplated changing my name to something less imperative, like Anne. Fortunately, as the years passed, I realized that *The Promise* was a myth conjured up by her from too much wine, and I was in charge of my own life. I gave up hoping and waiting for her empty promises.

Maybe that's why I love reading mysteries so much. They fulfill me by giving the answers. I never got hers. I never did discover any sparkling moment of, "*You'll know when you know,*" but I really didn't care. I've lived a fascinating, full life. I'm a widow and plan to stay that way for the rest of my years, enjoying what I do and who I see. My husband passed away too young, leaving me with three children to raise, who have gifted me with three grandchildren. After retiring from a career in Public Health, I turned my free time into writing and have published a three-book Young Adult mystery series. Being an author is the perfect second career because it allows me quiet time in my home office without distractions disrupting my dancing brain. I know, *crazy*, but my mind buzzes with a million thoughts and ideas for new books.

My life is comfortable, and my friends—the few I hold close—are my support system. I have a shaggy brown dog Oscar and a mean black cat living in the barn. The skinny stray showed up last summer. Against my better judgment, I felt obligated to take care of her, and now, mostly only get greeted with hisses of ingratitude. Yeah, thanks. My 100-year-old farmhouse is antiquing just as I am. We are well-kept and young on the outside but feeling the years on the inside. My kids hate it when I say this, but my mantra is, "Who cares?" Even my two horses, Maverick, and Speed—*not so speedy anymore*, are growing older and less rideable. On Facebook people say that old age is a gift, and I'm trying to stick with *that* promise and not dwell on the inevitable downside of aging and ageism.

At only three-quarters of a mile in, I groaned when

"The Way We Were" piped out of my phone. *Uck. Merle.* I'd jazzed up my cell to identify friends and family by ringtone, and this was a caller I hoped to avoid like dog poo on a shoe. My childhood friend *knows* this is my gym time, but she's likely gotten herself into some sort of pickle again that I have to hoist her out of. Her *many* not-even-surprising jams were often about some boyfriend. She's seventy-five and never changes. So, why get tangled in yet another one of her misadventures? It zaps my energy hearing her go on and on about it. What was it *this* time? Well, whatever it was, I knew for a *fact* the Big Reveal wouldn't be short. I gritted my teeth, steeled my eyes, and kept right on walking. She can wait. I have things to do. Barbra stopped singing out of my phone but immediately began again. I growled at the device, cursing the day I'd set that tune to her name. Ruined the song forever. I promised myself to change it when I got home. Maybe it should be "Who Let the Dogs Out?" next.

Ever-relentless, I knew she'd never stop. I slowed my speed, set the phone to my ear, and tried to sound more out of breath than I was. "Yes, Merle. I'm at the gym. Call ya when I get home." Oh, no. Her sniveling that turned into a blubber stopped me cold. "What's the matter? Are you hurt? Did you slip and fall again?"

"No, it's...it's Karl. He...left me," she wailed.

Yep. Boyfriend troubles. Knew it! Karl. Karl Hendricks, her latest prospect from Silver Love, a supposedly elite dating site for seniors. They've been seeing each other for a few months now, but *I've* never met him. I scrunched my eyes, pondering, *Has anyone?* "I'm very sorry to hear that, Merle. I truly am,"

I said, nodding at my own I-told-you-so. I did not have time to comfort her right now. "But I'm—"

"I was so in love. I thought...I thought... He seemed so..." She coughed. "Ugh. I cannot...even believe this."

"I know. We can talk more about it when I get home, all right? I know he was sweeping you off your feet and everything, making you dream about the future, but I *told you* that that Casanova was too suave, sophisticated, and slick, far too good to be true, and that online dating would only be a waste of your time, heart, and energy, but ya didn't listen to me. You never listen to me."

"I know. I am such a stupid fool, Izzy. *That*...is not even the worst part."

"What? What is the *worst?*"

She scoffed and seethed. "I am just so embarrassed. My kids are going to be *livid.* They'll never stop griping about it till I'm in the grave."

"Livid? About what?"

"The money," she blubbered and sniffed hard, twice.

"The car repair he borrowed last week in a pinch when he left his wallet in a cab? Did he not pay you back?"

Her voice cracked as she said, "No, that was just *one* thing, the *only* thing that I told you and the book club ladies about, actually."

My stomach dropped. I gasped and pressed the down arrow on my treadmill and slow-walked as it petered down to stillness. I stepped off onto the carpet with the side of my hand pressed to my forehead. "Oh, *no,* Merle. Tell me you didn't. How *much* did you give that clod? How much?"

"Um, a bit. *Thousands.*" As she winced, I could just see it.

"*Thousands?* What! Why?" I shouted in shock. "Why on earth would you—?" Far too loud and shrill, I bit down on my lip, as I was drawing eyes. "Err."

"I...don't know, Izzy. Please don't yell at me. I *know* what you're going to say. I already feel dumb enough. He sounded so smart and had great ideas, which, at the time, in the moment, made sense, but now, I can see he was only trying to swindle me. He scammed me and robbed me blind!"

All I could do was shake my head while wanting to hit hers with a 2x4. "Merle," I choked out.

"Can you help me?"

"With what? How? What can *I* do? Call the police."

"I did. He's gone. Like a ghost. Poof. So, there's nothing *they* can do. They said this sort of scam is pretty common and warned to be more wary in the future. Doesn't help me *now,* though. I willingly gave him the money. I did leave my contact information, and all of his, that I knew of, but they aren't hopeful."

"I can't help you with *this. I* don't know what to do, I'm sorry."

"You're a mystery writer."

"Yeah, I *write* mysteries; I don't *solve* them. This is way above my pay grade and skill set. Maybe your daughter can track something down. But *I* don't know how to do that. I will call you back later. Maybe we can brainstorm, but I don't even know what to say right now. I am...*stunned.*" Not surprised, though, given her impetuosity, but, I *did* expect her to have much better sense than *this.* To fall for a scammer?

I *warned her* to be on the alert! Unbelievable! "I have a busy day ahead and really need to think. I'll call you later."

After walking two more miles on the treadmill, I'd had it. Good enough. I fulfilled my obligation and was eager to head home to my office and complete the last two chapters of my new novel. I promised my agent the manuscript would be ready next month, and she's been nagging me for the final draft. Leaving the gym, I ran to the car, feeling like the wind would topple me. I'm a creature of habit, and before I turned towards home, I drove to the drive-thru of Dunkin Donuts to pick up a small, iced coffee. Not surprising—no line. Too cold to be out. Speaking of, I cannot believe Merle fell for that leech who'd left her out in the cold, holding an empty bag. What was she thinking? Giving him all that cash? I can't even get over it.

Gym. Coffee on the run. Next up, work. And this was only my morning.

*T*wo hours later, I was sitting there in my home office, stuck, staring at my laptop screen. Engulfed in daydreaming and worrying about zany Merle instead of writing, I couldn't focus at all. The only thing I'd drafted thus far was a big headache. Wind still howled as winter screamed its displeasure about meeting its end. Just the kind of day that squelched my creative juices. I was spinning my wheels, trying to create meaningful dialogue between a hero and his nemesis as they searched for buried treasure, but nothing decent was emerging. I leaned back in my chair and ran my hand through my hair. *Nope. Nothing. Face it.*

I rubbed my eyes, finding myself with writer's block. I stretched and yawned, trying to shake away the fog. My dear friend Sylvia's words came to mind. *"There's no such thing as writer's block. Write the first sentence, take a deep breath, wait for the surge of inspiration, then do something else if that doesn't work."*

She was right. Going nowhere fast, I decided that that "something" was getting out of the house—freezing cold or not. I needed to clear the cobwebs and get out of my funk. With a huge sigh, I lifted myself from the chair to change out of my comfy gear of baggy sweatpants and a loose sweatshirt into something more presentable. I couldn't leave the house looking this shabby.

Once good and all bundled up for Alaska, I eased my car out of the garage and turned onto the road. The comfortable, heated seat was relaxing, and with no radio playing or idle chatter with friends to distract me, it was just what I needed to let my imagination run wild. I visualized several plans for creating suspense and mystery. Oy! Too many plots danced in my head. I needed to write them down before they floated away. It was too early for dinner and too late for lunch but the ideal time for a happy hour cocktail, and as it so happened, I was close to my favorite haunt. Pulling into the parking lot, I knew my timing was just right. But for a few cars, it was empty. "Perfect. No disruptions." The Carriage House Restaurant has been my go-to zone to work. My office can get boring, and a change of scenery was just the ticket. Not to mention, sitting too long in one spot for long periods of time was not good for these aging bones.

As I entered with a gust blowing my hair every which way and a chill zipping down my spine, I was greeted with a wave from Dale behind the bar, a UMass student. I slid into a comfy leather booth in the corner, swiped my hair smooth and took a deep breath. Except for two older men sitting at the far end of the long bar, the lounge was empty from what I could tell. I scanned the room for other hardy souls who'd braved the bite.

Nope. A basketball game was playing on the TV mounted behind the bar, but the volume was low. Those patrons did not appear to be watching. Instead, they were engaged in a deep conversation, hunching close, but I couldn't hear what they were saying. Happy for the quiet, I collected my thoughts and put pen to paper to scratch out a few detached ideas.

Dale approached me with his friendly, broad smile. His shoulder-length dark hair was tied back and his blue shirt sleeves, rolled up, as per usual. He worked here part-time to pay tuition. Whenever I came in, we enjoyed prattle about his courses or my writing. "Hey, Izzy. What'll it be on the coldest day of the year?" He glanced at the yellow pad and pen on the table. "While you get some work done."

"I know. Crazy weather. But here I am. Had to get out and clear my brain fog. How's business been on this frigid day? I only see those two guys at the bar."

"Well, it's quiet now, but it gives me time to work on a paper that's due early next week. Think the chill has kept most folks home, not that I blame them." Dale had a pleasant way of making everyone feel welcome. He knew the regulars like me by name, and it was easy to see why they liked him. I knew he depended on tips and a thin crowd didn't help. Having waited tables myself while I was in college, I knew having plentiful customers was what paid the bills.

"A slow day is good for me but bad for you. The morning meteorologist said the wild wind is supposed to settle down by around four, so that *should* help around dinnertime."

Dale shrugged his shoulders and glanced at the two men

at the bar. "Yeah, it'll get busier later, I'm sure. Working on something special today?"

"Yes, trying to plot out two chapters, and I needed the change of scenery, cold or no cold."

"Sounds good. We strong ones soldier on." He lifted a fist. "Well, let me get your drink, and you can relax and enjoy the quiet. The usual?" He flashed me a lopsided grin.

I nodded and smiled. "Yep. You know me well. A cosmo and small Caesar salad with chicken. No rush on the salad."

"You got it, Izzy."

I'd written down a few more concepts by the time Dale returned with my cocktail.

"Here ya go."

"Thanks, Dale." I raised my glass to him. "Here's to a quiet hour and an early spring."

"Indeed. You read my mind. Spring can't come early enough for me. Enjoy. I'll wait a bit on that salad." He gave me a quick wink and returned to the bar.

Time to get to work. I savored a sip before jotting some scene notes. And then some more. Good. At least I was making headway and finally on a roll. Had to admit, this *was* the perfect plan to get out, clear my brain and start anew. I gazed out the window. The hazy sunlight looked promising, but it wasn't enough to bring any warmth to the day. The time change had increased the daylight hours, but the sidewalks were empty of the smart ones who'd stayed home where it was warm. I caught Dale out of the corner of my eye, placing the salad on my table. I looked down at the shallow bowl, then up at him. "Thanks so much."

"No prob. Water with lemon and lime to go with your salad?" He'd read my mind.

I beamed and nodded. "Yes, please."

The salad was the perfect size to quell my appetite. My focus traveled to the bar where the two men had finished eating and were draining the last of their beer. For some reason, they piqued my interest, and I wondered who they were and what they were talking about so intensely. As a writer, people intrigued me, and at times, I conjure up crazy stories about random individuals and the secrets they might be keeping.

The men, still conversing quietly, slid off the bar stools, grabbed their coats, and headed to the door.

"So much for that," I murmured, as I stabbed fork prongs into a piece of chicken.

The lounge was now empty except for Dale and me. After a good half hour of solid productivity, I looked up and watched as he ran his cloth over the bar. Catching me staring, he gestured to ask if I wanted another cocktail or a top-off on my water. I raised my palm and shook my head no. My phone chimed. Merle, again? Damn! Won't she ever stop?

Can't you just LOOK into this criminal? I could actually hear the nails-on-a-chalkboard whine behind those words, like a pterodactyl's screech.

I texted: *I'm out to lunch. And working! Nothing I can really do. But talk to you later.*

What the heck does she expect me to do? I'm not a private investigator or crime solver just 'cause I write mystery novels. For teens.

I can remember our exchange and her words of protest so clearly when I brought it up months ago.

But, she had *insisted*, "I'm a smart, seventy-five-year-old woman, and I'm *certainly* aware of the scams, but other ladies I've talked to tell me this is a legit service. What's the harm in looking at photos, talking to other singles, and meeting with a man now and then? And by the way, where's a woman my age supposed to meet a man for companionship? These men are in the same boat as we are."

Merle had had me there. Many singles have met partners online, but I was not convinced. "Nurse or purse," I had reminded her. "Why do you need a man in your life to make you happy? You constantly complain about how busy you are and enjoy a comfortable lifestyle, thanks to your wealthy deceased husband. You travel all the time, too many places to count, and your life is full, from what you've shared at book club. So why do you need to complicate it by meeting up with strangers?"

"I can't explain it," she replied, "but I find talking to the men on Silver Love entertaining, and I look forward to meeting them in person. Back in the day, after work, we could go to a bar where everyone hung out and meet someone. No one does that anymore. Everything is online, and that is where people meet. It's the modern way of dating. You need to get up to speed, Izzy."

"I *am* up to speed, thank you very much, and online dating would be my *last* choice for meeting a man. Seems they tell you all the things you find appealing, but who's to say if their intentions are honest. I bet most women post the same.

They want someone to hold hands with and walk in the moonlight as they listen to the soft chirping of crickets." I knew I was piling it on, but I couldn't stop. "Or to sit by the ocean with cocktails while a handsome, silver-haired gentleman is rubbing lotion on their back." Merle's eyes had rolled up in a pooh-pooh way. I knew she was thinking I was judgmental, but I was trying to be honest. "Men looking for an easy mark know exactly what to say to pull women in, and just because they're past seventy, it doesn't make them any more trustworthy."

My words landed on deaf ears, and the ladies in our book club didn't help a lick because they relished her tales, hungry to hear one crazy saga after another. She had the floor and their attention, and they, in turn, lived vicariously through Merle's various escapades. Most of the men posted younger pics or lied about their height or weight. Some of her meetups had been so hilarious, they could serve as fodder for stand-up bits. She left a lot of men alone at restaurants before meeting this charming schemer, Karl Hendricks. He'd schmoozed his way into her life months ago, and she, apparently, *willingly* gave him all this cash? *Thousands?* The critical word being, *willingly*. And for what? How? Why? It left me gobsmacked.

I wanted to stuff cotton in Barbra's mouth when her lilt came from my phone. *Oh, come on!* I answered and clenched my jaw as I quietly spat, "Merle. I can't help you. I am busy and out. Call me later."

"You're a *writer*, for God's sake. You have a great imagination. Can't you, at least, take a little time out of your *busy* day to help your oldest, dearest friend out by tracking this Casanova down and making him pay?" The tone in "writer" was a low blow because she believes writing a novel is so utterly easy and has incessantly bragged about the book she'll write someday. "All the book club ladies agree with me. You are the best person, with your savvy skills, to help me. And, as I said before, the cops, and even the lawyer I consulted, say there's nothing they can do. I'm not the first woman to be swindled."

I let out a long grumble. Guilt. Something I've lived with my whole life. She was wearing me down. To a nub. I had warned her of *exactly* this, but she claimed it was just for fun and she was lonely. "Not sure how *I* can help. I really gotta go, Merle," I said, sweeping the last breadcrumb around with my fork. I popped it into my mouth and crunched it into dust. "My meal's getting cold. Bye, Merle. Talk to you later."

Since we were kids, she has loved the attention of boys, and, later in life, men of all ages. Even worse, at seventy-five, she believes she is still a flashy, sexy sixty-year-old woman. Granted, she looks younger and is still attractive. Her thick, short red hair and stylish clothes give her a youthful appearance, but really? I know she lies about her age to the men on Silver Love. And as young as she looks, she still does not understand that most available older men who post on dating sites are attracted to younger women. After all, most men never see themselves aging, and when they look in the mirror, they see a younger version of themselves staring back. Lucky for them, they can look more youthful and grow a beard or mustache to hide the lines, and bald heads are in style. But, unfortunately, a woman has only so many options.

PLEASE HELP ME! she texted.

I did not reply. A moment later, she called back.

"The Way We Were" stopped short as I tapped Decline. I drained the last of my water in peace and crunched the scant ice chips until they dissolved. Just as I pulled out my credit card to pay the check, my phone rang again. "Damn," I muttered. "Why didn't I turn it on silent?" I felt trapped. Looking at my empty cocktail glass, I took a deep breath and answered. "Yes, Merle."

"Why are you brushing me off, Izzy? Stop hanging up! *This* is an *emergency!* A Code Red. You are the *only one* who can help me. Please!" All her rapid-fire words hit my ears like a rat-tat-tat.

I give up, literally lifting my hands in surrender. "Okay, okay. I'll *think* about, it, okay? That is the best I can offer. I'm not even sure what to do yet, and I can't hash it out now. I don't know. Maybe I can go on the site, poke around or something. But, as I said, I'm *working*. I will call you later. Good. Bye." I clicked off.

Without any clue on direction, or know-how, I already felt like I was in way over my head. I signaled Dale for another cosmo. I needed the heat. This was setting up to be a far stormier day.

*W*ell, looks like my novel's gonna have to wait. With two ladies from book club giving me even more specifics on Merle's dilemma over the phone, this unexpected hunt had obviously fallen into *my* reluctant lap, even though I'd never fully committed to anything with Merle.

Krappy Karl—*my nickname for him*—had schmoozed, wined, and dined my friend to con her into giving him money. And God knows what else he gave her to lower her red-flag alert. Uh, that's a sordid little tidbit she can keep to herself, thanks. At least she hadn't handed over *all* her savings —the sorry fate of some, and her bigger assets were under her daughter's name. Krappy Karl had promised her that an investment in the joint purchase of a building in New York City would easily be doubled within a month from the rents collected. Since he worked in finance, or, said so, and was the so-called expert, she totally believed him when he said several seniors were now pooling resources together in a "shelter" to buy properties for residual income. And, she could always get a buyout for her portion if she later decided it wasn't for her. It's a wonder he didn't just say she was investing in the Brooklyn Bridge. Crazy what lies, promises, and sex can do to loosen your grip on reality.

It was no surprise to me that the authorities were not going to pursue it, so I have to try to do *something*. I have that little, niggling issue that tends to plague my waking hours: *guilt*. There'd be no rest for me till I, at least, looked into it.

I pulled into my driveway, grumbling, then parked in the garage and pressed the fob to lock up. I rushed towards my home's warm embrace. My faithful companion Oscar greeted me at the door, and I left it open for him to go out for his last run. He'd been alone long enough. Oscar meeting me at the door and patiently waiting, no matter how long I've been gone, was always comforting. He raced past me in a hurry to do what dogs need to do. While he was outside, I mixed his food and set it down for him. He barked to be let in and, gentleman that he was, waited for the okay to gulp down whatever I put in front of him.

My turn. Coffee. And, oh, how I needed it. I zipped to my coffee machine, and after filling my mug, headed upstairs to my bedroom to change into my comfy jams. I groaned a sigh of relief as I pulled off my bra. "Why can't they design a bra that's actually comfortable?" I muttered. I slipped my tired feet into soft, old slippers, sidled to my office, dropped my butt into my worn chair, and rolled up to my desk. Leaning forward, I took another sip from my mug, fired up my laptop and wondered how long it'd take me to find the elusive

Krappy Karl. My nerves prickled under my skin at the task ahead. I had low expectations for finding him, but I could at least tell Merle that I did my best and hope she'd let it go. I typed 'Silver Love' into Google. It only took a second for results to return. *Wow. Quite a few* .

I clicked on the first link and cringed to be greeted by men far too old to be showing off *all* their stuff. *Whoa. Yikes.* Not much glory anymore. Porn? Well, *this* couldn't be it, could it? I gaped in shock. *OMG! This is crazy. Guess not all Silver Loves are the same.* One wrinkled body looked to be a hundred, and the man's crooked smirk was snarky and creepy. Did he really believe that anyone would find him attractive?

"No! Stop the madness!" I shouted to the screen, as tears of laughter welled up in my eyes. Having never been on a porn site, I was glad I'd never been subjected to this sort of eyesore before. *Yuck! Disgusting! Where's the bleach?* The more smiling faces and awkward poses there were, the harder I busted a gut. Was this a comedy show? Tears were rolling down my face. *This is crazy.* These pics of farty old men should never be hit by the sun. You needed to post your credit card to see more. Well, *I'm* not doing that. *JOIN SILVER LOVE NOW.* This can't be it. No. No way. Can't be.

I Xed out, rubbing my eyes with my knuckles for a reset. "Oh my God! What the hell, Merle! Ya should'a warned me," I muttered, wiping my cheeks dry. "Why would a dating service choose the same name as a porn site? And who had it first? Is that even legal?" Wonder how many women got slammed with the same shocker while searching for the dating site instead. Likely scared the bejeezus out of 'em.

I scrolled till I found the listing that seemed right, as it advertised, *Just for seniors! Welcome to SILVER LOVE, the only true ELITE dating website, dedicated to helping seniors connect and find happiness in the golden years. Are you looking for simple companionship, casual or serious dates? Are you searching for love, partnership and romance? Join today and take a chance at finding your silver love.*

"Ah, *this* must be it." I clicked in. A header of well-dressed couples in extravagant places flicked on by in slow fades, one after another, with messages on them. "That's more like it. At least everyone's in clothes here." Before I clicked through the tabs to see what I could actually explore for free, my focus was disrupted by the doorbell and the loud barking of Oscar. "Who'd be crazy enough to be out in this bluster?" I snatched my robe from the door hook, slipped my arms into the fuzzy sleeves, then marched to the door, annoyed by the intrusion. Oscar was in full warning mode, barking wild, and I signaled for him to sit and wait so I could see who'd be banging on my door without calling first. The porch lights were on. Surprise, surprise. "Of course! Merle." Oh. My. God. I'm helping! I'm helping! Give me a break! Will she ever stop?

I'd hardly cracked the door open when she shoved her way in. Her hair, usually perfectly styled, was sticking out from under a purple knit hat, and her face was beet red from the biting wind. Before I could even speak, she brushed right past me, untangling her scarf and yanking off the hat that matched. She quickly patted Oscar's head and dropped her gray coat, accessories, and handbag on the sofa.

"What the hell, Merle! Can't believe you came out in this

weather. The wind has not lessened any, as it was forecasted. Lies. The air even almost smells like snow now, too."

"Yeah. Tell me about it! Here," she said, spinning and holding out a bottle of wine to me. "A gift for your help. Your favorite, *Riesling*." Her red hair, filled with electricity from the knit cap, stood straight on end, making her look like a comic book character. "Despite the freeze, I couldn't wait a minute longer for you to make up your mind." She flipped me a beady-eyed glare of vexation. "You didn't answer my latest text. *Thinking* about helping me does not mean you *will be* helping me. And you must! You could've saved me the trip if you'd responded with a simple, "*Yes.* I am on it, Merle." That's what friends *do,* you know."

"I literally just got home." I stifled a laugh, trying not to look at her. "Don't blame *me* for your decision to come over. You could've called again, *instead.*"

Oscar's head bobbed from Merle to me. He had enough of the woman with the flaming wild red hair and left the room. Dogs are fortunate like that. They can walk away.

"Well, you were being far too fickle and elusive. I need action. *Today.*" Merle tromped to the kitchen sink and turned on the faucet, running hot water over her wrists. "Wow. This is the best way to warm cold hands after you made me stand in an outdoor freezer. It's a wonder I didn't solidify in place waiting for you to let me in." Merle had a way of exaggerating any situation to her advantage. "*Gotta warm the blood,* as my mother used to say." She dried her hands on the kitchen towel and reached for a tissue to wipe her red, runny nose. "You *clearly* needed a little...*pushing.* Face-to-face. You have no idea how important this is to me," she said, opening the refrigerator door and removing the half-and-half. "And why are you staring at me? I need a hot cup of coffee, and fast. Oh, and, *by the way*," she said as she reached into the cabinet to retrieve a mug, "you're *lucky* that I braved the Arctic blast to buzz over here, besides."

I felt like I was watching a comedy show, and my mouth was beginning to quirk and quiver into a smile. Merle was a tornado, zooming around my kitchen, and she never stopped talking. I couldn't get a word in edgewise if I tried. She thinks *I'm* lucky? Of course, she does. It's always about her. There was no winning when Merle was on a tear, and it was better to let her rant than try and defend myself for not responding to her text. I leaned against the wall, keeping my mouth firmly shut, and just watched her buzz around like a bee.

She helped herself to a coffee pod in the K-cup holder and dropped it into the coffee machine. As the coffee brewed, she turned to me with a scolding voice and said, "I knew you'd need my password for the dating site to get in, and navigation help, and I thought we could search for Karl, the Snake, together."

"You mean Krappy Karl?" I said, hiding my grin. "I may as well grab another coffee, too. Looks like this is gonna be a long night."

"Krappy Karl or Karl, the Snake. He's all the above." Merle's eagle eyes swept over my messy hair, lack of makeup, and baggy clothes. "Thank goodness you're *not* in the market for a man. Your failed fashion sense would never work." Her lip quivered into a half smile.

"Think you need to take a gander of *yourself* in the mirror, chickie. Not lookin' as coiffed as usual. Your old Glamour Shot meets Glamour Not." Laughter was bubbling up, and once it started, I knew I couldn't stop. "Hope Krappy Karl never saw you on a cold, windy day."

We stared at each other for a millisecond, and I don't know if it was the time of day or our bedraggled appearances, but peals of laughter erupted from us both.

She grinned as she patted a frazzled section of hair. "Yeah. Not a good look, huh?" she said, wiping the tears from her cheeks. "Wind-worn Chic?"

"Nope. Which is why I have no interest in bringing a man into my uncomplicated life. My dress code of simple staples is fine by me. Pass me a tissue, please."

After gaining control of ourselves, we headed to my office and set our mugs on the desk.

Merle dragged over the spare chair, so we were both sitting in front of the screen.

I clicked my mouse to pick up where I'd left off. "Well, I found Silver Love, but, um, did you *know* there are *porn sites* with the same name?'

"Know? Of course. You are so naive, Izzy," she said, rolling her eyes and shaking her head at me, as if I were some pitiful imbecile. "That's done on *purpose* to let women visually sample what they can get if they join the dating site."

"Oh, stop! You don't really believe that, do you?" My jaw dropped open.

Merle's tattooed black eyebrows raised in surprise. "It's true!" She rattled her lips at me. "Get with the times, Izzy.

That's what is called a *lead-in,* in the business world." Her lips stretched into what passed for a smile as she looked at me.

"You have got to be kidding me. Do you *actually* find those pics of sad-looking bag-a-bones with knowing grins on their faces appealing?" I could feel another belly laugh rising, but I didn't want to make fun of her. On the other hand, maybe she was just teasing me.

Merle looked directly into my eyes, and I could see that she was dead serious about her crazy assumptions. Her tone was humorless. "Sure. Think about it. There are too many websites and apps for dating. How does one stand out and make yours *the* one that older ladies enjoy? You gotta tempt 'em and *start* the trends. Those sites are set up with the same name on purpose."

I leaned over and pinched the bridge of my nose to regain my composure. I felt like whacking my forehead in disbelief. Where does she get these outrageous ideas and information?

"You'd know I'm right if you looked into it. Did ya know there are websites that use this sort of stunt on places like TikTok where their mature content can be found? Parents should be checking what their kids are searching for, even if it's for a school paper. Results can land you into something highly inappropriate, like, searching something simple like hamsters leads to an entirely non-innocent kind of Hamster."

"Oh. Ya know, Merle, I agree with you about being careful with searches, but I just can't buy that this porn site is linked to your dating one. Come on. That's a bridge too far for me."

Merle gave a short laugh and shook her head at me. "Well, it is. You know, Izzy, for a modern older woman, you are just not up-to-speed with today's world. You don't know how anything works."

My lips pursed at the slight. "Okay. If you say so." I had to stop while I was ahead. I knew I'd never win this battle. Changing Merle's mind once she got something in her head was challenging. Her heels were dug in and held firmly in place by cement. I could never convince her or reason with her. And why should I? Maybe she's right, although, I find it hard to believe. But, the women on them conversed with each other in a language I did not know, so it was better to move on. And God knows who she follows on TikTok or any social media site. So, I decided not to touch that subject. I opened the login page and entered her email. "And...*password.*"

"Hotbody75," she said, puffing up her shoulders.

"Yeah. Figures," I mumbled as I typed it in.

The paywall lifted. "We're in." Photos and bios of all sorts of men popped up. It was amazing that so many older men were posting to a website to find love, a soulmate or a companion. The variety of ages and backgrounds blew my mind. I was dazzled and overwhelmed. "Gosh, Merle. How do you settle on who to contact? Must take hours to weed through all these profiles. Are you on more than this one dating site?"

"No. Some women are, but I picked this one because it had good reviews, and it was the priciest."

"Pricey? How pricey?"

"Well, I'm a *Diamond* member," she stressed with pompous flare, "which is three hundred a month."

I gawked. "Three hundred? Wow. That's a lot for a senior

online dating service. Must think we're *all* rolling in dough, huh? But, it's probably the perfect hotbed for the predator losers out there. They're looking for women with money."

Merle took another sip of coffee, her eyes locked on the screen. "Izzy, don't forget there are women looking for men who are well-off, too."

I nodded. She was right. But I bet more women than men were searching for a companion. We do outlive men, which was why she dated men younger than herself.

"Search 'Karl Hendricks'. See what comes up. I tried before, and, *nothing*. And he's not answering his emails or calls."

"So, why try again? I don't know. You think *I* can find him better than *you?*" I asked, typing Krappy Karl's name into the search bar anyway.

"Just try it, Izzy! Maybe he made a small switch-up or I did something wrong."

"Okay. Guess we can try variations in spelling and the things you know about him. I know on some of these sites, you can research qualities or what people are looking for." We leaned closer to the screen, expecting Karl's photo to magically appear. Nope. No Karl Hendricks. An hour passed with us entering everything we could think of, and Krappy never came up. I felt defeated.

"Hmm. Now what?" I turned to her, lips pursed, hoping she had an idea or two because I was clean out.

Merle dropped her head into her hands, then sat up. Rolling her shoulders to release tension, she turned to me. "Uh, I don't know. That's exactly why I need you to help me figure this out. *Think*, Izzy."

I rubbed my tired eyes. It was getting past my bedtime. "I *am* thinking, but the only thing that comes to mind is that he must've changed his appearance, his name, his bio, or is using another site now. Maybe he's moved on to another mark. He's got to know you are presently searching for him."

Merle almost jumped out of her chair. "See?" she screeched. "That makes sense! *This* is why I need your input. You have good instincts and ideas. You are a writer and dream this kind of stuff up all the time. Bet you could even be a PI."

My eyes popped open. "Merle. I'm no PI, nor do I want to be one. This is a big ask from you, but *you* need to do some of this work, like join some other dating websites so we can lurk and see if he's on the prowl elsewhere, going by Karl Hendricks. At least eliminate this possibility. *I* can't do it *all*. You can join with another name and photo. Otherwise, he'll quickly know you are trying to track him down."

For the first time, Merle let out a swear I hadn't heard from her before. "You're right, Izzy. Maybe he *is* on some other dating sites as Karl. Bet I'm not the only woman he's conned. And I never would've thought of that. But, since I can't be me, using my own name and photo now, how 'bout I use yours?"

"What!" I shouted, moving my chair back and standing up. "No. No way. I don't want any part of that."

"Really? Because I was thinking it'd be perfect for *you* to post and interact, as well. As a writer, you can dazzle men with your words and, hopefully, find Karl. I can work on some, as faux-you, but I can't do it all."

"Me? No way. I don't think so! People know me, and it's not something I'd ever do. Find another friend to help with that piece. Besides, he'd never contact someone from the same town. He's not *that* dumb."

"Pleeease….Izzy. I need you." Merle's voice was sober and imploring. "You use a *pen name*, so if you use your real name, your readers won't even know." She was spewing out words as quickly as they came to her head. "And, *for your information*, I used my address from my condo in Boston and that's where we met up, mostly. He doesn't even know I have a home here. He told me he only dates Silver Love women in-state, cause he lives in Boston. And we can find a younger photo of you. No one will associate you as the author of kid's books."

"A younger photo? Now you're insulting me as well."

Merle was pacing in circles and wringing her hands. "Izzy, everyone posts younger photos. And it's not like you're actually looking for a date. We need to find Karl, the Snake, and you're my only hope. You're the smartest, cleverest friend I have. It'll be fun. Think of it. I believe we *can* find him. He's gotta be out there somewhere, with a dangling hook, and we just need to locate it. Maybe you can even write a book about his epic take-down once it's all over. Will you, at least, *think* about it? Going undercover? For *me?*"

My mind was spinning. I couldn't take the drama anymore. I was bone-tired and wanted her to leave, but intense rage coursed through my body. I hated that Merle had been swindled out of money and her dignity. Krappy duped her, broke her heart, left without a trace, and is probably, right now, reeling in some other vulnerable woman looking for love. I just had to help her. I couldn't bear for him not to be held responsible for it. *Nope. Not today, buddy. Not on my watch!* How many other women had Krappy, or whatever his name was, sucked in with his schmaltzy charm and words of love? A lot, I'll bet. He's probably got a whole system down in this scheme of his. I thirsted to find Krappy Karl and make that no-good, filthy-rotten bloodsucker pay. Undercover? Yeah, I guess. I just *had* to do something. So, against my own intuition and better judgment, I was pulled into Merle's pleas like a kid in a candy shop.

I was awoken by bright sunlight streaming through my bedroom window and hitting the pillow where my head lay. After a fitful night's sleep, I wasn't ready to begin the day, and all I could think of was coffee. I rubbed my eyes and glanced at Oscar, still asleep on his doggy bed. What time was it? As I glanced at the clock, it hit me that I'd actually slept in for the first time in months. It was Saturday, my day off from the gym. I turned my head and stared out the window, focusing on the giant oak tree. Branches weren't moving. A good sign. Bright sun, no wind, and a prediction of calm weather to come suggested that winter's grip was finally breaking. The bitter cold wind lasted two days, and with the bright sun and melting snow, I was in the mood for tacking up Maverick for a short trail ride. It would give me time to gather my thoughts and plan a strategy. I still hadn't entirely decided that signing up to dating sites or apps was the best path for me. It eeked me out.

I stretched and rolled out of bed with a burst of motivation, but I really needed someone else's input. Sensing I was awake and moving, Oscar came over to greet me. "Hey, there, old boy. Did ya sleep well last night?"

He nuzzled my hand and, in his doggy way, said, "Yes, but I need to go out."

After visiting the bathroom, I threw on my bathrobe and padded downstairs with Oscar hot on my heels. He was at the door before I could toss a pod into the coffeemaker. My usual morning routine. Feed Oscar, sit with a coffee, catch up on the news, dress, and prepare for the day. After he went out, I quickly moved to fill my mug and waited at the machine. When Oscar returned, I opted to run my dilemma by him as he ate his breakfast. I was still talking as he licked the bowl clean, but he didn't seem very interested in my plight. He failed to advise, unless his tail wag counted as a prod. I was still vexed by the idea of joining a dating site, regardless of Merle's appeal, *insistence*, really. It didn't feel right, and each time I thought about it, my gut told me, *Don't do it.*

When I swallowed the last drop of coffee, I knew this would be a two-cup morning. After so much drama last night, and finishing off a bottle of wine with Merle, I was left with a huge problem.

She had tossed her plan into my lap, and I wouldn't say I liked her control and had no faith in her, but it had to be *my* plan if I was going to do this. I didn't mind helping her search for Krappy, but pretending to be an enhanced, flirtatious version of myself, someone else really, seemed like overkill to me. On my second cup of coffee, I was still contemplating what to do and decided to call someone for guidance. Milly, my best friend, was just the person. With a good head on her shoulders for solving problems, she offered me the sure ground to walk me through Merle's minefields.

Milly's a retired family therapist, and her skills often come into play when I need advice for one of my books. And now that the sun was finally out, and the air, warmer, we can tack up the horses and take a trail ride while we discuss options. There's nothing better than a relaxing ride on the back of a horse to help thread ideas together. Milly has been on horseback since she was young, and her home is in a town that borders mine. She lives in an old Victorian house, and her yard is stunningly landscaped into a showplace of exquisite flowers and shrubbery. In the summer, the lovely flowers grown in her greenhouse are nestled along her walkway and planted in beautiful garden beds. Of course, with her knowledge of all things flowers, since her retirement, she has found time to teach others and is president of the garden club in her town. At one time, Milly stabled her horse at my barn, but her beloved Thunder died five years ago, so now she rides my horse, Speed. When I travel to visit my children, Milly stays at my home and cares for all the animals. She shares my love of horses and does barn chores when I'm busy writing. Riding keeps us fit, and occasionally, we meet a group of horse friends and ride the longer trails in the state forest. Our friendship and commonality keep us happy and balanced. Milly's not a member of the book club. She has told me more than once she has her limits. I know what she means. Merle can be difficult, but the ladies love her.

As soon as I was dressed, I phoned her. Milly's ringtone for my listening pleasure was set to the melodic voice of Gene Autry, singing, "Back in the Saddle Again." She picked up on the third ring. "Hey, Izzy. What's up today at the farm? Did you ever get back to Merle?"

I texted her that Merle had been driving me crazy all day yesterday and was trying to rope me into her latest calamity. "Get back to her? Oh, she came over. Fun. At least the wine she brought was better than I thought." Milly understood our history and how Merle always turns to me for help. It was no secret, by now, that Merle had been bamboozled by Krappy because she never kept anything private. She was an open book. "She was here, hounding me, till late last night. Too complicated to get into details over the phone, but I need your perspective on her plan for *me* to find the guy who swindled her out of money and disappeared."

"*You?* OMG. I hate to say it, but she reeks of desperation and is the perfect target for such a scam, so I can't say it surprises me." I could picture the tsk-tsk on Milly's face. She didn't hold Merle in the highest regard but tolerated her like all of us. Merle did have a kind heart, but it was difficult to notice because she was annoyingly stuck on herself, and when she entered a room, she sucked the life out of it. I knew Milly would never say no for a ride on Speed, so I added another enticement.

"I need a second opinion," I answered. "And the day's warming up. I'm considering taking Maverick out for a short trail ride later and wondered if you wanted to join me. I have lasagna in the freezer. If you have no plans, we could have a late lunch, or early dinner, when we return." There was a pause at Milly's end. I knew what she was thinking, and I also know she loves to ride, and the added enticement of lasagna— *her favorite*—was like frosting on the cake.

"Of course, I'll help you. Sounds fun. It's a lovely day for a ride and you don't even have to add the lasagna, but that sounds perfect, too. I'll see ya later then. Around 2ish?"

"Yep. Good." After disconnecting, I leaned back in my desk chair and took two deep breaths. I rubbed my eyes, tired from the long evening of searching for Krappy online. Too much screen time had my eyes burning, and, admittedly, too much wine, sampled from the bottle that Merle had brought, left me muddled. I'm not a fan of more than one glass of wine, and beer, cosmos, or martinis are my libation choices. However, the wine seemed to disappear sometime in the middle of our search.

Even though it was later than I usually start my day, I still needed some sustenance. I'd need more than just coffee to get me moving. Cereal would do just fine. So, I scarfed down a bowl of Cheerios, then set off upstairs. I took a long hot shower, and it felt good not to be rushing to the gym. My day off. Yippee for me. I put on my riding clothes and headed to the barn to tack the horses. Getting Milly to join me took no persuasion, but the lasagna temptation had sealed the deal. She was as eager as I was to get outside after the grumpy start to spring, and I could feel the change in the air.

Oscar followed me to the barn and waited as I slid the heavy door open. "Ahhh, the pleasant smell of barn and horses," I murmured as I paused to turn the light switch on and took a deep breath. The mingling scent of horses and hay has a calming effect on me, and it fills my soul with sweetness each time I enter. I know horse lovers everywhere feel the same.

My horses have the barn to themselves, and it's open for

them to go out and come in as they wish. They also have a large run-in shed in the upper field, and the outside feeder is kept filled with hay when the weather doesn't allow them to graze in the vast pastures behind the barn. At one time, my ten-stall barn was filled with horses and barn cats, but times changed when my husband died, and two horses were plenty for me to care for. Maverick is my riding horse, but Milly loves Speed, who has only one speed—*slow*. Horses need companionship, and Maverick and Speed are best buddies.

They welcomed me with low neighs.

Cat greeted me, and I bent to pet her. She rubbed against my legs, purring as most cats would. "What? No hiss today? You don't fool me." Since the day she appeared, she took ownership of this place. She decided the barn was hers, and hers alone, and allowed no other feline to invade. Once her claim was staked, she and Oscar ended up making a shaky peace agreement, deciding to just tolerate each other. They'd come to a standoff early on and now knew when to back off. But woe to any kin invader who attempts to enter her kingdom. I've watched that queen in action. She believes she's a lioness and becomes a wild beast chasing any and all other cats from her territory. I'd placed a comfy cat house in an empty stall with her food and water bowl, and she was free to roam. Each day, I expect her to be gone for good, so I never officially named her.

She stayed close as I opened a new bag of salmon-flavored cat food crunchies. Like most of my pets, the stray took advantage of me, and I tossed out a wide variety of cat food she refused to eat. She was still bony, even though I had wormed her, and she had a new tick collar around her scrawny neck. When she arrived, I trapped her in a cat carrier and had the vet check her out. She said she was healthy, and I shouldn't worry about her. I tempted her with a wide variety of cat food to get her to eat, only to have her sniff, turn up her nose, and walk away. My only thought was that she was living on mice. "Okay, Cat. Let's see if this suits your fancy."

I poured the food into her bowl, and she gave me the usual stare and then sniffed it.

"You know, Cat, you sure have a fussy palate for a stray. You think you'd eat anything I put in your bowl and be grateful." For the hundredth time, I wondered why I cared this much for a finicky creature. I watched as she sniffed at today's offering, and to my amazement, she began eating. "Yay. Finally found something you will eat." Felt like celebrating. If I didn't know better, she understood human language and was trying to please me for the first time. As I stared at her, I realized she seemed destined to be a forever barn cat, and I should call her something more fitting than Cat.

When she first arrived, I couldn't get near her, but now, watching her gobble down the cat food, I wondered how long she must be a squatter here before she gets named. I couldn't help but smile. "Well, you've finally won me over. Maybe today's the day I will officially name you. Milly's coming, and we can think of a proper moniker. You came here with a chip on your shoulder and allowed no one to enter your sanctuary, so I think it's time." A name suddenly spilled from my lips. "Chip! That's it."

She looked up at me when she heard me call, "Chip."

"OMG. I'm going crazy. Here I am talking to a cat, not to

mention myself, and I think she understands every word, and *likes* her name."

I closed the stall door and walked towards the end of the barn, blocked with a gate to separate the front from the rear. There was an opening on the side leading to the pastures, and both horses, hearing its rumble and creak, had come to the gate. They nickered softly to greet me and waited for their treats. "Hold on, I'm coming," I said as I approached them. "Hi there, big guy," I murmured as I ran my hand over Maverick's smooth velvet nose. "Wow, you are really shedding your coat. Spring is here. You're gonna need a good brushing before our ride." I pulled a cookie from my pocket and his lips gently took it from my flat hand. Maverick is a chocolate-colored American Curly Paint who is very handsome and as gentle as they come. Not to be forgotten, Speed, my sleek palomino gelding, was nosing his way in for his own cookie. "Here you go, Speed," I said, kissing his soft nose.

Milly had called and said she was on her way. Good. Good.

I told the horses the plans of the day. Brushing and saddling these two took time, but I wanted to be ready when she arrived. Today would be our first trail ride in some time. Short rides were the most Milly and I did during the cold, gloomy days of winter. But with spring on our doorstep, the length of time we could take the horses out without freezing our butts off will only increase. When we were younger, we rode the trails for hours, freezing cold or not. Now we still enjoy riding but have learned to pace ourselves. No more jumping fences or taking chances on green horses. Slower always wins the race. They were saddled and standing at the crossties when Oscar bolted from the barn. I knew Milly had arrived. "Hey, Milly," I shouted, looking up the hill to the driveway where she had parked,

She was already headed my way, waving back. "Hey, you." She was dressed for riding in jeans, boots, and a heavy jean jacket with a Sherpa lining. Milly, an attractive seventy-two-year-old with shoulder-length brown hair, sprinkled with swatches of gray, was shorter than me and blessed with beautiful olive skin. Her hair peeked out from a black knit cap covering her ears. She is my very best friend and has been for many years. What impresses me most is her quiet competence. She's a listener, whereas, I often have too many thoughts firing up in my brain simultaneously and tend to rattle on. Milly has taught me to listen more and choose my words wisely. I still tend to be a chatterbox, but I have become a quieter, more thoughtful woman as I've grown older. And, of course, I say that, tongue-in-cheek.

Milly met me at the barn door with a hug and a huge smile that spilled over her face. She stepped back, her curious dark brown eyes, creased at the edges, were perked for the Merle saga. Looking at Milly was like looking at myself. My friend seems ageless, but I can see the beginning of tiny lines on her cheeks and a slight drooping of her eyelids. She is still beautiful, but time is moving us forward, and I can feel its incessant tug. When I was young, I asked my grandmother how it felt to be ninety. She was a very witty and modern woman for her time. *"Well,"* she said, *"The years pass so quickly, you don't see physical changes as they occur. Inside, I feel the same, but when I look in the mirror, I often don't recognize myself."* Many of my friends, who've now traveled eighty years around the sun, say the same thing. Now I understand what my grandmother meant with her definition of aging. I'm seeing it firsthand. Milly and I talk about aging all the time. Think it's a woman thing. Men don't seem as obsessed about it.

"So..." Milly sang, as she unclipped Speed from the crossties, "shall we enjoy the ride and talk about Merle later?"

I nodded my agreement and smiled. *"Yes.* Sounds like a plan. Why waste the first beautiful day discussing Merle's fiasco at the moment? It can wait. I'd rather enjoy the sunshine and the horses."

Merle led Speed out of the barn, and I followed behind leading Maverick. We mounted our horses, and Maverick led the way towards the trail to the back mountain range. Speed's pace was too slow for Maverick, but he was forced to keep up, not wanting to fall behind.

I settled into the saddle and took a deep breath. My whole body began to relax for the first time in days. It was early afternoon, and the sun's rays were intense. The temp had reached fifty-two degrees and I could feel the heat penetrating my jacket. I wore my gray knit cap pulled down over my ears, and it felt snug and cozy on my head. My fingers grew warm inside my riding gloves, and my winter socks in these riding boots were creating the same result. I wondered if I should've dressed lighter with the sun so strong. Nevertheless, it was our first spring ride, and I was happy to be on it.

Milly and I rode silently, occasionally interrupted by soft blowing sounds from our horses as they relaxed into a rhythmic walk. *Everything is perfect,* I mused. *The air, the sun on my face, riding my horse, and feeling Mav's warmth beneath me, life is good.* Just as I was thinking all good thoughts, a touch of uneasiness swept through me. My gut told me something important was coming. I didn't know exactly what, but I had a strong hunch that things would soon change. *Stop! You're worrying about something you haven't even taken on.*

Luckily, Milly called out to me, and the worry about what may never happen slipped away. "Hey, Izzy. Even though this is fun, I might be at my limit. Ready to turn towards home?"

"Yep, I'm ready. Enough saddle time today."

The ride back was just as delightful. I'd set the timer on the oven, and our lunch/dinner would be ready when we entered the house. The horses picked up the pace as the barn came into view. The hour-long ride had indeed cleared my brain. We untacked Maverick and Speed and turned them out.

Inside the house, we eagerly shed our outer layers and boots, set the table, and talked about horses and the weather as I got everything served and we sat down to eat. The lasagna was hot, the crusty bread, warm, and the coffee, strong, and we were famished. Having agreed to discuss Merle once we finished, we were able to eat in peace.

I sighed at the heft of the responsibility and insane spy mission that had been suddenly thrust upon me as we settled into my living room. At least the wine and a stack of glowing logs in the fireplace provided a good atmosphere for me to dish and unload all my concerns. It reminded me of some Medieval battle.

Only Milly could give me the clearest direction in hunting down this Krappy Karl. I absolutely dreaded what I knew I had to do, but I also almost couldn't wait.

I eased out of my chair to toss another log on the fire, and as I turned, Milly lifted her goblet for a refill. I had relayed to her what Merle wanted me to do—*go undercover for her*, and then, we sat in silence. I studied Milly as I filled her glass.

Her wide eyes and headshake said so much, even as I'd rendered her speechless, and I hadn't even gotten to the porn part yet. She is gonna *flip!* Her face made so many expressions of shock and horror as I went on to tell her what I'd found and what Merle and I had done so far. I kept going until I was drained of words and my throat grew chalky and dry. I found the whole thing ludicrous. All of it. It felt like a bad dream. Merle handing over money like that. All those wrinkled butts and dingle berries. Her begging to use my ID and pic and expecting *me* to make a profile *myself.* I could feel a grin forming as I pictured Merle, her hair standing on end, and the password she gave me for Silver Love, like it was nothing.

Milly finally broke her silence with a scoff of stupefaction. She leaned back in her chair and took a sip of wine, then set the glass on the side table next to her. She choked back a laugh, rolled her eyes, and sucked in a deep breath. It was just so funny, but also...incredibly insane. *Who knew what I was getting myself into? I had to do something. But this? Uh, I dunno.*

"Yeesh, Izzy. Unbelievable. That woman never fails to amaze me with her shenanigans, but this is the *worst* mess she has ever been snookered into. It's a cross between belly-laughing hilarity and a dreadful bamboozle."

"I know," I shrilled.

"The crazy thing is, like you, I feel empathy for her and understand why you feel compelled to help her, but I'm not sure I could do what she asked. It could be dangerous."

I nodded with an "exactly" smile. My mind was running on overdrive again. I sipped the last drop of wine from my glass. "Honestly, Milly, I do feel drawn to helping her. This time is different, and she is frantic. She's never been conned out of money before. Or humiliated like this. On one hand, I feel like walking away and letting her learn a hard lesson, but on the other, I hate what Krappy Karl did to her and I want him to pay. But I loathe the idea of going on a dating site and pretending to be someone I'm not. I'll need to post a picture and my name and contact information. And write a bio. I pride myself in privacy, which is why I use a pen name for my books. The exposure frightens me. And meeting up with men I don't know doesn't appeal to me at all. Now that you've heard the whole story, I need some real-time advice. Should I risk my privacy and become involved with finding Krappy?"

Milly got up from the chair and stretched, then sat down and looked directly into my eyes. It was her serious stare.

"I don't see a problem with signing up for a dating site. Millions of people do. It's the thing nowadays. As for contacting you, you can get a new email address for messages. And buy a burner cellphone with a new number for any calls. You don't have to give your address, and from what I understand, you can meet up in public place like a restaurant, park, or whatever. If you do set up a meeting, I could be there to keep an eye on you."

"So, you're saying, *yes,* then. I should help? But, with precautions. And you'll be my backup?"

"As long as your password isn't Hotbody75, I will."

I laughed. "You know that's not my style. None of this is."

"You've got to promise to continue to call him Krappy, though. Target code name: *Krappy.* I love that." The dam broke, and Milly began laughing uncontrollably.

We laughed so hard, I couldn't catch my breath. And just when one of us stopped, we'd start up again. It was the wine. It was Merle. It was Krappy. I finally was able to stop and get a box of tissues so we could wipe away tears and blow our noses. I regained my composure and took in a deep cleansing breath to quiet my thoughts. "Well, if I'm going to do this, I need a plan to entice Krappy into my snare." I felt my mouth twitch into a tight smile to stifle another fit of laughter. "I have a feeling he's on another dating site and that he no longer uses Silver Love, but we still need to begin there. He must've changed his appearance by now, but I bet he uses the same bio and basic info. He's a cocky guy but lazy."

Milly put her hand over her mouth. Her eyebrows raised and I could see she was choking back another laugh, "Krappy is cocky you say?"

I looked away from Milly, trying to gain my composure, but couldn't help myself from adding, "Well, *that*, according to Merle's description, is what she found most irresistible. Krappy Cocky Karl knows how to snag a woman. And if it isn't about his good looks, what is it? Maybe cocky is his best feature. *Cocky*, yes!" I couldn't stop the laughter bubbling up, and the flood gates tore open.

Once again, we burst into unrestrained kicking, hooting, and laughing.

We spent the next hour discussing how to find Krappy, and after tossing the empty wine bottle in the recycling bin, we decided it was best that Milly stay overnight since she was feeling a little tipsy. My guest bedroom should've been named Milly's Place because she often stayed with me when we went on long trail rides or were inclined to load the horses into my trailer and meet up with our other horse friends to ride the state forest trails.

The following day, after sleeping in later than usual, we had a light breakfast of English muffins with marmalade. Since last evening's wine had the same effect on Milly as on me, it took some time to get us going. It was a two-cup coffee morning for us both. The caffeine kick worked, and we filled our mugs once more and headed to my office to begin a search for Krappy. The chair Merle had pulled out was still beside mine, and I placed a small table next to it for our coffee mugs. I rolled out my chair and opened my laptop. "Krappy is probably not on Silver Love anymore, but you never know. He may have changed his appearance and figured Merle couldn't do anything legal even if she did find him. Okay. What's first on the list?"

Milly checked the list we made last night, before our bottle of wine was drained. "Let's create a new Gmail address. That's the easy part. I think we've got this. Next, let's sign up for exclusive types of dating websites."

I set up the new email address, and Milly checked it off our list. "Okay, let's check out Silver Love, and I'll create an account." I felt a surge of excitement and was feeling like a real-life detective. "Maybe Merle is right. I've missed my calling, Milly. I feel like a real-life PI."

"A new career for you? Don't count *me* in." She grinned as she took another sip of coffee and watched me. "Wow, there's lots of websites with the same name," she said, leaning in for a closer look.

I scrolled down the names. "Now you see how I unknowingly clicked on a porn site with the same name." I logged into Silver Love and clicked on the page to set up an account. I scooted over so Milly could move closer to the screen.

She adjusted her readers for a clearer view. "Wow. They really have a nice presentation. It looks professional and has a great page. And look at all those photos of happy couples and their testimonials for Silver Love. Unbelievable."

"I question how many of these photos are real. Seems anyone can Photoshop now, and it's hard to believe *this* many singles are so pleased with the site and find it beneficial, but these success stories help prove it works. Wonder how many women have been rooked out of money by the likes of Krappy but are too embarrassed to report it. I asked Merle if she and Krappy had put *their* photo on the site, and she told me she sent a photo of them in, but it never got posted."

Milly scanned the photos. "I don't know why they didn't post Merle's photo that she sent in, but they probably receive hundreds from couples who've found love. Isn't that what they're selling to lonely seniors, brave enough to sign up?"

"You're right," I chuckled. "After we set up a Silver Love account, let's look at some other websites that cater to seniors who are willing to pay high fees to join." I searched elite dating websites for seniors. The list was surprisingly long and after clicking on several, we came up with three sites requiring high membership fees and only bona fide members were allowed to join.

We sat back, trying to understand how dating sites *knew* the trustworthiness of members and concluded that they must be configured with an algorithm that verifies if the person is legit or not. Which must mean Krappy had to be legit somehow, somewhere, or he would've been rejected at the jump. As I scrolled down the Silver Love membership page, it asked for approximate income, if working, former profession, if retired, whether you own your own home, divorced or widowed or never married. In addition, a tab for security data brought you to a page explaining how you are protected, promising they never sell or share your personal information with third parties.

"Well, that's reassuring." Milly grinned. "But I still don't understand how they can tell if you're legit and *elite* or some poor slug. Or worse, a con."

"They have powerful computers and coders to feed data into the system. Nothing is *that* difficult today. People can find whatever they want about you. It's scary. I remember when I was a teenager and worked at a retail store. I worked behind a desk and opened charge accounts. To decide if a person was credit-worthy to open an account, we used a card that gave points to certain questions on the application. One of the questions was "Do you own your own home?" That was given a high number. Also, steady employment received good points. To qualify, I added up the points, and I forget the exact number, but if it reached the required amount, I then opened a credit account for them. I had friends with *no credit* come in and answer the questions correctly to qualify. They did *not* own their own home, but merely *said* they did, and they were all able to open their accounts. Now, how crazy was that?"

Milly squinted at me. "Wow the things about you I am learning. Okay, what other secrets do you keep? Do you mean, you *prepped* them? Ha! I find *that* hard to believe. You are very high-minded and righteous."

I choked back a laugh and nodded yes. "Milly, I bet you have a few secrets of your own. And it isn't a secret. It just popped in my head looking at the information on the website. Some things are simpler than they seem, and with technology today, they can learn anything about you. I was sixteen years old, and I didn't see anything wrong with it." I could feel my cheeks pink up. I shrugged my shoulders. "Who cares now anyway? At the time, I thought I was helping my friends. It wasn't as if they were criminals."

"Damn, the things we did when we were kids," she laughed. "I think we are getting too involved in the process. Let's just set up a membership and forget about the rest of it."

"Agree. We are thinking too deeply. I am all in, but I hate the thought of getting emails from tons of senior dating sites. It seems once you do a Google search, they flood you with ads and crap." I typed in all the information, including a credit card that is current, but I never use it. "Merle said she will reimburse me for all expenses, and I will hold her to it. This is only the beginning."

Once I was signed up, we used the same bio details as Merle, but I fluffed it a little to make it sound different. *I am a retired seventy-two-year-old woman, healthy and in good shape. People say I look much younger than my years.* "Oh, boy. That's a lie," I chuckled. I had scouted around my old photos on my computer and uploaded one taken five years ago that was a little blurry. I was holding an ice cream cone and sitting on a rock wall, the ocean behind me. Merle's profile said she loved the ocean, seafood, romantic movies, and was a good cook. She also enjoyed long drives to mysterious places and was looking for a man who could keep up with her energy. I added that I loved ice cream. I had to change it up some. I continued typing my version of Merle's profile, keeping her same likes but tweaking it a bit. *I enjoy romantic walks in the moonlight.* "Geesh, they all say the same thing," I muttered. *And I love back rubs, especially by the ocean. If you like hot tubs and body lotion, I could be the match for you. If you need intelligent conversation, sprinkled with adorable flirting, email me.*

"That seems good enough to me." Milly snickered then let out a huge sigh. "Uh, this is exhausting."

I kept going, building my fake Merle persona, and then snickered as I read it aloud to Milly.

"*Intelligent conversation?* For *you, yes,* but her?" Milly stood with a sigh, then cranked and wiggled her back to work out the kinks. "Are you sure *that* is what she posted?"

"It's there," I said with a smile and a nod.

"I just don't see her truly caring about that. The "hot tubs" thing is probably what won out, but I guess you should include that bit in yours as well, just in case."

"Yep. Done. I *definitely* left off where she talked about wild fun under the covers, though."

"Oh, no! Yes, yes, lop it off. Smother it, *fast,* and burn it with fire. Don't you *dare* put anything like that. No wonder she ended up with Krappy. She sounds kind of slutty for her age. Well, I don't know about *you*, but I need a break, or I may never stop laughing."

"Good idea." I pushed my chair back, got up, and stretched big. "I agree. Let's have a slice of the apple walnut cake you brought. And another hot cup of coffee may be just the thing. I'll switch to decaf this time."

"Tea sounds good to me. Three cups of coffee are more than I drink in the whole day, never mind, first thing in the morning." Milly followed me to the kitchen while Oscar led the way. "One thing for sure, I am learning all about dating websites and what one needs to do."

"Thinking about joining one?" I teased.

"Ha-ha, no. I think Merle has jaded my feelings about them. I know that's a good way for seniors to meet, but after what happened to her, I wouldn't want to subject myself to a possible gigolo thinking I'm his match. And besides, my profile would be so boring, no man would look twice at it."

Catching Milly rolling her eyes, I quickly turned my head so she wouldn't see my cheeks pull into a smile. "I can help you spice it up if you change your mind. I have plenty to go on after reading Merle's."

Milly's head snapped as she looked me straight in the eyes and gawked. "Oh, and just *what* would you say for *mine?*"

I feigned indifference with a shrug of nonchalance but I couldn't stop my puckish grin. Creating a profile with Milly would be so much fun. "Hmm, well that may take some puffing up. I could say you enjoy riding horses and gardening, and you are looking for a companion with the same interests, but I agree, it would take a little more spice to attract a suitor. Do you want to add anything?"

"Well, not *hot tubs!*"

I laughed.

Milly swept a strand of hair out her of eyes that had slid loose from the crinkled tie at her nape to behind her ear, then turned to fill the teapot with water. I could tell she was trying to think of something witty with some zing to say. "Hold that thought. I need sustenance to fuel my brain into coming up with something that fits." She reached into the cabinet and removed a floral teacup and a coffee mug. "A decaf for you?" she asked as she popped a pod into the drip machine.

"Yes." While my coffee dripped in the mug, I set place mats on the table, forks, small plates, and the cake. Milly's apple walnut cake was the best. Unlike me, she was a great baker. I made everything from a box or bought desserts from the local bakery in town.

"Where's the honey for my tea?" she asked with a smile, placing my coffee-filled mug on the table and the container of half-and-half next to it. "I dare not fix your coffee, since it must be just the right color. Dark, no sugar," she joked.

"Uh, spice cabinet by the stove." I gave her a thumbs up. I admit, I felt wiped out, so I let her finish the serving.

She set the honey and tea down by her plate. Her brown eyes looked tired, but it was no wonder. The screen on the laptop made my eyes burn if I worked too long staring at it.

"Think I'll stay off the wine for a week or so. For some reason, it has made me very lazy today, and I haven't showered or dressed, which is unusual for me."

"Who cares? Have somewhere important to go? I was up early and already at the barn. So, chores are done."

"Oh, thank you! I appreciate that so much."

"Well, I really wanted to clean your plate and lighten your load so we can finish up the profiles and see if someone takes the bait."

"Let's take this break and then get back to joining the other three dating sites for elite seniors. Seems like the best we can do today until we get a nibble of some sort. Then, we can pull ourselves together and go shopping. I need to buy a group birthday gift for one of the ladies in our book club, and you can help me pick something out for her."

Milly placed a slice of cake on her plate and sat down. "Gift fairy? How'd you get *that* job? Bet you volunteered." She flashed me a playful smirk.

I groused and took a sip of coffee. The stark truth was fairly obvious. Milly was constantly reminding me not to volunteer for everything the book ladies asked. She pointed out that they took advantage of me, and I agree, they do, but I find it hard to say no. To avoid answering, I stuffed my mouth with a forkful of cake and changed the subject. "The weather looks good next week, so if you want to go out for another short ride on Speed, I'd enjoy the company. I think spring has finally arrived."

*A*fter a long, hot shower, I felt renewed and ready to start fresh. It was time for a new outlook and clearer heads to prevail. I had been in my jammies long enough, and so had Milly. Merle had given me a copy of Krappy's profile, and copying- pasting my profile, a version of Merle's, to Silver Love was the simplest way to begin. Milly and I decided to work two angles. One, wait for emails from men attracted to my profile, and two, see if we could recognize Krappy on any dating sites he may have landed on. Merle told me Krappy only joined elite dating sites, so we would begin there and stretch the net further if we had no action. We found a clearing house for dating sites catering to elite seniors that promised to simplify the process. It listed ten that fit our search. We chose three from their list and determined that if we did not find Krappy after two weeks, we'd add three more. This method, although time-consuming, was the simplest starting point I could think of. My biggest hurdle would be screening the respondents, trying to pinpoint Krappy.

But even if I *did* get him in the mix, *then what?* Since the odds of finding him were scant, I tried to not get tied up in knots, worrying about something that probably would never happen. As Milly said, I would fulfill Merle's nagging request for help, but we both concluded that the creep was long gone and would not chance another scam on a dating website.

We trekked to my office, ready to set up profiles on the three new dating sites. I felt much better sitting at the computer dressed in workout clothes, my usual dress code now that I am a gym member. Ready for the day, Milly had tied her hair back and pulled on jeans and a loose-fitting green T-shirt. She rolled out the spare chair and moved it beside mine, reminding me she didn't want to spend more than two hours on dating sites. Shopping and lunch were firm plans for the day. My biggest fear was that Merle would arrive to check on my progress, bang on the door again, interrupt us, and self-invite to join us for lunch. I knew Milly wouldn't be able to tolerate Merle leaning over the back of our chairs, repeating her "woe is me" again. And I didn't think telling Merle that Milly was helping me in the search was wise. I knew full well that she'd be calling and texting Milly if she couldn't reach me, and Milly did not have the same patience with Merle.

I typed in the first senior website, *'Perky Seniors Looking for Love. The Senior Dating Site Full of Adventure and Connections.'* "Geesh, that says a lot. Merle certainly went on an adventure of her life that she'll never forget."

Milly laughed, nudging my arm.

"Well, here goes nothing," I chuckled as I clicked on the membership page and entered my credit card and profile. It was much easier this time since I had copied the information from Silver Love. I pasted in the blanks and as soon as I clicked submit, the dating site opened. A banner slid across the screen, touting two thousand happy members, and growing. "Wow, do you believe this?" I was wide-eyed and so was Milly. I opened and perused some of the men's profiles. Milly leaned closer so we could check out their photos. Some members had added a video of introduction, but we didn't want to waste our time listening to men we had no interest in. "This seems more upscale than Silver Love. It's a slicker site, and like us, I bet some members are on multiple dating sites to find more matches."

Milly squeezed in closer. "Geez Louise! Some of these photos look like normal older men. Not the photos of ninety year-olds we saw on Silver Love. I am amazed by the number of seniors looking for a new mate." She sat back in the chair, her brows knitted together. "I know some women who have dallied in these websites for fun, but it must take a ton of time to look through all these profiles." She leaned in again to look at the screen. "How old do you need to be to be called a senior, and is there another term for real old? And what's the difference between elderly and senior?"

My eyes widened in amusement. "You're asking me? I am flying blind here and never gave it much thought, although, I do like the name *senior*, not elderly. The name and description of aging has changed now that we are living longer. I can't keep up with the new descriptions and categories." I stopped scrolling through the photos and rubbed my burning eyes. "Are we out of touch with the modern world, Milly?" I moved my shoulders back and forth and began scrolling again.

"Maybe. And I hate to say this, but that means Merle is better with change than we are, and that scares the hell out of me." A corner of her mouth hitched up. "I've got to admit, I am fascinated with these photos. I never saw so many men looking for matches in one place. I guess Merle is right. Most seniors, like younger people, are finding love online."

"Let's see if there's a search bar where we can find a match for Krappy. There must be one to weed out possible matches from what looks like thousands of members. Looks like this is a site that is world-wide." Merle had given me a copy of Krappy's profile. I chuckled as I read it out loud to Milly. *"Hello. I am a younger-looking, attractive sixty-nine-year-old businessman in finance, looking for a woman who thinks and acts younger than her age. I do not care if she is older than me, only that she enjoys cuddling, romantic adventures, staying at first class hotels, drives a luxury car, and has no responsibility to animals or children so we can travel on the spur of the moment. I am open to a long-term relationship and enjoy wooing a woman in the manner she deserves. If you fit this description, email me."*

"Damn," Milly muttered. "He's straight to the point. Karl, or Krappy, the name that sticks, thanks to you, knows just how to attract a woman to fit his needs. He has a way with words. A businessman looking to con women out of their money. I wonder how many replies he gets and how he homes in on the neediest. Krappy's profile says it all. He's looking for a woman, unencumbered by family or animals and has money. And enough for traveling in the style he expects." She sat back in the chair and sighed. I expected her to shake her hands into a pooh-pooh manner to chase away Krappy's bad karma. Instead, she leaned forward and nudged me. "And better still, is his wording, *I do not care if she is older than me.*" Milly snickered. "That's exactly what attracted Merle to his profile. She's always on the lookout for younger men."

I nodded in agreement. "I know. She thinks she is forever young. Honestly, Milly, the picture of Krappy and Merle, and why they hooked up is very clear. I'm getting more and more annoyed at Merle for drawing me into something she created for herself. And it's a good thing I didn't mention the horses, Oscar, or my still unnamed cat on my profile. I'm feeling a strong desire to quit the whole thing. Krappy is a creepy guy." I sat back and ran my fingers through my hair. A feeling of trouble washed over me. And it wasn't good trouble.

Milly rolled her chair back and got up. "Time for a bathroom break," she said, walking away. "And I think it's too late to back out now. I, for one, find it entertaining and maybe that's how you need to think about it."

She was far enough away that she didn't hear me cussing under my breath. She was right, of course, and she knew me well. I would never drop something I started, but I did need to find the humor in it, or it would drive me crazy. But, first things first. Try and find the dating site Krappy is lurking on, and, if we can't, at least I can tell Merle that I did my best and, hopefully, she'll be satisfied. But the unanswered question to her is if we find him, what is her next step? My role is to find him if possible, and her role is to take it from there and I need to make this very clear. Maybe I needed to be more like Milly and not worry about it. Just see it as a fun thing to do. Reading all the profiles and seeing photos of seniors full of vigor and looking for love might be interesting. I hoped I didn't see a picture of anyone I knew, especially if he or she was married. It made me wonder how many married men were on dating sites. I bet a lot. Maybe it puffed them up to find women who still found them attractive. I suddenly had the feeling I was diving into parts unknown. My mind began filling with all sorts of visions. I remembered seeing a documentary about a man who lived two separate lives until someone who knew his wife turned him in after seeing his profile on a dating app. I was still musing with all sorts of crazy thoughts when Milly returned. "I'm back. Let's finish this up."

"My turn for a bathroom break," I said scooting away from the desk. "While I'm up, can I get you anything, like, coffee or tea?"

"No, thank you. Let's sign up for the other two websites and be done for today. We set the bait and now we wait. Hey, I just made a rhyme," she laughed.

On the way back to my office, I made a side trip to the kitchen and picked up two bottles of water. I handed one to Milly before I sat down. "Time to down a bottle of water and finish up. We need to stay hydrated."

Milly set the bottle on the table next to her. She frowned and rolled her chair closer to me. "Why, are we in a desert, or do you plan on sitting here longer than I'd like?"

"No, it's just that time passes quickly, and we need to drink something other than coffee and tea." I twisted the top off the bottle and took a long sip. "I am as ready as you are to call it quits after we apply for membership on the last two sites. And, besides, my eyes need a rest. I just used some drops to stop the burning. We'll finish up then get out of here before someone we don't want shows up." I typed in the next name, *Seniors with Gusto*, '*The Dating Site for Seniors with Get-Up-and-Go.*'

Milly's need to avoid Merle at all cost went skyrocketing. "Hold on." She grabbed my hand "You don't think Merle will show up, do you? She has a habit of doing that."

I felt my lips pull into a tight smile. It was fun watching Milly's reaction at the possibility of Merle barging in before we finished our search for Krappy. "Well," I said, bemused, "it's a possibility, so we better get with it."

Always contained and calm, Milly looked like a cat on a hot tin roof. "Well, if she does, you can count on me leaving right away, and I'll text you when I get to the Brown Dog Tavern." She was already planning her getaway.

"Okay. I'm ready to finish up before any interruptions," I chuckled. "And I just thought of something to relieve your mind. If Merle drives by, she'll see your car and think we are on a trail ride. And you know how much she wrinkles her nose when we even mention horses. I think we are safe to finish up."

"Good thought." Milly took in a deep breath and relaxed. "What's the next site we're signing up to?"

Seniors with Gusto, Over Sixty Elite Dating Site, with the subtitle, *Energetic Seniors Looking for Love.*

I clicked on the name, and it opened to a page with a colorful background of seniors on adventures of all sorts. Camping, fishing, backpacking, skiing, tours of wineries, the Eiffel Tower, and more. It was dazzling and I wondered how anyone would have this much energy, never mind, seniors. I was in awe and a bit stunned.

Milly started laughing. "I don't know how anyone has the

time and energy for love after all that activity. I would be ready for bed. And, I mean, *bed and sleep*."

I laughed out loud but tried to stop myself before I fell apart. "OMG! This is really funny. I can't imagine Merle on this site. She'd be in fear of messing her hair or chipping her nails, or worse. She is certainly not the right profile for this page, but from what she told me about Krappy, this may be the perfect one for him. Merle said Krappy had a lot of energy." Milly's eyebrows lifted and her eyes grew large with amusement. I could see she was trying to hold herself back from peeling over with laughter. "Stop it, Milly. I can't keep going if we can't control ourselves." Milly placed her hand over her mouth to stop, but when I said, "Merle told me she didn't take him up on any of the outdoor physical activities he suggested, and she said he was content to take her lead."

"Are you implying that she only wanted indoor physical activities because that *does* sound like Merle."

That did it for me. I had to stop. I couldn't concentrate, never mind, talk. We got up from our chairs and left the office and gave in to uncontrollable hysterics. When we were spent from laughing, I handed Milly a tissue and we returned to my office where I finished typing in my membership information. "What's the next site we need to enroll in?" I asked, trying to be more serious and composed.

"Seniors with Spirit," Milly replied, biting her lip to control herself and remain focused.

I opened the page to Seniors with Spirit. Once again, the page background was filled with smiling faces of seniors staring into each other's eyes, holding hands, snuggling and more. The subtitle was *'Are you looking for pleasure with spirited intentions?'* I sat back in my chair and stared at the subtitle. I glanced at Milly. Her brows were furling, and I knew she was trying to decipher the subtitle too. "What kind of seniors have spirited intentions, and what does that mean anyway?" Visions of seniors frolicking and spooning flooded my mind. I mumbled, "Stop!" and pinched my lips together to stay on task. I didn't believe I could stand another minute on these silly websites, and I knew if I didn't stop myself I would keel over with laughter and never complete the form.

Milly appeared as confused as me by the site's description. She leaned back in the chair, thinking about the subtitle. A puzzled look washed over her face and her voice turned serious. "The only thing I can think of, Izzy, is that this is a double entendre. The wording sounds serious and may mean *'are you ready to find a soul mate'*, but another meaning may imply a sexual connotation that is too awkward to write. I think this is a site where member profiles will tell us more." She pushed back her chair and got up. "This has certainly been a learning experience, and a lot more than I expected, to put it mildly." She smoothed back her hair and twisted the navy-blue tie tighter. The Brown Dog is calling me, and I don't want to spend any more of my day exploring dating sites. I have laughed enough to last a lifetime."

I rubbed my forehead. I didn't realize this would be so exhausting and crazy. "I agree. My mind is frazzled, and I can't take looking at one more picture of energetic men with spirited intentions searching for their soul mate." I moved my shoulders back and forth. "Too much time staring at a computer screen is bad for the back and legs, and at this point, for the brain."

Milly suppressed a wry smile. "Duly Noted."

After finishing my membership page, I logged out of *Seniors with Spirit* and closed my laptop. "We are done with Krappy for today. Maybe tomorrow, there'll be a few emails from men interested in my profile. Then we can check out their photos and see if they look anything like Krappy." I lifted myself from my chair. "Give me a minute to change into jeans and sweatshirt. I still need to shop for the book club birthday gift and my stomach is rumbling for food. Too much coffee and not enough sustenance isn't a good habit. My trainer Jackie would have a fit if I told her that donuts, coffee, and more coffee were my breakfast of the day."

It didn't take long to change from my sweats to jeans and slip on a passable dark blue sweatshirt. I dropped my slippers by the bed and pulled on my warm mukluks. Yesterday was a treat, but winter hasn't finished with us yet. The wind had picked up and the outside temperature of forty- five degrees felt more like twenty. I tossed a treat to Oscar and spoke to him in my doggy voice. "I'll be back soon. Don't wait up for me." I smiled at him.

Oscar tilting his head to the side told me he understood what I was saying and believed it. That made me wonder if any strange men who actually chomp on our lure will buy anything I'm saying just as easily.

*M*illy and I found a parking spot close to the Rose Flower Boutique. The last gasp of winter was smattering us with gusts of cold air and a sun that couldn't break through heavy clouds long enough to warm a groundhog. Spring was teasing us, weaving in and out like a wispy silk scarf, and I was growing very weary of winter's dark, cold days and the need for heavy coats. We rushed to the shop and entered. The bell at the top of the door jingled, and the shop owner Phyllis greeted us with a cheery hello. After a moment of chatter, we quickly moved to her beautifully displayed shop. In the short drive, we had discussed a few ideas for the ideal gift and settled on a piece of jewelry or a scarf. Either would be perfect.

I finally settled on a green silk scarf with small white flowers that reminded me of my Magnolia tree just beginning its spring bloom.

After paying, we said our goodbyes to Phyllis, and hastily settled in the car for the drive to the Brown Dog.

"I'm famished," I said to Milly as I started the car. "A late lunch-early dinner is beckoning me."

Milly turned the heat on high, even though we would be at the tavern before we felt the warm air. "Uh-huh. Sounds good to me. A whiskey sour to warm my blood and linner. I'm thinking chicken pot pie would hit the spot right now."

Linner was a new name for a combined lunch and dinner in our vocabulary, but the book club ladies laughed when I told them I had heard it and now used it. "Don't you wonder who came up with that name, Milly? Linner, linner, linner. The name linner flows off the tongue. At the last book club gathering, I told the ladies the new definition, but they said it sounded foolish and they wouldn't use it." *Just call it a late lunch or early dinner. Why does it need a name?"*

"I was a little disappointed that they pooh-poohed the name. I told them I was so intrigued that I Googled the Urban Dictionary to learn more about the definition. But their curiosity wasn't piqued, so they returned to discussing the book. Can you believe it? Their interest in learning something new is that of a gnat."

Milly let out an exasperated sigh. "This is why I refuse to join your club. They are too stuck in their ways. Damn, Izzy, promise we will never get that way. Closed to new ideas and thinking. We must keep evolving. I personally think most of the book club ladies are smart enough but are they wise enough? And even though linner isn't common yet, we are using the word and maybe we are ahead of our time. I like that," she grinned. "It's so simple. We have brunch, a combination of breakfast and lunch, so why not name the combination of lunch and dinner, linner? Most seniors combine lunch with dinner anyway. People don't want to eat after six o'clock anymore. We're all on diets or whatever."

I nodded in agreement. "Honestly, Milly, I enjoy the ladies and being in a book club encourages me to read books that I would not pick for myself. I have learned a lot listening to the members and find their company enjoyable. We've been meeting for fifteen years. However, I admit that Merle can annoy me. She shares far too much, but they get her back on track. Most times she reads the book, but her interpretations of it are usually very different from ours. Since she started dating Krappy in Boston, she wasted a lot of our time talking about him. When their romance was in bloom, she shared intimate details and the ladies loved listening about her dates and her after-dessert. She bragged incessantly about what a great lover Krappy was and how young he made her feel. That was bad enough to listen to, but now at meetings, all she talks about is what a lousy lover he was and how happy she is that he is no longer in her life. Of course, she wants revenge. She is exhausting. At the next meeting I think we should make a rule that she only gets ten minutes to talk. And now I fear that she will be talking about me and online dating. They will want to know all the details. *She* may be an open book, but *I* am not, and it's only because she guilted me into helping her that I'll be the center of attention this time."

Milly said nothing and that said everything. She lived by the motto, *"If you can't say anything nice, don't say anything at all."* Milly shrugged. "I suggest you leave her out of it, and this should be your agreement with her, or you won't help. Tell her you'll let her know when you need her input; otherwise, do not bother you. And I'd be adamant about it."

"You are so right. I alluded to this when I agreed to help her, but she has a way of turning a deaf ear and only hearing what she wants to. Before I go any further, I am going to have a serious talk with her and tell her if she breaks these terms, I am out."

"And don't let her guilt you into letting her be in charge. You set the terms."

The Brown Dog Tavern sat on the corner of Vine and Elm Street. The parking lot was to the right of the old brick building, and it looped around to the back. "Let's see if we can find a parking spot close to the door. It's four o'clock, and we're just in time to beat the crowd."

We pulled into the parking lot, already crowded with vehicles. "Guess everyone has the same idea," she said, her eyes scanning the area. We were almost to the end of the lot when she pointed her finger at a spot between two vehicles. "There's a spot. Can you squeeze in?" I eased my car into the tight space and turned it off.

We hurriedly exited and quickly jogged to the door of the Brown Dog. Opening the door, we were hit by a blast of warm air and the clinking sound of glasses.

My mouth began to water as I watched a server pass by with a plate of fresh baked bread and small bowls of dips. "Do we want to share appetizers or are you in the mood for the special of the day?"

Milly's attention was on finding a booth. "Let's head to the back and grab that empty booth before someone else takes it. It's away from the door. Then we can decide on food once our drink orders are in."

"Good thinking," I whispered as I followed her.

We passed the bar and made our way to the last booth. Three bartenders were busy taking drink orders and setting plates of piled-high chicken wings in front of regulars who stopped at the tavern at least once a week. The Brown Dog was noted for its variety of chicken wings and ten dipping sauces. The blue cheese dipping sauce is my favorite, and seeing and smelling the plates of wings made my choice of appetizer easy. Appetizers varied weekly, with at least one special a month. Customers voted on their favorite starter; if one did not get a substantial number of votes, it was replaced with a new dish. Milly slid into the booth, and I followed on the opposite side of the table. The tavern was beginning to fill with people looking for a familiar place to gather for drinks and food.

"I love this tavern and that it's local. Even though it can be noisy, sometimes I enjoy being with lots of people."

Milly smiled wide, nodding in agreement. "It's my favorite. My second is the Whiskey Sour Tavern. You can't go wrong with either. It all depends on what you're in the mood for. You really like the Carriage House, too, right?"

I picked up the menu, looking for the specials of the month. "I do. It's not busy before dinner hour, and I enjoy a break from my office. I find it's a good place to plot my next story. I usually bring my laptop. It helps me gain a new perspective. Isolation in my office only goes so far, then I need to be around people."

"I know the feeling. I can only be alone for only so long and then I crave company."

"The Carriage House is quieter, and Dale, you met him, makes the best martinis, and knows just how I like them."

I scanned the room, looking for anyone familiar. Thank goodness Merle was not inclined to frequent either of the places Milly and I liked. She preferred the Carriage House for dinner and was not fond of taverns. Although she would never admit it, Merle was an elitist with a snobbish taste. We slipped into the booth, and Bill, who we both knew, arrived to take our drink orders. The tavern, still standing since the 1800s, was noted for Dirty Martinis and craft beer. We ordered beer and a plate of wings with sides of dipping sauces. "Those wings looked so good when we came in and a frosty mug of beer fits just right. I love the blue cheese dipping sauce. Have you decided what you want to eat?"

Milly was studying the menu, then closed it and pushed it aside. "Yes. I wonder why we even look at the menu. We know it by heart, except for the weekly specials or a new appetizer." She shrugged her coat off and laid it next to her on the seat.

I had removed mine before sitting down and hung it on the hook next to the booth.

Bill returned with our beer and announced our wings would soon follow.

We toasted to a well-done day, and I added, "Here's to an early conclusion to the hunt for Krappy, whether we find him or not." I drew a long sip of beer and set the mug on the table. I glanced at the bar and noticed it was packed with customers, stools filled, and some standing behind. My eye caught two men we knew sauntering toward our booth. The taller man was Gus Olmstead, a widower I had met a few years ago while working on a political campaign for a friend. He's also a local artist. Many of his watercolors hang in the town shops. Gus is a tall, rangy, seventy-three-year-old retired accountant who worked for the FBI. His wife died a year after my husband, and we often talked about our spouses and how much we missed them. Gus is a horse lover, too, and when we have time, we tack up the horses and ride the trails behind my farm, and when I'm busy, he rides alone. In return, he mucks stalls, and helps stack hay in the summer. Gus also checks fences and repairs them as needed. A man of many talents, he got my old tractor running again when I was about to dump it and buy a new one. He has a rugged, handsome face that's easy on the eyes, and I must admit that if I were younger, I would have considered pursuing him. His gray hair was usually tousled spilling over his ears or hidden under a ball cap. He told me that he promised himself that he would never get his hair close cut again after retirement. But it was his alert, piercing blue eyes that I found most appealing. If someone were to ask me his best trait, I would say that his face always held a smile that welcomed you in. It was easy to see why he attracted a woman's interest. As he came closer, I could see he was dressed in his usual casual wear of jeans, western boots, and his well-worn leather jacket.

His friend Bob Earley was with him. Bob was close to eighty and didn't look a day over seventy. Sadly, his wife was in an assisted living facility suffering from dementia. He and Gus hung out often, playing cards, going to sports games, and mostly eating out. Gus had told me he lacked cooking skills and preferred to eat out or happily join our monthly friend's dinner. Gus and Bob were like Milly and me—best buddies and company for each other.

"Milly, Gus, and Bob are heading our way."

Milly turned to look as they moved closer to our booth. "I don't see another booth empty, and the bar looks full. Do you want to ask them to join us?"

"Of course. I don't see any empty booths and I haven't seen Gus for a couple of weeks. I think he's been in Florida with his daughter's family for a well-deserved vacation. It's something we should consider this winter."

Milly nodded in agreement. "We need to plan better. I'd like to head south in March of next year."

"Hey, young ladies," Gus said, smiling. "What brings you out on another beautiful day in New England?"

"Same as you. Fun and drinks," I replied, jokingly. "And Milly and I loved the cold wind snapping at our faces as we ran in. How 'bout you two? I haven't seen you around in a while. Did you head to Florida with your family?"

"Yup. Just got back Monday. We took the kids to Disney for a few days and the rest of the time stayed at their condo and used the pool. Got to the beach twice. It was great to get out of the cold, but I'm glad to be home," he chuckled. "Those kids have more energy than I can keep up with for more than two weeks."

I nodded. "I sure know that feeling. After a week, I am exhausted and wonder how I managed a family and work years ago. Wish I had the same energy as I did then."

Gus's eyebrows were raised in amusement. "What're you talking about? Aren't you a gym fanatic, and aren't you the one pushing me to join? You should have twice as much stamina as me. And I see you ride horses and lift hay. You ain't no weakling, that's for sure."

I lifted my glass to toast his teasing complimentary words.

"Thanks for your support. Now that you're home are you thinking of joining? The gym has a special price for new members to celebrate their ten-year anniversary."

"Let me think about it. Doc said I *should* exercise more. Gotta keep the body in shape." He grinned. "And with spring here, maybe I should get in better shape for the greens. Enough of that. How are the horses doing? Bet you were out riding yesterday with the teasing day of warmer weather."

"Gus, are you deflecting?"

"You got me there, Izzy." His blue eyes crinkled at the edges, and he gave a lopsided grin.

"Okay. I'll see you at the gym next week," I said, not counting on it. "But talking, "horses," you are right about that. Milly and I took Speed and Maverick out for a short ride yesterday. They seemed to enjoy it as much as we did. Even Speed picked up his pace. Warmer days are coming, and you are welcome to ride any time. Or just stop by and bring them some treats. They always look forward to that."

"I'll be taking you up on that and call you. So, make some time, and we can hit the back trails."

We bantered for a few more minutes. Horses were our common connection, and we had the same sense of humor. Grieving the loss of our loved ones had made us fast friends. We understood each other's pain.

"And you, Bob? How are you?" Milly asked. "Did you take a winter vacation?"

Bob shrugged his shoulders. "Too damn many doctor appointments to make plans. I need to be smarter about when I make them so I can do some traveling."

Milly nodded. "I didn't take a winter vacation either, but I am planning to stay at the Cape for a few weeks this summer. Izzy and I were just talking about heading south to break up the winter next year. The cold, gloomy days really took a toll this winter. I think Covid changed everything. Those two years of worry and isolation have changed all our thinking."

"Okay," I said. "Change of subject. Let's talk about food and drinks." Talking about the two years of despair felt too heavy for me to lean into.

The mingling of voices got unmistakably louder. Seems that everyone had the same idea.

Bill, our waiter, arrived carrying a tray of wings and dips, and Gus and Bob moved aside so he could set the plates on the table.

I asked Gus and Bob if they'd like to join us.

"Thanks, ladies, we'd love to," Gus replied, motioning to Bob.

Milly and I moved so they could slide in.

"So, what can I get you two gentlemen?" Bill asked.

"Beer, and I'll have the same as they're drinking," Gus said to Bill.

"Make it two," Bob said.

"You got it," Bill said. "Have you decided on what you're going to order yet, or do you want me to come back?"

Gus looked at me. "We were thinking wings and pizza, but do you ladies have something else in mind?"

"What do you think, Milly? Pizza does sound good. I could do with pizza and more wings."

"Agree," she nodded, placing her mug of beer down on the table. "When I first came in, I was thinking chicken pot pie, but wings and pizza sound perfect with draft beer."

An hour later, we had finished two orders of wings and a sizable stone-baked pizza.

Gus and Bob ordered another round of beer, and we spent the next hour catching up on life events. As I listened to Gus and Bob talk, a thought occurred to me. Although Gus had been only an accountant in the FBI, he may have some insight he could share with us on Krappy. So, I decided to tell him about Merle, how she was conned out of her money and ask if he had any ideas we could pursue. "Gus, can I run something by you concerning our friend? I know you were an accountant at the FBI, and your professional point of view may help me. It's about money that she was cheated out of."

Milly's eyebrows raised. I wasn't sure if she was surprised that I would ask Gus's opinion on Merle and Krappy or because I had said "*our* friend." I quickly turned away from her questioning eyes. "You can say no, but I think with your professional background, although not an investigator, you can give me some needed advice."

Gus gave me a puzzled look. "Sure. I will help, if I can. What's going on?"

Gus listened intently to my shortened version of Merle's tale of woe. He and Bob almost choked on their beer when I tole them I'd renamed the man known as Karl Hendricks—Krappy Karl. "Seriously. Karl *deserves* the name Krappy. And I'd call him something worse, but Krappy fits just fine. You guys get the picture, don't you? He *is* a crappy man who did crappy things to my friend," I said with a growl.

Bob's eyebrows raised, and I could tell he was on the verge of laughing and was trying hard to remain serious. A smile pinched the corner of Gus's eyes each time I said the name. Finally, a chuckle started deep in Bob's belly and grew louder until he could hold back no longer.

Then Gus began to laugh, and Milly and I joined in. I don't know if it was the name Krappy or the whole damn crazy story about Merle being duped by a loser lout, but Krappy Karl had us all in stitches, and even more when I announced I had joined four dating sites to try and find him. Gus gained control first, then his expression grew grim, and a stunned look crossed his face. His eyes met mine as I wiped the tears from my cheeks. "You didn't *really* join a *dating* site, did you? *Tell me* you're kidding," he said, not even bothering to mask his surprise...nor the subtle shades of disappointment, if I'm not mistaken. He *knew* this wasn't a real search for love.

Before I could answer, Milly chimed in. "Yes, yes, she did. She *always* falters under the pressure and jumps in to bail Merle out of one predicament after another."

Gus raised an eyebrow in disbelief. "Forgive me, Izzy, but I just can't picture you joining an online dating site. It takes *a lot* to put yourself out there, and it doesn't seem like your kinda thing at all." I immediately saw him rethinking the words he'd just spit out. He quickly blurted, "I mean, you *are* a very attractive, interesting woman, but to meet up with strange men, just to find Krappy?" He grinned, studying my reaction. "That takes a certain amount of intention."

Bob and Milly sat listening, seemingly, waiting for my response. My mind immediately went to, *Is Gus concerned or does he think I'm not up for the job?*

Milly's brows lifted. She saw me hesitate and knew I was rolling his words around in my brain.

So, what? Now it's about me and not Krappy. I didn't want to overreact, but Gus's opinion of me counted.

The look of regret on Gus's face said he realized the spider's web he'd just stepped into. "No, no, no. Don't get me wrong, Izzy. But, I've known you for some time now, and you always gave me the sense that you're not interested in dating *anyone,* never mind, a stranger. Everyone knows you're not available. I'm just surprised, that's all."

I quirked my lips. "Guess you surprised me with how

you see me. And who is *everyone,* exactly? Gus." Now I had *him* cornered, but I was feeling defensive. Since my husband died, it's true, I've had no intention of dating, but since a young girl, I've always been comfortable hanging out with boys, and I enjoy their company, just as I do now. I can take their joking and teasing and have no problem returning it. But was I the topic of conversation when I wasn't with them? My mother's words flashed through my mind. *"We never see ourselves as others do. Take a long, hard look in the mirror."* Was I just a cranky widow? I thought I was fun to be with but dating scares the bejeezus out of me. Worse still, if Gus is correct, how would I ever handle meeting a man I had no idea how to connect with, and flirt with, to gain information? Maybe this is not for me, and I should cancel everything. How can I pretend to enjoy a date when my friends believe I'm not up to the task? Doubt began to soar through me. If men see me as unapproachable, how will I ever be able to con a con?

Gus reached across the table and placed his hand over mine. He looked genuinely concerned about what he had said. "Izzy. You are my friend, and I don't want you to get into something that will make you uncomfortable. Is Merle truly worth leaving your comfort zone?"

Oh no. I can't take Gus feeling sorry for me. He sees me as insecure and fragile. Get a grip, Izzy. But I hated the thought running through my mind that the man I enjoyed being with, riding horses with, and laughing with, was seeing me as *weak* or worse yet, *boring.*

Milly knew by my tone of voice that I was questioning myself and it was time to break in, as she interjected, "Listen, Gus. Izzy is no shrinking violet. Anyone with her background and common sense is up for the job. Plus, I am her backup. I'm going to keep an eye on her, and we're in this together. She's not alone and we are both up to the challenge."

Gus's eyes twinkled with amusement. "Fair enough. So, how can I help?"

Bob sat quietly, taking it all in. He took another swig of beer and leaned forward. "Well, after listening to all of this, I agree with Milly and Izzy." A slight smile crossed his lips. "Gus, I don't think these two need to hear your doubts or unease about how Izzy will hold up dating men she meets online. What they can use is your input. You did work as an accountant for the FBI, and this is about money, something you have experience with understanding. And, you may have some expertise to share with them." Bob was making sense and I appreciated his advice. The heated exchange between Gus and me took a backseat. "Once more, after hearing about this guy Krappy, I'm angry too, and interested in seeing if they can find the jerk, who by the way has earned the damn name. No man should be allowed to swindle a woman out of her hard-earned money. Maybe you can use your old contacts and get some insider information on how many seniors on dating sites are bilked out of money? And I would bet there are men as well who are scammed too. I never gave it a thought till I heard the Krappy story."

Milly and I nodded our agreement. Gus's eyes and mine locked in a stare. I wasn't sure what it meant, but I held his gaze until he looked away. He looked down at his folded hands, then choosing his words carefully, he looked at me again. "Bob's right. I've been retired for a few years now, but I still have some contacts and I can send out some feelers. It's a white-collar crime, and difficult to take legal action if a man or woman freely gives the money to scammers like Krappy." I felt my mouth quiver into a half smile as Gus said the name, Krappy. We were all using it now. "Most folks are probably too embarrassed to report it. Don't want their kids or friends to know they were conned. But in this case, you have Merle trying to find the guy. Or should I say, she has Izzy and Milly trying to. But, what then? Have you decided what action you will take if you *do* manage to flush him out?"

Milly eyeballed me as if I had all the answers. Truthfully, I knew I didn't. I had contemplated the vague possibility that I might uncover Krappy's new identity when I first agreed to help Merle. But, what then? I had brushed away my concerns if that scenario happened with my gut feeling that he was long gone and we'd never find the scoundrel. I only decided to help Merle because I couldn't take her hounding me, and the book club ladies sided with her. Plus, I knew other women out there were just sitting ducks, and it made me sick. On the other hand, this was like finding the proverbial needle in a haystack, and Gus was only admitting what was sitting in the back of my mind. What if we *do* uncover where Krappy has set up a new con? What do we do then? "Well to be honest, Gus, in the remote possibility that he responds to my profile, it's up to Merle to figure out what to do next. I have no idea. I told her I would join the dating sites, but I promised nothing after that. And this is only a short-term project for me. I'm only doing this for a month or so. If I don't find him by then, I don't think I ever will. I am not wasting my time meeting up with Krappy lookalikes when I have other things to do."

Milly nodded her approval. "Well, I for one, am all in.

And, Gus, don't be so hard on Izzy. You don't know Merle. She is like a dog with a bone. She will hound Izzy for the rest of her days to do this." I knew by Gus's expression he was still finding the whole plan amusing. And it was more about me dating than finding Krappy. Only Bob showed seriousness by his solemn face and demeanor. Milly leaned forward and looked squarely into Gus's eyes. "And, I will never leave Izzy alone, and I will check every guy who replies to her profile. We will scan everything he says, and have Merle check out the guy first to see if there is a resemblance to Krappy."

Gus straightened. For a moment, he said nothing. I wished I could read his mind. Then, he leaned forward, placed his hands on the table and smiled. "Well, sounds like you ladies have it all figured out, but I'm glad you ran this by me. Just keep me updated, and I'll let you know when or if I hear something back from my contacts." His eyes met mine. His face was somber and still held a concerned look I had never seen before. Our friendship was always fun and easy. "And, Izzy, I don't doubt your ability to take this on. I have confidence you will make it work and I am sure you will have many tales to tell us after meeting up with crappy men for coffee." The beginning of a smile softened his concern look. "Plus, Izzy, I'm *sure* you will get a lot of responses from men looking for love. I mean, just look at your photo!"

I could feel my face flush. My throat worked around a small, tight swallow.

"Even though you say it's a younger version of you, you still look the same to me. Take it from me, you are a strikingly attractive woman. If you were available," he grinned, "I'd ask you out on an official date myself."

What? Was he serious or jesting? No, no, I knew he was only kidding, but that was out of the blue. We discussed my feelings about dating again before, and his feelings were the same. He wasn't ready either. I have no energy or time to get to know a man. Seems too exhausting to meet new family and friends. I like my life just the way it is. Besides, I've found most men needy, except for my late husband. He spoiled me. Another man could never match up. I mean, look what happened to Merle—canoodling with men from dating sites. I flipped the subject. Redirecting uncomfortable conversations, that's how I operate. "Did you guys know there are high-end sites that cater to well-heeled seniors? Merle is a Diamond Member of Silver Love. These elite senior dating hot spots are exclusive and pricey to join. She said people can be matched up according to wealth, profession, and status, and Silver Love feels safer and more secure because it costs so much."

Bob wiped beer foam from his mouth and set his mug back down on the table. "Well, we see where that got her. Safer? Please. Her good friend Krappy just conned her out of money, and he was supposedly "*safer*" because he matched her needs on this "elite" dating site? Gimme a break. It's exactly the site swindlers would join. If *I* wanted to fleece someone, I sure wouldn't waste my time on some free site. I'd go right where the rich ladies are and zero in on who likes to travel or owns extravagant real estate. It only makes sense."

Milly and Gus nodded in agreement.

"I can see that," Milly said. "Merle did say on her profile that she loves luxury resorts and traveling in style. And you know, she owns a condo on Bolton Street in Boston where she and Krappy stayed during his supposed courtship. Thankfully, she never told Krappy about her deluxe condo in the town next to ours, or Izzy's made-up profile would never work. Merle screams money, in her home, clothes, and travel. I bet, Gus, that in FBI lingo, she would be called a mark."

Gus's penetrating blue eyes held a spark of mischief when he looked from Milly to me. His voice was a low rumble as he asked, "So, Izzy, did you copy Merle's profile when you joined these sites then? Or add a video introduction?"

I knew he was baiting me, and my smile tightened for a moment. Two can play this game. I paused then smiled sweetly. "Yes, we thought I should use her profile, with a few changes to make it about me. I need to stick as close to who I am without turning Krappy off. Of course, no mention of horses and kids. And I did not post a video, no. I like to meet my men in person." I grinned wickedly.

Milly chose to save me from myself, changing the subject. "Izzy, remember when we stayed at the hotel in Florida and there was that guy, full of himself, prancing around the pool, always on the lookout for a woman? We nicknamed him, "The most interesting man in the world" because he thought he was." Milly's nose wrinkled in disgust as she told the story.

Bob and Gus feigned interest in the narrative.

"And, guys, for your information, he was at the pool every day. He couldn't keep his eyes off Izzy. Strutting his stuff in his tiny tight swimsuit, by our chairs, every morning and nodding hello. You should have been there, Gus. I have never seen Izzy blush so much. And this guy was built, looked to be in his seventies. You know, *Gus,* Izzy is *quite* attractive in a swimsuit. Have you seen her?" Milly beamed.

His jaw tightened and brow crimped. "Uh, no, *no*, can't say

I've had the pleasure. Except for receptions we happen to be attending, our clothing of choice is casual, as today."

Bob rolled his eyes and smirked. He knew the game was on, and it was between Gus and me. The heat of Gus's gaze rattled me, but I couldn't stop teasing him.

"Oh my God, Milly! He thought he was so damn sexy. That's what happens when two women travel alone. The male wolves come out. But he wasn't my type. Bet Merle would find him attractive." Now I had Gus's attention. I glanced at Bob. His grin said he was enjoying the game. "But I'm ready to *pretend* I'm looking for love. I can do that. Now that we're talking *dating*, for everyone's information, *if* I were to date, for real, I'd pick a man with gentle brown eyes and lots of muscles so he could help at the barn." I laughed. "Of course, he'd have to like dogs, horses, and mean cats. He'd need to be intelligent, well-read, older than me, and more experienced in dating. He'd also have to know his way around the kitchen so I wouldn't have to do all the cooking, or subject him to just boxed desserts. And, most importantly, he'd need to care more for me than I did him. That's the only way I'd feel safe in his care." There. I said it. Most of what I described was *not* Gus, especially the caring part. Let him mull that one over.

Gus gave me a devilish grin. "Damn, Izzy. Never thought dating would've entered your mind, but you've clearly already considered what you want and need. I think you *are* ready to date again, and, *in a backhanded kinda way*, are using Merle's profile to sort of test the waters. And who knows, one of them may fit your wish list. If it works out for you, *I* may give it a try. My ideal date would be my age with grown children who likes horses and *enjoys* cooking." He was sure to stress that.

"So far, I've been out of luck. Seems like all the good women are taken. Not that I've actually been busy looking, but it'd sure be nice to know if there are options." His squinted eyes and playful simper as he studied me for something made my head tingle and neck feel warm.

Options? Gus was considering...*options?* Was *I* an option? What did he mean? Stalemate. We had met a stalemate. This cutesy volleying, bordering on flirtation, *maybe*, could go on forever. Our conversation was turning into part teasing, part serious nature, and I didn't even want to know the percentage of each. Given my unexpected reaction to this banter—a faster pulse and, indeed, butterflies, I knew I was way over my head with Gus. We'd never had this type of conversation before on the subject of romance, but it added a defined shift and new dimension to our friendship. And a tad bit of awkwardness. And...heat? Uh, *maybe?* Aw, what the hell. It didn't matter. For right *now*, I had to focus on two things: finishing my book and searching for Krappy. I didn't have the time, or the will, to spar with Gus anymore. But, something had changed.

Milly broke the standoff. "Okay, guys. It's been fun, but it's time for me to head home. My car is still at Izzy's, and I have some work to do, like paying the bills that have been sitting on my desk for a week. Are you all set?"

Bob motioned to Bill for the check. "I've really enjoyed this. We've got to do it again. Maybe we can meet here when Gus has information that will help you, Izzy. In the meantime, good luck finding Krappy."

"Thanks, Bob, for your words of support and thanks even more for joining us. The pizza was delicious, the beer was great and the company even better."

"I couldn't agree more," Milly said.

Gus stood up to let me slide out of the booth, and Bob handed his credit card to Bill, who'd arrived with the check.

Milly and I reached for our credit cards, too, but Gus held his hand up to stop us. "Treats on us, ladies," he insisted. "Payment for sharing the booth and giving Bob and me lots of laughs today. You two make a good team. And, yes, I'll keep you updated. It may take a week or two for me to hear back from my old friends, but I'll stay on this. And, one more thing, Izzy. Be careful. If you're looking for a man who defrauded your friend, you may find more trouble than you think."

I nodded. Sliding out of the booth, I grabbed my coat.

Gus stood behind and held it for me to put on. He leaned in close and whispered in my ear. "I'm always here if you need me, Izzy, any day, or any time. Please do not get in over your head. I am your friend. Don't forget it."

*O*n the drive to my home where Milly would pick up her car, we chatted about Gus and Bob and how valuable their input was. A crowded tavern, a chance meeting, and sharing a booth with the guys had opened a discussion and advice from two men whom I trusted and enjoyed being with. At first, I was skeptical about telling them about Merle's fiasco and my promise to help her. I wasn't sure if they would laugh at me for joining dating websites to try and lure Krappy, or if they thought it would be a fool's errand. But I was surprised at the support they gave me and even more pleased that Gus would reach out to some of his friends at the FBI. It was good to have two men, who were friends, and now, confidants, to reassure me that my plan was reasonable, if not a bit crazy. What *wasn't reassuring* was Gus's concern about me meeting men looking for love on dating sites. Even though I explained it was the only way to find Krappy, he was right. What then? If Merle couldn't take him to court to get back her money, what was the purpose of the whole thing?

After Milly left the driveway, I made my way inside the house, greeted by Oscar who rushed past me to skedaddle outside. Since he didn't even pause for my greeting or any welcoming pets, I knew he'd picked up the scent of an animal and I prayed it wasn't a skunk. A small herd of deer was scavenging branches from my apple tree. It was slowly becoming naked, and I doubted I'd have apples in the fall. Between the deer and a colony of rabbits, Oscar was continually on alert. The rabbits showed no fear and could scoot away faster than Oscar could come close to catching one. They were eating everything, and although I love animals, I was glad Oscar was able to scare them away.

I stood by the door and waited for Oscar to return. He ran past me, tail wagging, proud he chased the intruder away. After talking with Milly, Gus, and Bob, I realized there was much to absorb and more to plan than I expected. It was a lot to process. I headed to the kitchen, popped a K-cup into the coffee maker, and took out the half-and-half, still mulling over the conversation. Gus said, for now, I need to close my social media accounts. I wondered if I should snooze them for a month or delete them. Closing and opening each site would be a pain in the butt. One of my Facebook pages was for my books, which was essential. Wait a minute. Books? Oh, boy. I need to close everything down for at least a month. I headed to my office with my coffee to delete anything connected to my real name. Merle can pay for someone to open them again. I knew it would be time-consuming, and the thought of closing them made me angry and dismayed. All this work to find loser Krappy was becoming overwhelming, and I was rethinking my offer to help her. I backed everything up on an external hard drive but disliked deleting it all. Too late. I was already a member of several dating sites, and time was of the essence. I can't go back now. What happened to my quiet, organized life? Damn, Merle! I'm doing all the work to help her out of what? I quickly opened my social media sites to see if my pen name was posted anywhere. I'm not a FB fanatic and only use my page for photos. Yikes! Horses were all over it. I deleted my page, along with Instagram.

I worked for an hour, covering all the bases as Gus had suggested. Luckily, he had me write everything down before I left the Brown Dog. Gus had talked me through critical steps to guard my identity, schooling me on all I needed to do. I took a break and sat back. Whew! I was sure lucky to have a former FBI employee as a friend, even though he'd only been an accountant before retiring. Then I thought of something else. Oops. No one knew, except a few close friends and family, that my pen name for my books was Phoebe S. Malave. Thank goodness I used a pen name for writing.

I finished the checklist that Gus had me write down and was just about to close my laptop when I checked my new Gmail address to see if I had any activity from a lovesick member. I didn't think someone would be interested in my profile this quickly, but I needed to keep up with emails to ensure the plan worked and would have an end date. A month to me was long enough. I told Merle I would delete all my memberships at that point, and she had better not try and talk me into searching for her conman any longer than that. Opening the new Gmail address for the dating websites, I was startled to see I already had ten men interested in my profile. What? I couldn't believe it. I didn't know whether to laugh or cry. I felt like the chickens had come home to roost, and I was the hen house.

In my wildest dreams, I never thought my profile would be answered this fast. My stomach churned, and my fingers shook as I debated opening the emails. No. I was not doing this right now. I needed Milly to be with me when I read them. She was the one who had my back and would help me write the response after we read the invitation. I closed my laptop and walked away. It was barn time. The stray cat needed to be fed, and evening chores were waiting. But, more than that, I craved to be in my place of comfort, my barn. In other words, I wanted to be as far away as possible from Merle and Krappy and their twisted relationship.

I slid my arms into a warm jacket, stepped into my barn boots, pulled my knitted cap over my ears, and headed to the barn. I opened the barn door, and the black cat greeted me. I bent down to pet the fluffy stray weaving in and out of my legs. "Hi, Chip." She purred her acceptance of her new name as she rubbed against my leg, and I knew I had chosen the right one. Half laughing, I picked her up and held her close. She snuggled against me as I scratched her ears, tilting her head and purring louder. "So, you like the name, Chip? You came with a chip on your shoulder, angry and untouchable. Now look at you. A cat that likes to be cuddled. I never would have guessed that." It occurred to me that now that she had a name and a forever home in the barn, I could bring her into my confidence, and she would never repeat what I said. Since she made no move to jump from my arms, I began talking to a cat. I bet most animal owners do the same thing. "Now that you're an official family member, and I've named you, I would like to run something by you. You don't have to answer, just listen." Chip snuggled deeper into my arms and lifted her head to look at me. "OMG. I think you understand." There was no stopping me. Words spilled from my lips to a cat, no less. "Well, Chip, here's my huge concern. You're such a smart cat and a survivor. I'd like to think we're somewhat alike in that way, and, yippee, you no longer hate me. So, here goes." I had Chip's full attention and knew she wouldn't butt in with quick advice or give me a wide-eyed judgmental attitude. An audience of one cat to listen to my tale of woe but not give feedback was what I needed. It was time to empty my thoughts to a cat and the two horses staring at me, wondering what was happening. I poured my gut out to Chip, and listening to myself talk about everything from start to finish brought new questions to ask Merle that might help in the search for Krappy. Why hadn't she filled me in on her time with Krappy in Boston? Where did they go other than her bedroom? Did she ever go to *his* place? Did she ever meet any of his friends? What made her believe his con? After all, Merle wasn't that dumb, or was she? Did she ever check on where he once worked? After a short time, Chip grew bored listening to me rattle on and on, and she wiggled from my arms and jumped out of my arms and down onto the floor, where she walked away. This sudden departure didn't shock me because I, too, was tired of listening to my voice drone on and on, but crazy as it sounds, it had helped. The downside was that I was coming up with more questions than answers.

I finished my barn chores and returned to the warmth of my cozy living room. It was time to toss a few logs in the fireplace and enjoy a cup of hot chocolate. The last cold days of winter have passed, and according to the weather forecast, a warmup was predicted for next week.

I changed into my jammies and readied myself for a relaxing end of the day. The fire was glowing, Oscar was lying beside my chair, and I had a cup of hot chocolate on the end table. Life was once again uncomplicated and quiet. I was tempted to turn on the TV, but instead, I thought about the list of questions for Merle. I had grabbed a small yellow pad and pen before I sat down, and after another sip of hot chocolate and licking the marshmallow from my mouth, I began writing. There was too much I didn't know. I had a nagging feeling that I had glossed over what Merle had told me. Her story had too many missing pieces, but I rushed to join websites without the complete picture because I had been in a hurry to appease her. Did she do that on purpose? Or had I not asked the right questions? I am not a Private Investigator, so how would I know what questions to ask? But if I am going to get answers, I need to think more like a PI, not a friend. No wonder Gus had given me the "look." He believed I didn't have enough information from Merle to cause me to jump so quickly into finding Krappy. I took a sip of hot chocolate and added another question to the growing list. I placed the pen down and called Milly to see if she could stop by the next day to help me decipher the new emails. Next, I called Merle's cellphone and left a voice message asking her to meet me for dinner at the Carriage House. I had more questions for her.

Milly said she would be at my home early the following day, and we would check out the emails to see if any of the guys looked or sounded like Krappy. I would need to pass the photos on to Merle, but I wanted to interact with her as little as possible. She would be at my home twenty-four hours a day if I opened *that* door. An hour later, the fire was out, the last drop of chocolate in my cup was gone, and my list was completed. I was drained. It had been a long, insightful day, and I was ready for bed. I trekked up the stairs, Oscar at my side, feeling like I'd accomplished something today, but I wasn't sure what. Tomorrow would be an exciting X on the calendar, yet I was sure it would be my last day of rest for a good, long while.

I heard Milly's car pull into the driveway. After early morning barn chores, I ran to the local bagel shop and awaited her arrival. Before we opened any emails, I wanted to talk about our strategy over bagels and coffee. I wasn't sure if I was stalling, but I was.

Oscar bee-lined to the door to greet her when I opened it. "Off, Oscar!" I scolded. As old as he was, he still got excited when his friends arrived. Oscar had decided long ago that my friends were his best friends, and he did anything to get their attention.

Milly gave Oscar a friendly rub on his head. "Hey, buddy. How ya doing?" She was dressed lighter this morning. It was shocking how the weather had changed from windy and cold to sunny and warmer. It's not late spring weather, but it's warming up. I was ready for the change, as most people were.

"Hey, Milly. Thanks for coming by so early. Toss your jacket and cap on the chair in the living room and join me in the kitchen."

I was happy to see her. I needed her beside me when I opened the emails. I wasn't the most courageous soul to be doing this. My mug of coffee was sitting on the table where I'd left it. My first cup of the day wouldn't be my last. I'd refill mine as soon as Milly was all set with hers.

She came in and fixed her coffee while I popped the bagels into the toaster. "So, you got several responses last night?"

"Yup, but I haven't opened them yet."

The bagels popped up, and I placed them on our plates.

She leaned over the warm bagel and moved her hand to swoosh the delightful aroma to her face. "Ahhh. My favorite. French toast," she said as she reached for the cream cheese.

Mine was Snickerdoodle, and it smelled sweet. I smothered it with cream cheese. Neither of us spoke a word, preferring to bite into our crunchy, warm bagels first instead. We knew it was time to enjoy the moment because trouble lay ahead.

We finished breakfast, rinsed our plates, placed them in the dishwasher, and headed to my office, Oscar trailing behind. I wondered if he thought he could smell a rat online sooner than I could. Probably so. He's a better judge of people than I am. I opened my laptop and Milly pulled up a chair. To our amazement, there were even more emails in my account.

"What the hell! So many lonely men are out there looking for love. What in my profile attracted them exactly?" My hand hovered the mouse as I cringed at the bursting inbox. I shook my head, already overwhelmed. "Holy moly! It's like spaghetti. How will I ever be able to read and weed through so many responses just to find one that matches Krappy?" I looked at Milly, and she rolled her eyes.

"Oh, my Lordy loo! Did you go back in and add something

sexual after I left?" she teased. "You've been without a man for —how long it has been now?" In her count, her eyes tilted up.

I gasped and elbowed her arm. "Oh, for God's sake, Milly! We haven't even opened one and you're thinking the *only* reason they're interested me is for sex? Or that I'd sneak in some spicy teaser on the sly? I'm fine, thank you very much, and on a mission. Maybe they liked my photo or my profile, huh? Did that ever occur to you? Now you have me worried."

"Just read the damn emails. Can't wait to see what they say. This'll be the most fun I've had in a long time. Hurry up."

I double-clicked the first to open it. He looked nothing like Krappy. From Seniors with Gusto. *Hi. I'm Teddy. My lady friends call me Teddy Bear because I'm so huggable, and I have a ton of gusto. I love to camp and spend nights in the deep woods listening to the owls. I see from your profile it's what you enjoy also. Please email me back so we can plan some cozy trips and cuddle through the night."* The sender's pic was grainy, but he looked too old to be driving, never mind, camping, and cuddling with him was his crazy dream. I wondered how many replies he had received. "Ew, ew, no! *Delete.*" A puff of humor left my nose as I vanquished him.

"You mean you don't want to cuddle with *Teeedddy Bear* in the dark woods and listen to the owls? Hoo-hoo, coo-coo cachoo?" Milly couldn't hold back her peel of laughter.

"Please, Milly. I am begging you. Stop! Do not even get me started or we won't be able to get through all of these. But I guess you're right. This is kind of fun."

Sniffling to regain her composure, she said, "Kay. Just don't look at me if you don't want me to keel over with laughing. Open the next and let's read what he says."

"Okay, this one is from Perky Seniors.*"*

Milly lost it again, just at that name.

"Stop. Let me read it. *Hi, Izzy. How are you? I like your profile. Your photo is beautiful. You look great for sixty-nine. Never would've guessed. Is it current? I'd love to take you on a ski trip if it is. We could fly down the mountains of Aspen, sip martinis in my favorite lodge, head to a room with a fireplace, and enjoy room service. And each other. Can you keep up with me? If so, please email me back. Frank.*"

"I dunno, Izzy, *can you?*" Milly teased. "Keep up?"

"Oh, please. Even Speed could best him. I mean, *look.*" He *said* he was sixty-seven, but in his photo, he looked much, much older and he was very obese. I wondered how he could put shoes on, never mind, skis. Delete! I clicked the next response. It was from Seniors with Spirit. *Hi, Bonita. I'm so happy you've joined this dating site. You are someone I've been waiting for all my life. I am a spirited seventy-nine-year-old man who loves to travel on the spur of the moment, and I'm looking for a long-term relationship. I love to pleasure women and have been looking for the right one. You seem perfect. Can we meet? Georgio.* Too Latin in the pic. Delete!

"Milly, do you think they're *all* like this on these supposed "elite" dating websites?" I opened another from Seniors with Spirit and read it aloud. "*Hello, Izzy. My name is Omar, and I was impressed with your profile. I see you like to travel and go on spontaneous adventures. I only vacation at first-class hotels and can cuddle all day. And, like you, I enjoy long massages while overlooking the ocean. I am looking for a long-term relationship. Email me if I fit your heart's desire, Omar.* Oh my God, Milly," I gasped. "Look at this one. Does he resemble the description of Krappy? Only, this guy is bald with a mustache and beard. Sounds like Krappy's profile."

Milly moved closer to the screen to look. "Damn. I guess. Why doesn't Merle have any photos of this guy? You'd think."

"She said she was too busy, being *otherwise engaged*, and that he hated posing anyway, but she *did* have *one* a fellow jet-setter took of the two of them at a resort. She lost the SD card it was on after sending it in to Silver Love Success Stories through the contact form, and it weirdly never posted."

"Well, that is ridiculous, and this is asking too much. We are flying blind, trying to find a man matching the description she gave. Too many emails sound like him, except they don't match his description. I don't get it. What's wrong with these guys? Do they just copy other men's profiles because they can't think up one of their own? Honestly, Izzy. You need more information from her. She's out of touch with reality if she thinks you, and now me, can keep looking at bogus emails that may not even be him. It just doesn't make sense to me."

The pic of Omar was printing out as we spoke.

"Can't agree more. Reading all these is a waste of time and I'm gonna tell her so. It's probably a game to Merle, the big chase, but to me, it's a ton of work that I don't even have time for. She hardly gave me anything of worth. Aside from one holiday in the Bermuda where she got the picture, they only met, or I should say, *rendezvoused*, at *her* condo in Boston, and she had only been to his place once." I leaned over and took the photo from the printer, aggravated that I'd let Merle push me into a fool's errand. I handed the picture to Milly. "Hate to say it, but I'm beginning to dislike Merle and her arm-twisting. Is she my friend or, as you always say, a user?"

Milly glanced at the photo then at me. "Are we having a breakthrough here?"

I blew out a deep breath. I knew where she was going. She'd warned me about Merle since the two met, but she didn't share our history. Even though Merle was hard to take, my loyalty to her outdid loyalty to myself. Was I just a glutton for punishment? I ignored Milly's comment. "I'm writing down questions for Merle, and if she doesn't have any answers to help, I may just drop this whole crazy investigation."

Milly looked at me wide-eyed. "Now you're calling this an investigation? I think Merle got it right. She has you now thinking you're a PI," she chuckled. "I've gotta get goin' in a bit. You can fill me in when you get back from dinner with Merle. I hate to say it, but I think I'm as sucked in as you."

For the next hour, we sat reading emails from men, waiting for my reply. The more we read, the funnier it became, and soon, we both had tears of laughter running down our cheeks. The responses from these lovesick men made creating comic remarks about their photos or messages easy. I couldn't believe the explicit sexual content of some of the emails. Who are these elite single men? At one time, I had to get up and bring back a box of tissues. We had already gone through the box next to my laptop, and my stomach hurt from laughing so hard. Reading the emails was better than any Seinfeld episode I had watched. After a while, we both grew weary of the same song from different men and agreed to quit. We were through for the day. Enough already! My index finger was numb from pressing the delete key so many times.

As Milly and I left my office, we were still chuckling about the crazy emails from men looking for love. Or, so they said, but we both knew it was more than love they were searching for. As Milly left, I promised to call her as soon as I got home from meeting Merle and gained more vital information about Krappy Karl Hendricks. The biggest question I would *need* to ask was, why did she not have any photos of him if they spent *so* much time together that he could gain her trust *enough* for her to part with her money? Crazy!

I entered the door of the Carriage House Restaurant. The six o'clock dinner reservation patrons had yet to arrive. Merle and I chose to meet at four thirty since we had not made reservations, and she did not want to go to the Brown Dog Café or the Whiskey Sour Tavern. She considered both places not up to her standard for dinner. Since she said she was buying, I agreed to her choice. Merle clarified that this was a business meeting, and I was officially on her payroll. I wondered if that meant she was paying taxes and if I was earning sick time. Was I on the clock? As she emphasized, reimbursing me for my expenses made her feel better, and she insisted that I keep a running account of the hours I put in, but I wasn't sure if this was good or bad. But as her paid employee, I was now obligated to find Krappy. I didn't sign a contract, but I know how she thinks. She is a cunning businesswoman who knows how to reel in customers and keep the hook in them. However, she wasn't clever enough to recognize a con, and Krappy had outmaneuvered her. To be taken advantage of and sold a lie was her driving force and her obsession to find him. It wasn't about money. It was about her pride and self-esteem. That, I could understand. She wanted payback, and if she could not get her money, she had another plan for him. At this point, I did not want to know what it was, and I doubted I'd ever find him on another dating site. He was way too cagey for that.

Merle was already seated and waved to me. I walked past the long bar where Dale served a patron a drink. He smiled and nodded his head in acknowledgment. Merle stood to hug me, and my eyes swept the lounge. It was filled with customers, but the booth she chose was at the end of the aisle and against the wall. It was the same one I selected for privacy when I came alone. I slid into the booth, slipped my jacket off my shoulders, and placed my small bag beside me. "Damn, Merle. Have you gone daft? I thought you would be seated in the main dining room, not the lounge. As I recall, the lounge differs from where you usually ask to be seated." I loved to tease her about her penchant for only dining in the most upscale restaurants, and the lounge didn't seem fitting. The Carriage House dining room was the only place I had ever seen her enjoying dinner. "Did you even know there was a lounge here?"

Her beady eyes looked directly at me. "Are you making fun of me because I don't like the lounges you frequent? I thought this would be more private. We have a lot to talk about, and the dining room is much too open, and people can overhear conversations if they are listening and not eating. And besides, I know you like it here. I saw that bartender nod to you. How often do you come here? He's a bit young isn't he?" Her mouth curled up into a sly grin, and her eyebrows were raised. She picked up the menu, faking riveted interest.

I knew I had her on the defensive, but she was quick on her feet. Only two long-time friends can take the back-and-forth teasing we give each other. "Merle, do I detect a bit of

jealousy in your voice? Didn't you say you like younger men?
I can't help it if younger men find me attractive."

"Touché," she said, raising her glass-free hand to toast me.

Our usual give-and-take prattle ended with a stalemate. It
was then on to business.

A young waitress, whom I knew casually, approached us to
ask if we'd like a beverage, and Milly and I both ordered a
glass of wine.

Merle scoured the menu and closed it. "I want something
simple. Do you want to share appetizers?"

I agreed, and when the waitress returned with our wine,
we ordered several appetizers.

"Okay, Izzy, have you had any luck yet?"

"Believe it or not, I've had *too much* luck. Using your
profile and tweaking it has been enough." I reached into my
bag and pulled out Omar's picture. *"This guy* sounds a little
like Krappy, which could be him from your description."

Merle was dumbstruck, eyes popping open in amazement.
She grabbed the photo from my hand so fast, it almost tore.
"I can't believe it!" She pulled her reading glasses from her bag
to study the picture more sharply. After a moment, she said,
"Well, Karl had a lot more hair, no mustache, and this guy has
a light beard, but this kind of resembles him. Most of our
relationship happened over phone and email, though, and we
spent a lot of time in the dark."

I dipped my head and held up a palm to stop her there.

"It stands to reason he'd change his appearance. His eyes
look to be the same shape but are a different color, and his
eyebrows are bushier. What did this man say in his email?"

"He wants to meet. We talked about that possibility of

Krappy altering his look. I doubt he'd present himself as the same persona. This is not from Silver Love. It's from Seniors with Spirit." I reached into my bag and retrieved the copies I'd printed. "Here, I copy and pasted your bio with minor changes. You can read your/my profile and this response to see if it sounds like the one you first found so endearing." I stifled a laugh and added, "From Krappy."

Still studying Omar's photo, I doubted Merle was even listening to me, but she looked up with a glare. "*My* profile? I think I know what I wrote! I don't need any reminders."

"Listen, we need to see if you think there's a correlation between what you wrote and what Omar, if that's his real name, responded to." I read it once more and handed it to her.

Hi, I am a sixty-nine-year-old, flirtatious, professional woman, but I easily pass for fifty. I drive luxury cars, enjoy high-end spontaneous vacations, and love massages by the ocean, feeling the warm saltwater breeze caressing my body. I have nothing to hold me back from an impulsive trip to Europe or one of the islands. I prefer Hawaii, but I am willing to try something new. I enjoy cuddling, romantic dinners, and candlelit meetings in secret places. I have no animals or children to cramp my style, and I am looking for a long-term relationship with someone like-minded. Write me soon. Izzy.

As she scanned it with a scowl, I pretended to search for something in my bag so Merle wouldn't see me trying to hold back my snicker. One would've thought I was desensitized to it after having read it so many times. Thank goodness, the waitress had arrived with our appetizers. Milly and I had almost peed our pants before, and I was biting my lip now.

As soon as the waitress left, I read Omar's email aloud.

Merle listened carefully and then took it from me to study.

"Yes, I do think this Omar guy is one you should reply to. It sounds a lot like him. A lot. The cuddle all day thing, and the heart's desire is the Snake's kind of language. He's worth dating at least once. When you *do* meet up, try and record his voice. I will recognize that for sure. Or, better still, I can perch out of sight to spy, and I'll know if it's him or not."

"What? Oh no! You are not doing that. What if he sees you? What'll you do then? Krappy is a grifter, and who knows how he'll respond if he sees you."

For once, Merle had nothing to say. She took a deep sip of her wine, wiped her mouth with a napkin, and leaned across the booth as close to me as possible. "You're right." She spoke low and in a conspiratorial voice.

I strained my ears to hear what she was saying.

"We need a better plan."

I tossed and turned all night. Merle's problems were now mine. Finally, I'd had enough, sat up, and looked at the clock. It was four in the morning. OMG. I will need a nap today. Oscar, sensitive to my every move, sat up too. "Sorry, boy. Didn't mean to break your sleep," I mumbled as I went to the bathroom and emptied my bladder. I returned to bed and lay there reviewing everything Merle had told me at dinner. For the life of me, I couldn't get it into my brain why she had left out these essential details of her time with Krappy.

"You didn't ask me," was her answer.

Like that was a good enough explanation. I realized it was my own fault. I wasn't thinking like a PI, but rather, a friend. I needed to find my way into my new career. As tired as I was, I smiled. Me a PI? This is crazy. Now I believe everything that Merle says to me. But, I had taken on this task. Why can't I say no to her, or anyone for that matter? From the many mysteries I'd read, I considered how the crimes were solved. What did the PIs do to break the case? They asked questions, of course, which I did not. I had to get a grip and think like one. So, it's not Merle's fault that she didn't fill me in on everything. I never asked the right questions. I know I can't continue investigating until I learn how to decipher the tangled web of deceit. *I'll review my notes when I get up*, I told myself. I reached for my iPhone and tapped Podcasts. The lulling of voices may drown out my thoughts, and I could fall back asleep. It usually worked, but not this time. After a half hour of listening to The Moth, I couldn't stop going over Merle's answers racing through my mind. I was still wide awake. My brain was too wound up even for a podcast. Too encumbered by more questions than answers dancing in my head, I rolled over and got up.

I sat at the table with a decaf coffee next to me.

Oscar decided once I was up, he was too, and I opened the door for him to empty his bladder as I had mine. "Ahhh, to be a dog. Not a worry in the world," I mumbled.

Merle made me promise to answer the email from Omar and set up a meeting. She seemed satisfied at my refusal to have her in the same place I was meeting Omar. I was taking no chances with her. But somehow, I didn't believe this was Krappy. More to appease her, I agreed to the so-called 'first date.' I shuddered to think about it.

I had recorded our conversation, and when I returned home, I transcribed it onto my sizable yellow pad. I needed to see it written down for the puzzle to make sense. It was what any good PI would do. Scanning my list of questions and Merle's answers, I began to put the pieces together.

1. Why don't you have any photos of Krappy? "I told you, he didn't believe in photos. You know there's a type of

person that hates having their picture taken. That was him. The one I got of us was taken on the sly, and I stupidly lost the card it was on. He insisted we didn't need any photos, that a picture did not do me justice anyhow, and that we were building memories through lived experience. He said I was much prettier in person than in my photo on Silver Love. Besides, we are not teenagers who capture everything for our Instagram, and we were too busy...*enjoying each other.*"

2.   Didn't that make you suspicious of him? "No, not at all, because we all know people like that."

3.   Where did you stay in Boston? Any details? See his work place? "No, no office stop. As I said, we mainly went to my condo. Once at his place, a condo also, and it was absolutely gorgeous. Fit him perfectly."

4.   Did he have any photos in his condo? Family? Sites? Anything on the fridge? "No. It was a beautifully decorated place with priceless paintings. But no personal photos."

5.   What is his address? "I do not know it, nor could I even tell you *where* it approximately is in Boston. Let's just say, I was busy doing things when he drove us there."

6.   Did you ever meet any of his friends or colleagues? "Oh, yes. We met up with a friend of his for dinner. Karl was eager to introduce me. He was very personable and told how lucky Karl was to have found such a fascinating woman."

7.   Is the friend the only person he ever introduced you? "No, I did also meet a cousin who came to Boston for a business meeting. Oh, dear, I forget his name now. Anyway, we met at his hotel dining room for cocktails. He was very pleasant and he stressed how lucky Karl was to have me."

8.   Where did you travel and who paid? "Just Bermuda,

spur of the moment, split cost. We took turns with dining and entertainment. We also stayed at a luxury B&B in Vermont. I already called, saying I forgot, thinking I could gather info, but he paid cash. We had *planned* a cruise before my life fell apart. We both had enough money to not worry about costs."

9.   Ever see his credit cards? "No. He was a cash man."

10.   Are you *sure* you have no photos of Karl? Think. "I already told *you*, no! I lost it! The one, and *only one*, I had."

11.   Ever double check his job details? "No, no need to."

12.   You were with him for three months. You have to have something, Merle. "Oh, wait. I forgot. I *do* have a photo of his cousin. I didn't tell Karl because I wanted to have it framed and surprise him. They said they hadn't seen each other in ages. I took it secretly on the way back from the ladies room with my cellphone. I was a distance away and they were too busy talking and laughing to notice."

BINGO! Yes, finally, I had something to work with. Merle had taken a photo of his cousin? And Krappy was unaware? Perfect. I seriously doubted that guy was his real cousin, but Merle adamantly believed that he was. She said she'd go through her cellphone and send me all of Karl's texts for any possible clues. Not really sure I wanted to read three months' worth of yuck and blather, but something was off about the men she met, and I might be able to find further allusion as to what was making me itch. I sat back in the chair, studied the list again, and began making notes for each response.

Had Krappy played this same scam on other women? Of course, yes. Merle was set up from beginning to end. Were either of the men Merle met who they said they were? Alarm zipped through me. If the three were working together, this was more serious than a lone guy conning one woman out of money. One man swindling a woman happens all the time, but a group? We all think this only happens to someone else, to the gullible, but, sometimes, *we are* that someone else. These predators know how to play the game well without conscience or empathy for their victims. Can happen to the brightest of us. Another of my friends, pretty, intelligent, and aware of all the red flags, met a man who conned her out of her money, and it was all she had from the sale of her home. The police never found the bastard. It affected her self-esteem, never mind, the loss of the down payment she had saved to purchase a new home. She never told her daughters or sister about having been duped by the creep. She, like most women bilked by a con, was too embarrassed. That was giving me a boost of motivation, also. Someone had to pay for once.

I rubbed my tired eyes. Do I dare have another cup of coffee? So many thoughts were racing through my mind. And what would I do with the photo Merle sent me of Krappy's cousin? How would I begin to find another stranger if I couldn't even find Krappy? I didn't have a facial recognition program on my computer. Was it legal to search for one at the app store and load it onto my computer? Do I need an official PI license to purchase these types of programs? I brushed that thought away. This case was getting too complicated, or I was too tired to evaluate what I could or could not legally do. I scribbled down a note to Google information for a PI license. Oops! And one more thing came to mind. I would begin a search for the question of how many women are taken for a ride, not a fun one, on dating websites.

I squeezed my eyes tightly and rubbed my forehead, trying

to plan my next step. Oh, right. I had set up a meeting with Omar for lunch today. Milly and I chose the Brown Dog Café to meet him. He responded right away and said he was eager to meet me. EEEKKK! Omar lived three towns over, or so he said. I told him we could have coffee and something light to eat because I didn't have more than an hour to spare. I had a meeting to attend. Of course, this was a lie, but even an hour was too long to converse with someone I didn't know. He agreed. Milly would sit at the bar across from our booth, keeping an eye on me and taking a photo of him when she had the opportunity. Later, I would meet Merle and show his picture to her to see if it matched Krappy. I dreaded the lunch date, and if I didn't get some sleep, I would not be on my A game. I couldn't meet him with dark bags under my eyes. I wondered if I should go back to bed and see if I could sleep for another couple of hours. Unfortunately, I was wide awake. I couldn't shake the feeling that something was off with Krappy, his cousin, and friend. Maybe I should run this by Gus after I meet with Omar. He may have some ideas for me. I trusted his advice, but he still hadn't gotten back to me about any information he had discovered through his old FBI contacts. He probably thought this was a petty Merle debacle and saw no rush in contacting former colleagues. But I think he'll be more interested when I fill him in on Merle's latest info about the secret photo and meeting with Krappy's friend and cousin.

Suddenly feeling drained, I couldn't stop yawning. I might fall asleep if I go back to bed, turn the TV on low, and clear my brain from concentrating on Krappy by thinking of my current novel. I still needed to finish it, but that was on hold.

This wave of intrigue was becoming crazier and crazier, sweeping me along and making me imagine all kinds of conspiracies and twisted outcomes I couldn't foresee. I reminded myself again that this was Merle's debacle and her doing. She was caught up in a simple con job, but the two men she met with Krappy were more than likely who they said they were. Lots of friends and family didn't know everything about whom they trusted or their own relatives. Who truly knows anyone anyway? Normal families spawn criminals and never find out until they are arrested. Look at Bernie Madoff and how he alone bilked millions out of people who should have known better. His investors were high-net-worth individuals. They were bright, educated people who fell for the big con, and it was perfect until he confessed that it was all a pyramid scheme. So, maybe Krappy's cousin and friend were legit people who didn't know anything about Krappy's criminal racket. Damn. Something my mother used to say to me ran through my tired brain. *"You allow your brain to run amuck with nonsense. Take control of yourself, Izzy!"*

Maybe my mother was right. After all, who knows you better than your mother? I am dreaming up all kinds of conspiracies now, especially since Merle has planted the seed that I have the potential to be a PI, and I am currently taking on that role with passion. What happened to my quiet, organized life? I usually play it safe and steady, and now, I'm drawn into dating strangers, looking for a con man, thinking I'm a PI, and creating chaos in my life. What would my kids think? They would be shocked. I chuckled when I pictured their faces if they found out I was on dating websites and looking for a man whom I nicknamed Krappy.

Not in a million years would they ever believe their mother would do something this reckless and impulsive. And I will never tell them! It's a good thing my daughter and her family are away on vacation. Although she asked me to join them, I was glad I had turned down her invitation because I was having enough fun, right here at home.

Sarah needs to talk to me daily and send me photos and short texts, which I dutifully reply to. I am glad she is out of state, so I don't have to lie to her. As a lawyer, she would give me all sorts of legal advice I wanted to avoid hearing. And I picture her wagging her finger at me, saying, "Ignorance of the law is no defense." My sons are busy with their careers and live far enough away not to check up on me like my daughter does. It suits me fine. But in all their eyes, they see me as their quiet, retired, happy mother who writes adventure mysteries for young people as a hobby. *Surprise, kids! Your mother is now a PI.*

I picked up my notes and headed back to my bedroom while making a mental note to call Gus later. Then, I thought quickly about what to wear on my first date. I was out of touch with the dating world, but did I really care? The most important thing was not to get mired in any questions that may entrap me. I had to think like Merle but be myself. I would need to lie about my whole life. I had to be flirtatious and talk about my massages by the ocean. Merle had coached me, but could I take on a new identity? Thank goodness she had a rental Lexus arriving in the morning. I don't think my pickup or SUV could pass for luxury. No wonder I couldn't sleep. But sleep must come, or I will not have the energy to pull this off.

I was woken out of a deep, dreamy sleep by slurpy kisses washing my cheeks. I struggled to wake up, my groggy brain still in dreamland, feeling Max's arms wrapped around me, brushing my cheeks with his soft lips. My eyes fluttered open. I was suddenly wide awake. It wasn't Max's soft lips on my cheeks but Oscar's warm tongue licking them, pleading for my attention. Holy moly! I had fallen asleep after returning to bed at 5:30, and it was now 8:30. For a moment, I was in a fog. Oscar's dark eyes bored into mine, pleading for me to come to my senses and get out of bed to let him outside.

The minute I opened the door for Oscar, he sprinted out. I wondered how he had held his full bladder so long when I had to empty mine the minute I rolled out of bed. It made me chuckle to picture Oscar crossing his legs, patiently waiting for me to wake up. How long had he been sitting by my bed, slobbering on my face, trying to rouse me? Oscar, like me, was a creature of habit.

After finishing my coffee and feeding Oscar, I headed to

the barn to feed Chip and the horses. Thank goodness they were flexible, which is more than I am. I had so much to do today and no time to linger in my favorite place, the barn. My peaceful way of life was beginning to crumble brick by brick.

I showered quickly, threw on a robe, and ran a brush through my hair. It was time for a second cup of coffee and a bowl of cereal. Sitting at the table, I gazed at the list of To Do's I had compiled earlier. It would be a busy day, and I had no time to dawdle. First on my list, I called Gus's cellphone. After questioning Merle, I wanted to run by him some of the answers she gave me. I left a quick message for him. It was nothing urgent, just that if he had time, I needed his input. I glanced at the clock. My lunch with Omar was set for noon, and I still needed to decide what to wear. I felt like a high school girl going on her first date. My book club meeting with the ladies was at two o'clock, enough time to meet Omar, grab a cool drink, no martinis for me today, something light to eat, and then drive to Sue's. Check—check, and—check. I loved making lists and crossing them off when I completed the tasks.

A half-hour before meeting Omar, I was finally dressed in something acceptable. It had been a struggle. My wardrobe consisted of gym clothes, barn clothes, and jeans. Plus, I overslept and didn't have time to burn my anxiety off at the gym and pull myself together. I felt out of sorts by not maintaining my morning routine. Oscar had followed me everywhere I went. Does he know something I don't? After running a light-colored lipstick over my dry mouth, I glanced in the mirror. Staring back at me was a woman I almost didn't recognize. Was it the makeup, the hair I had taken more time with than usual, or the clothes? I liked the new Izzy look. Where has she been for the past five years?

"You're looking good, Izzy," I said as I ran my fingers through my hair. Hearing my voice, Oscar looked up at me and cocked his head. "No, I'm not talking to you. I'm talking to the woman in the mirror."

I had accepted the aging process as inevitable, which it is, but I had not realized how less and less I cared about dressing up and wearing makeup. It was easier not to bother and live in jeans and barn clothes. I didn't wear makeup or stylish clothes even when I met up with friends. I preferred casual comfort, but that was okay for home and barn. Something clicked in my brain. I need to try harder, to not fall into bad habits. Merle may be right. Fashionable clothes and makeup should still be a part of my wardrobe. After retiring, I was happy to toss vanity away and live a more straightforward lifestyle. Now, looking in the mirror, I liked my new look. And it wasn't overdone. My eyes looked more prominent with the slight mascara, and my cheeks looked rosier with the blush. It made me pause and take stock. Why, since Max died, had I only bothered to wear makeup for special occasions? A little mascara always helps make eyes look brighter and more awake. I had to admit, I looked good. The black stretch pants, low black boots, and white blouse made the difference. I hadn't worn them for some time, and, luckily, they still fit. I put on my sweater coat in case I needed to leave in a hurry.

A sudden flash of insight came to me. "Geez, Louise!" I'm being forced to become someone else, and it's Merle. I didn't know whether to laugh or cry. Pushing myself out of my comfort zone opened a door I had kept closed since Max died.

I drew in two deep breaths to gain my composure. Dating at my age was crazy. And even if I was only pretending to be a woman with Merle's profile while honing my PI skills, I still found it scary. My reflection in the mirror proved I didn't look as risqué as Merle, but as my mother used to say, *"You'll pass with a shove."*

"Stop overthinking this," I muttered. But it was all happening so rapidly that I felt jittery. Meeting a stranger to find Krappy Karl and worrying about my appearance took me out of my comfort zone and dropped me into the unknown.

It was almost noon when I entered the Brown Dog Tavern. My eyes flitted around the lounge until I spotted a man sitting alone in a booth who looked like Omar's photo. I added a sultry sway to my hips as I sauntered toward him and prayed I wouldn't topple over from my unsteady and unnatural gait—or my racing heart. A martini could be called for, after all.

The stranger stood and held out his hand to shake mine. "You must be Izzy." His baritone pitch came with a slight European accent.

"Yes, I am, and you must be Omar. Pleased to meet you."

"Here. Let me help you with your coat." I put up my palm before he moved behind me, but it was too late.

I tensed and squirmed as he gripped my shoulders. His fingers, tickling my neck like worms, seemed to linger for far too long. "Uh, that's okay. I'm fine." I placed my hands over his and glanced back, batting my lashes. "It's just my sweater coat, part of my outfit. I love the accenting colors in it."

"Oh, okay. You do look ravishing, with or without." He stepped back and gestured for me to take a seat. "You are far prettier than your photo on Seniors with Spirit. You take my breath away." He smiled crookedly while watching me slither into my chair in Merle's beguiling way, but I felt so silly.

I cringed on the inside. "Why, thank you!" Trying to sound more like her, too, I purred, "You look very dashing yourself." I forced myself to smile, but my lips felt frozen. I wasn't cutting it and wondered if he could see straight through me. The server saved me as he approached our booth and asked if we were ready to order. Against my better judgment, I ordered a cosmo. It might settle my frazzled nerves.

Once the server left, Omar asked if I had something special in mind for lunch. The thought of food did not appeal to me. My stomach was in knots, but I had to order something and move the conversation forward. This awkward silence was not something *Merle* ever would've let happen. Was this Krappy or not? Merle said Krappy had a slight accent and a low voice. I had to say something. *Get a grip, Izzy.* "My nutritionist has me on a light lunch diet, so I'll order a small Caesar's salad. I usually eat a larger meal for dinner. And you?" He did not reply. His eyes never strayed from mine, so I broke the stare first by reaching into my bag for my readers. As I searched my bag, I tried to clear my brain with a deep breath and settle into Merle's personality. *Is he analyzing me and trying to figure out if I'm conning him? If I don't step up my game, it's all over.* My bio said I was flirtatious and spontaneous. By now, Merle would have Omar under her spell. She could mesmerize any man with her serpentine movements. I've seen her in action. I *must* become more Merle-like. "So, did you decide on your order?" I smiled as coquettishly as I knew how.

Omar responded quickly to the new me, sitting taller. "Yes. Since I arrived a little earlier than you, I had time to look at the menu. The corn beef sandwich is appealing. I'll try that." He leaned over and intimately touched my hand.

Ignoring my instinct to retreat, I left it there and smiled coyly. "That sounds as delicious as you." Did those actually words tumble from my mouth?

His body language showed that he found my response alluring. He dipped his head closer and lowered his voice. His tone was more ragged, and his accent more pronounced, as he said, *"So, Izzy,* you said in your bio that you enjoy massages as you lie on a blanket beside the ocean. Rubbing a sexy woman such as you down with scented oils while she enjoys the sound of waves breaking is pleasurable to me, too. And the sumptuous smell of salt water revitalizes me in ways that will thrill you." He smiled seductively.

I was too stunned to reply. My silence left space for him to continue.

"Izzy, according to your profile, you and I are compatible, both, risk-takers. You're my kind of woman. I have an idea. Let's throw caution to the wind and take a trip to Bermuda. I am the man you're looking for, and I suspect your attraction is as strong for me. I know you feel our matched magnetism. There is nothing to stop us from enjoying each other."

I was gobsmacked. Omar's grin was rakish as he waited for my reply. My heart thumped wildly in my chest. I scanned the room, searching for Milly. It was apparent how *spirited* the man sitting across from me was, and my hands began to tremble, wondering how to continue a conversation with Omar, who oozed lust and sensuality. Suddenly, I felt a hot flash rising from deep within my belly and slowly flowing to my cheeks. It had been years since I'd had one of those, and it was unsettling. The air around me was suddenly steamy. My cheeks were on fire, and my body was melting. I ran my fingers through my hair. Was I sweating? My mind raced back to my profile posted on Seniors with Spirit. I *had said* I was spontaneous, and he was taking me up on my own words.

Omar's steely brown eyes bored into mine. I had not been in the company of a man who looked at me that way for so long that I felt breathless. Now what. What would Merle do?

My hands shakily reached for the glass of ice water our server had placed on the table when he first came for our order. The cold water snapped me back to my senses. I tried to answer in a soft, seductive voice. "That sounds *so* inviting, Omar, and perfect. Unfortunately, I have business with my accountant this week that can't wait. Another time?"

Hot breath fanned my face as he leaned close and whispered, "Of course, my darling. I can see you are as excited as I am to plan a getaway. It will be *all* that you desire *and more.*" Then, he kissed my hand.

Darling? Did he call me darling? I was stunned into silence.

Omar flashed a lustful grin. "When we finish lunch, we will look at our calendars and plan accordingly."

Thank heaven, our server arrived with our martinis and took our luncheon orders. It was the break I needed to pull myself together. My mind was spinning. If this *was* Krappy Karl, I can see why Merle had fallen fast and furious for him. Omar held his glass up and waited for me to raise mine. We tapped our glasses, and he made a toast. "To beautiful adventures with a beautiful woman. Let the fun begin."

I took a deep gulp of my martini. All I could do was mumble, "Yes. To us."

Lunch came, but I could hardly eat. He watched me lift the fork to my mouth, making me more uncomfortable with each bite. Who is this man? A bad feeling about him welled up in me. My red-flag alert was flying high. I needed to escape, *immediately*. Omar was becoming more and more salacious in his speech. Each time I tried to begin a new subject, he turned the conversation back to what was becoming more sexually explicit. I wolfed down my salad, drained my martini, and said I needed to fix my makeup. Rushing to the ladies' room with my bag, I passed Milly, seated at the bar. To her silly grin, I mouthed, "I need to get out of here, *fast*. Now!"

Milly nodded. This was the cue for her to drive to the back door and pick me up. Krappy Karl or not, I couldn't take it anymore.

I hoped she had photographed him when he first arrived as we had planned. I was walking as fast as I dared in case Omar was watching. When I reached the end of the bar, a woman wearing a black scarf wrapped around her long gray hair and a long, floral skirt that met her clogs caught my attention. Heavy makeup donned her face, but her tattooed black eyebrows were a dead giveaway. *Merle! What* was she doing here? She promised not to show up in case it was Krappy, and he recognized her.

I paused and whispered, "Why are you here, and what's with the disguise?"

"He's *not* Karl," she hissed.

"Good to know," I muttered before racing to the back door and out to the parking lot. Milly was there to pick me up. Hooking my seat belt, I was finally able to exhale. "Oh my God, Milly! I think Omar is a sex maniac. And guess what?

Merle, who thought she was in disguise, was sitting at the end of the bar watching the whole thing."

Milly gaped. "What? We *told her* to stay away."

"Well, that's Merle for you. She gets something in her head and all bets are off. Honestly, Milly, I didn't know how to act like her around Omar. I tried, but I need more practice. If all the meetups are going to be with creepy men like Omar, I quit!" I didn't realize Milly was speeding till I caught my breath and checked the speedometer. "Slow down. I don't think he's following us." I leaned back against the headrest and wiped my brow. I was sweating, and my hair was damp ringlets. "Can you turn off the heat, please?" I opened my window to let the cold air blow on my face.

Milly immediately let up on the gas." Crap! I didn't realize I was driving that fast. You were so shaken that I just hit the gas to get the hell out of there. What's wrong with you? It's too cold for the window to be down."

My breathing and heart rate finally slowed. The cold air had done its job. "I couldn't believe it. I had an actual hot flash talking to that guy, pretending to be like Merle."

"A hot flash? Izzy, women our age do not get hot flashes. I bet your blood pressure was skyrocketing. It's a wonder you didn't stroke out. What did he say that got you in such a state that you thought you were having a hot flash? Fill me in."

Milly and I hashed over the encounter with Omar. I didn't leave out any details, and she sometimes *even* blushed. Talking it over with her was calming but left me drained.

"Damn, Izzy, that man is good. If that was his honey trap to bait lonely older woman he sure poured on the charm with you. And a sexual honey trap to boot. And I bet it works for women like Merle, and odds are Krappy Karl used the same spiel."

"Honestly, Milly, I am *done* if all the men who email me are like that. One thing is for sure: Omar was straightforward with what he wanted, and he had my profile down to a tee. I believe there is something in common about that style of profile and men like Krappy. The average online guy doesn't behave that way, right?"

Milly was silent for a minute, giving a lot of thought to my question. "Having never met someone online, I don't know and asking Merle is like asking if grass is green. She thinks nothing of it. These are the type of men she is attracted to."

"Oy vey! This has been an eyeopener! I guess it's true that we should learn something new every day, but online dating was never on my list. Not to change the subject, but I was thinking that I might do a search for online dating scams. It makes more and more sense to me. I think specific women are targeted by what they say in their profiles. But the question is, how do they sort through hundreds of profiles to find women to con? Tomorrow I am going to begin working on my thesis."

"Well, Izzy. Makes sense to me, but my question is, are you ready to meet another man that matches Krappy's profile? You've survived your first date and honed your acting skills, but if you keep on going, you're going to have to kiss a lot of frogs. What do they call that? Trial by fire or something?"

If I hadn't been busy reliving the whole Omar debacle, I would have laughed. I knew I had to work harder on my Merle image to pull this off. I had stumbled and been too overwrought by Omar's sexual connotations. I hadn't left Izzy at home and morphed into Merle. I had taken Omar's words personally, and a real Jezebel would have brushed them off, and asked for more. I needed to improve my act.

Milly interrupted my daydreaming. "Hey, we're almost at Sue's house. Are you still up for the book club? You'll need to catch a ride to pick up your car at the tavern. You don't think Merle will be there already do you?"

"I doubt it. She's never on time. I'm okay now. Yes, drop me off. If Merle's there, *I* need to be, too. She'll blabber all this misinformation about my date with Omar. They feed off her stories like a deer to a salt lick. I'm not gonna let her overblown exaggerations of what she saw at the Brown Dog be at my expense. Merle can bring me to pick up the car."

"Are you sure?"

"Yes. She seriously drives me crazy, though. Merle gave me all this hope about having a pic of Krappy's cousin on her old cellphone, which I *thought* would be my first solid lead, but she can't even find it now. She was so angry and distraught when she got dumped, she thinks she might've tossed it out with the rest of Karl's things. Unbelievable!"

Milly cracked a smile and shook her head. "Typical." She entered the cul-de-sac where Sue lived and stopped the car to let me out. I could see by the parked cars that some ladies' had arrived before me.

"Thanks for the ride," I said. "Call me tomorrow."

Milly gave me a thumbs up, then motioned to the BMW and smirked. Yep. Merle's car. She had beat me here, darn it. "Have fun, Izzy." She rolled her window up and pulled away, leaving me to face Merle and the book club ladies.

Worse still, I hadn't even finished reading the book.

*A*fter a quick rap on the door, I entered Sue's home. I could hear Merle's voice, loudly blabbing about *the* escapade at the Brown Dog. I knew she'd stepped up on her stage, dressed in her outlandish costume, to spill the beans to a captivated audience. They didn't notice I'd entered the dining room. I stood silently, enjoying the scene. The ladies sat around the table, book of the month beside them and coffee cups filled. Merle had them mesmerized with her dramatic description of events and her role in my first date at the Brown Dog. Her hands were gesturing wildly, and her voice was giddy with enthusiasm. As I suspected, she was embellishing everything to enhance her performance. It didn't surprise me that she had driven to book club without changing out of her costume. She was in her element, and the ladies were awestruck by her tall tale. Merle was known for her grand entrances and had often voiced that she could've been a movie star if her wealthy husband hadn't swept her off her feet at a young age. We had all heard that story many times.

I stifled a laugh. Seeing Merle in the light of day and away from the tavern was breathtaking. She looked hilarious with heavy makeup covering her face, dark red lipstick lining her thin lips, and, most prominent, her ink-black eyebrows. The head covering wrapped around the gray wig didn't help. If anything, she looked her age for the first time. I cleared my throat to announce my arrival.

Everyone stopped talking as if surprised by my presence. Merle whirled around and shot me a warm smile, but I knew she wondered how much I had heard of the conversation.

Francie was the first to break the silence. "Hi, Izzy. Merle was telling us what happened on your first date with Omar, the look-alike for the jerk Karl Hendricks. She said you met for lunch, and were flirting with him, but she saw how uneasy you were. She said you looked panicked and escaped through the back door. Honestly, Izzy, I could never be as brave as you. I hope you find the scum bucket."

Lynn piped in, "Izzy, doesn't Merle look and act like a movie star? I bet no one recognized her at the Brown Dog."

I could feel anger boiling up inside. "Oh, really? I did." That should stop this nonsense once and for all.

Everyone rushed to Merle's defense. Janet added, "Merle said she knew right away Omar wasn't Karl."

I glared at Merle. "You did, Merle? Why didn't you tell me as soon as you knew? I would have left immediately."

Merle looked guilty as sin. She jumped up and rushed to me and air-kissed both my cheeks. Merle likes to act European. "Oh, Izzy. You were marvelous sitting there talking to that strange man. I admit he did resemble Karl, but unfortunately, as I told you on your escape out the back door, he wasn't. I could see how difficult it was for you to behave like me. You looked so uncomfortable, but your conversation seemed to be going quite well, and I didn't want to interrupt."

I glared at her until she looked away. I couldn't believe I had let her drag me into the unknown; now, she was making me feel inadequate.

She knew she had overstepped and quickly added, "Izzy, you looked beautiful. I almost didn't recognize you. No wonder the man looked bedazzled."

The book club ladies chimed in with one compliment after another, trying to change the subject. "Izzy, you look so lovely. Izzy, I love that lipstick shade. Izzy, that blouse and black pants are very smart looking. Izzy, your hair looks so pretty. Izzy, you should wear makeup more often."

I knew they were trying their best to soften Merle's remarks. Milly had prepared me for a strong comeback. We both knew Merle. Her description of events was rarely on target, and she was known to manipulate the conversation back to her. I put on my most generous smile. I was ready.

"Well, I must say, Merle, Omar was well worth every bit of the time and effort I've put in to find the man who took you for a ride. Everything about Omar screamed to me that he's your type of man, and a perfect match for you. I have his email if you'd like." The ladies hid admiring smiles, enjoying the moment. I finally spoke my mind but did it with a smile and teasing words. By the look on Merle's face, I could see she had no retort, and for the first time, I felt satisfied that I had one-upped her. I gave Merle the eagle eye, and she knew she had better stop while she was ahead. This conversation was over. She quickly cast her eyes away, and with her gray wig and head wrap, I felt a slight pull of pity for the older woman in Merle's body. In her way, she was bragging about me. Merle nervously kept talking and boasted that I was now her personal PI and went on about how brave I was to meet men I didn't know to help her out of a mess of her own making. All eyes were on Merle, the ladies fascinated with her costume and her embellishment of the meeting between Omar and me. When she finished her lavish praise, she blew me an air kiss and smiled her most enormous smile. The ladies nodded in approval, and we finally got down to business. It was time to discuss the book.

Merle and I left Sue's house together. As we walked towards her BMW, I told her we had some things to discuss before she dropped me off to pick up the rental. We paused at her car to talk. I needed to clarify our arrangement and remind her of her promise to let me work on finding Krappy and that she would stay out of it. She already broke her word by showing up at the Brown Dog dressed like her version of a Hollywood star. I could not have this happen again. Her only role was to look at photos and emails and see if the picture fit Krappy's description to warrant a date. "Listen, Merle." I needed to be firm with her, or this would never work. "I don't appreciate you blabbing about the emails or my dates with strangers when I am doing this for you. And do I need to remind you? I said it wasn't a good idea to show up and check the guy out because if it was Krappy, he might recognize you. Even in this crazy costume, your eyebrows are a dead give-away. And, more importantly, if you want me to find Krappy Karl, you've got to stop sharing the case with everyone. This investigation is private and only between you and me."

I gulped. I had already shared everything with Milly, Gus, and Bob. *OMG! Did I say* case? "And, Merle, if you can't follow these rules, friend or not, I am done."

Merle looked contrite. I could see she was on the verge of shedding a few tears. "You are right, Izzy, and I apologize. I was so excited watching how you handled Omar that I didn't stop to think that sharing your experience with our book club would sound petty and foolish. But, Izzy, they already know how awful a man Karl is, and they are rooting for you to find him. They, like us, want justice for me, and for him to be arrested. We want this case closed, and I want to look Karl in the eye, and then scratch it out." Her eyes sparkled when she said "case" and her arched black brows gave her a comical look.

I stifled a laugh. We were having a meaningful chat that needed to be taken seriously, and I forced myself to look past Merle's outlandish wardrobe and focus on the subject.

For a moment Merle was silent. She had no comeback for the dressing down I gave her. Although it's not my nature to allow myself so much anger, and I have never spoken sternly to Merle, I knew it had to be said. I could see a crinkly smile forming at the edge of her red lips. "Izzy, can I ask you a question now that we have reset our ground rules?"

"Okay, but I remind you, I'll hold you to your promise."

Merle rolled her eyes for the hundredth time. I swear she burns more calories rolling those dark eyes than I do walking on the treadmill. "Izzy, don't get upset, but I think you are finally acting like a real PI. You called this a 'case'. That's PI jargon. And, Izzy, this *is* a case for a PI, and I have a feeling you are morphing into one."

On the ride home, I called Gus. His message said he was away and to call later in the week. My wheels were spinning. I couldn't wait to get to my office and check my emails.

As soon as I'd drained the last of a delicious cup of hazelnut coffee in my kitchen, with Oscar having gotten up to speed on the situation, Merle texted. Just a photo, no words. I squinted, unable to make anything out. Well, it was a male figure.

I texted: *What? This is it??? The cousin?*

She sent back a thumbs up and a big, cheesy grin.

Ugh. Why is she so proud? It's useless! Just then, "A Horse with No Name" sang from my cellphone. It was Gus. Not only do I love that song, but one of the stanzas reminds me of him. *'The ocean is a desert with a life underground and a perfect disguise above.'* I told him all my friends, including him, have a particular song for their ringtone. He said he found musical ringtones amusing but couldn't dream up appropriate ones for his friends; it seemed like too much work. After telling him his ringtone was "A Horse with No Name," he shook his head and smiled. "You amaze me, Izzy." I took it as a compliment.

"Hi, Gus, I didn't mean to disturb you, and as I said in my message, it wasn't anything urgent."

Gus responded, "Hi, Izzy. It's A Horse with No Name." Picturing his grin as he said that, I smiled myself . "And please never hesitate to disturb me. I'll always return your calls, as soon as I'm able. What's up? Have you given up on Merle?"

"Uh, no. That's why I'm calling you. I wondered if you had time to check with any of your former colleagues to find out if other women are on their radar list for dating scams. And I have another piece of info to add. Merle told me about two men she had met in Boston. One said he was Krappy's cousin, and the other, his friend. She had no photos of Krappy, *but* she was secretly able to take a picture with her cellphone of his cousin. She just found it for me, but it's all a blur. I can't make anything out. Don't know if this helps any, but...?"

"Now *that* is interesting. Any luck finding this Krappy creep on dating sites? How's that working out? I thought Merle said she had no photos of Karl?"

"Correct. She was too focused on finding Krappy, but she *did* snag this one pic of his cousin. It's all we have, sorry."

There was a pause at Gus's end. For a minute, I thought the call had been dropped. Gus cleared his throat. "Send it. So, Izzy. I'll be out of town till next week. How 'bout I stop by the farm, we can talk then, and you can run everything by me. Maybe we can take the horses out for a ride. The contact at the FBI I was trying to reach is on vacation and will be back on Sunday. I'll see if he can give me any information on dating app swindles. Don't worry. I didn't forget. Okay?"

"Okay. I knew you wouldn't forget, but, *in case* these men are all working the con together, I just wanted to fill you in on that piece, that she met two associates of his. It could be nothing. Maybe *you* can decipher some clues in this photo? I don't know. I didn't know you were out of town when I called. We'll talk next week. Thanks for getting back to me."

"Anytime. Never hesitate to call me. I'm your friend and I care. I'll see you next week and you take care of yourself."

"I will. Bye, Gus." I texted him what she sent me. Junk.

"Bye, Izzy."

After ending the call, I headed straight to my office. I was on a roll. First, I Googled 'scams online dating.' Wow, a whole bunch of searches came up. I scrolled down the list and began reading. A half-hour later, I closed my laptop and leaned back in my chair. What I read was shocking. According to the FCC, online dating scammers are masters of disguise and may create fake online profiles. They may even assume real people's identities, study information people share online, and pretend to have common interests. That sounds exactly like what Krappy did to Merle. He fed right into her profile and targeted her. The big difference was Krappy met her in person, whereas, most scammers don't. That's wild. Most scammers never meet their mark and only talk on the phone or via email or vid-chat. Why was Krappy so bold? The article said that many swindlers pretend to be investors and con their new lovers by offering investment advice, wooing them with promises of high yields. Once they lured them in and took their money, they disappeared. I swore under my breath, and my anger towards Krappy reached an all-time high.

I hated this man. I wanted to find the bastard more than ever. I sat for another ten minutes thinking of my next move and decided to check my emails before stopping. Wow, wonder of all wonders.

After scrolling through at least twenty emails, one from Silver Love snagged my attention. Again, there was a photo of a man who could pass for Krappy. And his bio was a close match. I copied the image and forwarded it to Merle. There was no sense in replying if she didn't think he could be Krappy. I deleted the rest of the emails and left the office. I needed to clear my head.

I decided fresh air would declutter my brain and help me sort things out, so I grabbed my barn jacket and headed to my refuge, the barn.

Once in the cool, comforting outdoors, I paused, took a long breath, and slowly exhaled. "Ah, that helped."

Oscar followed close on my heels.

I was in no rush, and the cool air on my face perked me up. It was a beautiful spring afternoon, and the bare trees, brown and dreary, were beginning to bud. And I saw a robin for the first time. Change was coming, and I felt it in my bones. Spring meant rebirth and new beginnings. Once covered with snow and frost, the ground could not hold back the renewal of what lay beneath. I felt a bounce in my step and a quickening in my bones. My whole body seemed lighter as Oscar and I made our way to the barn.

Both horses were out to pasture, but Chip came to greet me. I sat on a hay bale outside an empty stall and ran my hand over Chip's soft fur. She began purring and moved closer to my legs, asking for more attention.

Oscar lay down beside me, and I let my mind run free. I was in my place of Zen, where I could become calm and rely on my intuition rather than my conscious efforts, which so far netted me zero. It was time to use my intuition rather than the thin facts of the case.

What did my instinct tell me about the missing pieces of the puzzle? Something wasn't sitting right. Something was out of whack. But all my questions were unanswered. Just as a scratch on a record caused the melodic music to be broken,

Merle's botched situation had a hole in it, and I couldn't figure out why. My intuition told me I lacked an important clue, but I couldn't put my finger on it. Was joining all those dating sites the right move? I sat for at least twenty minutes trying to decompress and think fresh. I could only move forward once Merle looked at the email and photo from the new guy who said his name was Gerald. Another fruitless date? Gerald couldn't be as bad as Omar, could he?

I was ready to leave the barn when I had a brainstorm. Why hadn't I thought of this before? My investigation required someone with access to information I had no path to. The name Carol Foxy came to mind. Known as Foxy to her friends and colleagues, she's a freelance investigative reporter for the local newspaper and can access information I can't. I met Foxy when she was working on a whistle-blower story of animal abuse. She interviewed me about equine care, and we occasionally met for lunch or cocktails. Foxy was seventy-three and filled with a plethora of investigative knowledge. She could help dig into dating site scams and find out if Merle was a blip or if other women had also been tricked.

I slid my fingers through my hair and rubbed my scalp, coaxing my brain into solving the mystery. Should I contact Foxy or not? Would she be an asset with her resources? But how much should I tell her? I wanted her to refrain from following me on dates and using my experiences in an article. I don't want to embarrass my kids. They would be appalled with this new me, dragged into a conspiracy and dating strange men. Merle would be mortified to have her private life blasted all over the news. How could I get Foxy to help me without writing a story starring Merle and me? I worried about moving forward in a whirlwind of publicity, unable to bow out when my life became an open book and out of control. Dare I open the door and bring Foxy in to help with the investigation? Would she give me her word to not use our names? I rubbed my face and came up with the answer to all my doubts about bringing in Foxy.

I'll take the advice I give to family and friends. *"When in doubt, do nothing."* But maybe this requires another thought process. *"Indecision is the key to flexibility."*

*O*nce again, I tossed and turned all night. This case was driving me crazy. I woke up in a sweat, my heart pounding, and my eyes popped open in fear. I had a nightmare of spectacular clarity. I was running through a wooded area, a man fitting Krappy's description hot on my heels. Wide awake, I picked up the pad and pen beside my bed and wrote down all the details. I knew from experience that dreams, although vivid in the moment, must be captured and recorded before they leave your consciousness. Somewhere in my foggy brain, I knew I had to sit up and get it down on paper while it was still clear. When I finished, I laid my head back on my pillow, trying to erase the vision of the evil that had been chasing me. Still shaking from my dream of terror and calming my trembling legs, I rolled over, got out of bed, and padded to the bathroom. Feeling calmer after I ran a cold washcloth over my face and drank a glass of water, I climbed back in bed and wondered if I could fall back to sleep, and that's the last thing I remember. Sun streaming through the window roused me, but I was still groggy and not energetic enough to get out of bed and begin the day. Instead, I closed my eyes and spent half an hour reliving the dream that was already fading. I could feel Oscar's warm breath next to me as he sat patiently by my bedside, waiting for me to roll over and open my eyes.

If not for Oscar, I would have stayed in bed another hour, but I knew he couldn't wait for his morning ritual, and my bladder was about to burst. After a visit to the bathroom, I threw on a robe and slowly made my way to the kitchen. Oscar ran outside and quickly returned to munch his breakfast while I filled my mug with coffee. I placed my coffee mug on the table, sat down, and picked up the yellow pad to decipher my scraggly penmanship. My handwriting looked like I had had too many martinis, but I was glad I had the presence of mind to jot it down. I once read advice from a famous author who suggested keeping a notepad and pen beside the bed because sometimes a dream will inspire a plot for a book. But it must be jotted down immediately because dreams fade once you are awake. I know I have had other terrifying nightmares, but this was the first time one had jolted me from a sound sleep, leaving me out of breath from racing to escape someone trying to kill me. Last night was my first out-of-body experience, and it terrified me. It was so real. After reading my notes, it was no wonder I had woken so suddenly. I rubbed my tired eyes and took a deep gulp of coffee. I don't believe in foreshadowing, but did my nightmare mean something dark and deep was lurking inside my psyche, and this was a warning? Did Gus's concern show up in my nightmare in a distorted way? Or is my fear of dating men I don't know, transforming them into killers, that caused my nightmare? And is my apprehension about moving outside my comfort zone causing anxiety and fear when I am lost in sleepless dreamland? I'm not a shrink, but I find it disturbing that this is happening to me. I will talk to Milly when she comes by later to groom the horses. Maybe she will have insight into dreams and their meaning. I'll read my ramblings to her; hopefully, she can understand and share some words of wisdom.

Speed and Maverick were shedding their winter coats faster than I could keep up with, and Milly enjoyed spending time with Speed. Grooming him was her favorite pastime. I swear she loves that horse as much as I do. I placed my empty mug in the dishwasher, stepped into my barn boots, and headed outside. Milly will be here later, and my second coffee will wait until she arrives. I am already running behind.

I had finished barn chores, showered, dressed, and was in the kitchen when I heard Milly's car pull into the driveway. Before I could greet her, Oscar bounded out the open door to meet his friend. "Hi, Milly. Thanks for coming by today to help brush out the horses. They're shedding like crazy."

Milly gave me a quick hug and rubbed Oscar's ears. "I should thank you for asking me. I'll take you up on any chance to hang out with Speed. Can you believe this crazy weather? It's supposed to be 60 today. Last week, we were freezing our buns off, and this week, I believe spring is here at last. I think winter is done for. I'm ready for the change."

"I know. For the first time I didn't wear gloves and my knit cap when I went to the barn earlier. It's almost lunch. Are you hungry? Or do you want to eat after we groom the horses?"

"I'm always hungry. What do you have?"

"Bagels and cream cheese okay? I also have homemade tomato soup."

Milly was filling her mug with coffee. "Sounds perfect. Emails, barn, lunch."

We were just about to head to my office when my cellphone began playing "Who Let the Dogs Out?" I quickly answered. "Hi, Merle. What's up?"

I glanced at Milly. Her lips curled into a smile, and her eyebrows raised in anticipation of Merle's long-drawn-out conversation. I shrugged my shoulders and dropped my head, exhausted before she even began talking. I would not have answered if I had not been waiting to hear her take on the picture of Gerald and if she thought he might be Krappy.

Merle didn't know it, but I put her on speaker so Milly could listen.

"Well, Izzy, I examined that picture carefully and read his email. The email sounds like Karl and Gerald's eyes look the same as Karl's. Gerald's face seems thinner than his, but it's hard to tell with the full beard and thick eyebrows. But as you said, men can easily cover up their real identity with more hair and they can always dye it. But the eyes stay the same, except if they wear colored contact lenses. And—"

I stopped her mid-sentence. Merle could go on forever. "So, do you think he's worth seeing? Shall I email him to meet me for lunch? Never mind. Cancel that thought. I am not going to do lunch with another sex pervert. Your profile is attracting all the wrong men. Change that from lunch at the Brown Dog to coffee at the Red Horse Tavern. I'll email him. And, Merle, you had better stay away this time." I heard Merle harrumph, but she agreed. "Okay. Got to hang up. Lots to do. I'll talk to you later." And before she got in another word, I tapped my phone off.

"Wow. I can't believe you stopped her yada, yada, yada so quickly. I bet she's still talking."

"I bet she is too. But I have too much to think about right now. Let's reply to Gerald and make a date before we do anything else."

I opened my laptop to find Gerald's email. We sat staring at his photo and profile for a moment. "He looks like a winner," Milly muttered. "If Krappy looks like him, I don't understand Merle's obsession. He must be hiding something we can't see," she snickered.

"Don't get me going, Milly. I'm dreading these dates."

"You only had one, and it wasn't that bad was it?" She put her hand over her mouth to stop laughing. "Think of it this way. Merle threw you to the wolves, and now you know how to manage these guys. You survived Omar, and you can handle Gerald just fine. And I'm always there as your backup, watching you and sneaking photos of the guy. Think of these dates as learning lessons on how to navigate the new world we've lost touch with. We found a lot about dating online and users who are attracted to profiles like Merle's. I bet most women don't post profiles like hers, and there are some nice guys out there. We're becoming too judgmental. I, personally, know two women who have found great men online."

"I know that, but with this crazy method I'm using to find Krappy, there's got to be a better way. To be honest, Milly, I don't think we are ever going to find him. I think he's long gone, and I'm wasting my time."

"But you're having fun doing it," she teased.

"Stop! You're supposed to be my friend." I tapped the keyboard as fast as my fingers could move and replied to Gerald's email, asking when we could meet. "Done!" I closed my laptop and pushed my chair back. "Come on. Enough already. I have a few more important things to talk about with you. Let's head to the barn, and after we finish grooming Speed and Maverick, we'll have lunch."

I clipped Speed and Maverick to the crossties while Milly went to retrieve the tack box filled with grooming tools. Chip moved in and out between the horses' legs, but they never stirred. Oscar lay snoozing in front of a stall, relishing the beam of sun warming his body. With each brush stroke, Maverick relaxed. I didn't turn on the barn radio, preferring the peace and quiet. Maverick made soft-blowing sounds through his nose, expressing his pleasure. He appreciated the massage. Brushing Maverick released my pent-up stress, and I finally began to relax. Grooming horses is therapeutic and good for the soul. We finished brushing them simultaneously and unclipped them from the crossties. I ran my hand over my gelding's soft nose and kissed it. Milly ran her hand down Speed's neck and spoke to him in their secret language.

We turned the horses out, picked up the brushes, and put everything away. Chip weaved between Milly's legs, rubbing against her for attention. Milly bent down and ran her hand over Chip's belly. "Izzy, this cat is finally putting on some weight. She was so skinny when she first came here, and we both wondered if she'd make it."

"Yes, she's finally putting on some weight. And it seems so sudden. Wait, you don't think she's pregnant do you?" I picked Chip up and felt her belly. "Oh, no. I think she is. Don't know why it never occurred to me. She was so skinny and scraggly looking when she first arrived I thought she was too old to have kittens. And I couldn't get near her for the first few months."

Milly nodded. "I remember. Guess a trip to the vet is in order. Just to be sure it's kittens and not a tumor or something else."

"Oh my Lordy loo! What's the old saying? No good deed goes unpunished. Kittens? Is it time for a glass of wine?"

"Sounds good to me and I am suddenly hungry."

"Me too. Let's rake up the piles of horsehair and get out of here."

After lunch, we settled in the family room with a glass of wine. I told Milly about my nightmare and read her what I had written. She listened intently. "No wonder you are a writer. Even your dreams are a story. I am impressed. But I think your nightmare represents your fear of the unknown, and now you are thrust into something you have no control over. Helping Merle is turning out to be more than you bargained for. The men you are attracting are not ones you would think twice about. They are Merle's type, and she knows how to deal with them. They give her what she desires, and you are appalled by their words, where she would be delighted. You are trying to become someone you are not, and acting is not your strong suit right now. This is more difficult than you anticipated, and I believe, your fears and doubts are manifesting in a nightmare. It's that simple."

Milly made sense, but I couldn't shake the feeling of foreboding. I took a sip of wine and mulled over her words and her interpretation of my nightmare. "I know that dreams can reveal our fears and I hope you are right, but I can't shake the feeling there's a dangerous undercurrent surrounding Krappy and his friend and cousin. Call it a premonition, or as you said, my own lack of control over the situation, but I feel it's something more than that. Do you think it's Gus's concern that I am internalizing?"

"Maybe. But on the bright side, hold on to your notes. You may finally, after all my cajoling, write an adult mystery."

I chuckled at that. True, Milly had been pushing me to write adult books, and I had a few ideas, but I could barely finish my last kid's book. My mind was so focused on Merle's dilemma that I couldn't concentrate on much else, never mind writing an adult mystery, which is totally out of my wheelhouse and very time-consuming. "Forget that idea for now. I want to run another thought by you."

Milly scooted forward on the chair. "I'm all ears. Give it to me."

"I was thinking of contacting Carol Foxy and asking for her help."

"That's an interesting idea. What made you think of Foxy?"

I placed my glass on the table and picked up my notes for the pros and cons of bringing Foxy into my confidence. When I finished reading, I put the pad on the table and got up to pour myself another glass of wine. I sat down and waited for Milly's input.

She took a sip of wine and leaned forward. "Let's go through your list one thing at a time and try and answer each with a pro or con."

"Good thinking."

It took longer than we thought and a lot of brainstorming before we came to a decision. We concluded the most important reason for bringing Foxy into my confidence was that she had more resources than me.

"But most important, Milly, is that Foxy must agree not to write the story until the end of the month. That's when I told Merle I was done with the whole kit and kaboodle, regardless of the outcome."

Milly nodded. "Don't forget to tell her if she goes with the story she must agree not to use your names. And who knows, Izzy, after investigating, Foxy may discover there is no story. Merle just happened to trust the wrong man. It will all depend on what she finds using her sources and special investigative software that you don't have access to."

"True. She may come up with nothing. And probably Gus won't either. But, before I ask for her help, she needs to agree to my terms. Most importantly, I do have faith in her skills and discretion. Hate to say it, but she is older and wiser than a newbie reporter who is eager to make a name for herself. Foxy is fair and has already proven her worth in the news world."

Milly smiled. "I guess that's a benefit of aging. We no longer need to prove ourselves and we can say it like it is."

I got up and stretched my legs. "Whew. Too much sitting isn't good. Maybe I need to increase my gym time to six days a week."

"And maybe I need to join ·one." Milly chuckled as she stood up. "Let's take a coffee break and conclude this so you can make the call to Foxy."

"Who knows, Milly, perhaps this isn't a story and not worth her time. I'm sure she has heard other reports like this.

The main difference with Merle's saga is that she dated Krappy over a few months and got to know him, or, so she thought. But he had a plan all along. He enticed her by getting her to invest in Manhattan real estate that ended up being nothing but a lie. We're talking *Merle* here. What would she know about real estate anyway? I just *know* she did if for the accolades. She wanted everyone to think she is *so* smart to be generating her own good money for once. She fell *hard* for him and trusted his *"financial expertise."* And, from what I've read, most women conned by these nefarious types are in their seventies, and they *never* in-person meet whomever catfished them. The catfisher may even live in another part of the world, but the woman becomes addicted to the flattery and the swindler's sad backstory. They send real money to a fake love interest. Merle's story was different. Krappy wasn't just a voice or an email. She *physically* dated him and met his friend, and a cousin even. I wonder if they even know about his criminal life. They could be involved, too, but also, not."

Milly gave a huge sigh. "This is all food for thought. But one thing I'm certain is, we are out of our realm and it's a tangled web of intrigue. I'm ready for a break from Merle. Dessert is calling me."

Milly and I filled our mugs with coffee and opted for a slice of apple pie to go with it.

I searched for Carol Foxy's number on my contact list and tapped on the call symbol.

The phone rang, and a familiar voice answered. "Hello, Foxy here. What can I do for you, Izzy?"

I gave a thumbs-up to Milly. Foxy's voice was low and gravely, thanks to years of smoking. I paused for a moment, thinking how to begin the conversation. "Hi, Foxy. It's so good to hear your voice. I thought I'd probably get your voice mail and here you are."

"Yup. Your timing is perfect. I'm in my car, on the way to interview someone for a story. Damn, Izzy. It's been a while, too long, and it's so good to hear from you, too."

I gulped. It had been a while, but since the COVID lockdown, life had to reboot for me and many others, and there were still people I hadn't regrouped with. "I know. My apologies. The past two years have melted away and I feel like I've been held hostage on a spacecraft traveling at warp speed. The COVID pandemic ate up time like Pac-Man, and I wonder where it all went." I chuckled. "Thank God we came through the other side of it, whereas, sadly some people didn't. We all know friends and family who were affected."

I could envision Foxy's serious expression in her tone.

"I know. Who would have thought we would live long enough to survive a pandemic in one piece? If someone would have predicted this I would have laughed at the thought. Makes me wonder when the next one will hit. On the other hand, you'll be happy to know that I spent the time reevaluating my life, and I quit smoking. Hurrah for me!"

"OMG. I am so happy to hear that. I see you are still working for the Times?"

"I am. Part-time but once a journalist, it's in your blood and hard to give it up completely. Still waiting for a big scoop to drop in my lap. So, Izzy. What have you been up to?"

I wanted to tell her I had a new career as a PI, but that would blow her mind. Isadora Rose Franklin a PI? That's too unbelievable to say out loud. "I know this is the spur of the moment, but I wonder if you have time to meet over a cocktail and dinner to discuss something I'm deeply involved with. I need your investigative mind and clandestine tools to help me sort it out. It's much too involved and lengthy to go through over the phone."

"Now you have me curious." I heard a car honk and Foxy cursing. "Damn people! Learn how to drive," she muttered. "Sorry, Izzy. People are crazy out here. Sure, I'd love to meet for a drink. It's been too long, and I'm always ready for a cocktail. When's a good time?"

"Well, I know how busy you are, and this is spur of the moment, but do you have time today. My treat for your time."

"Spur of the moment works for me and dinner on you. Only kidding. I'd love to see you and catch up. Can we meet at say four o'clock?"

"Four sounds perfect. Is the Carriage House okay for you?"

"Yes, see ya there later. Gotta go. These drivers are out of their effin minds," she yelled, blaring her horn again at some hapless driver. Foxy's spicy life as a reporter has consisted of dark bars and hanging out with the boys; thus, cursing is her second language. I, too, have been known to throw a few F-Bombs along the way, much to everyone within earshot's surprise.

Milly shook her head. She was still chuckling when I turned the phone off. "Love her," she said. "While you and I were raising a family and living mundane lives, she traveled the world, seeking adventure, living on the wild side. Got to admire her. And her name is so damn fitting."

My lips pulled into a tight smile—Milly's right. I *have* lived a life of standard fare. I had a loving husband, my children are grown and successful, and I retired from a fulfilling career, but I have never lived with unbridled adventure. The most daring ventures I had were riding horses and skiing. I envied women like Foxy. *Why couldn't I have had it all*, I mused.

Milly waved her hand in front of my face. "Earth to Izzy. Where are you?"

Felt like I was in a trance. "Sorry, Milly. My mind was elsewhere, thinking about Foxy and how she's lived her life. Do you think we are too old for new adventures? After all, nothing is holding us back. Are we in a rut, still doing the same old things. Something has changed in me since COVID. I feel my life is moving way too fast and I haven't accomplished half of what I want to. Do you feel that way, too?"

True to form, Milly took a moment before answering me. She sat back and blew out a sigh. "Now, those are deep questions. I'm going to be honest with you. Taking on Merle's problem has blown you out of your comfort zone, but you feel more alive than you have in a long time. You've shape-shifted from a comfortable, safe, routine-life Izzy into a new Izzy. Izzy, the daring PI, doggedly pushes out of her comfort zone into a new world of risk and chance. Sounds like a book title, doesn't it?" she smiled. "And although you feel that you have tumbled into this risky venture against your better judgment, the new Izzy is leaving her cozy cocoon and reinventing herself. And that's all one can hope for at any age."

And that's Milly. She is a straight talker and has no BS. She only offers advice if asked and then tells you like it is. "Whew. I feel better already. I guess it's never too late to start over, and now I need to take my own advice and your sage wisdom. I'm feeling lighter for the first time in what seems like forever."

"Okay, Izzy. Let's see how interested Gerald is in meeting you. And when?"

Back in my office, I checked my email, and Gerald had answered. "Funny, Gerald said he found me on Silver Love. Most responses have come from there. Looks like Silver Love attracts a lot of men looking for someone like Merle."

Milly stifled a laugh as she read his reply. "*Bonjour, Izzy. I am pleased you want to meet me for coffee. After reading your profile, we will make a good match.* Yeesh! Sounds like another studly guy very sure of himself," she rolled her eyes, then returned to reading aloud, "*I am at your disposal and willing to meet anywhere you choose. I am waiting for your rapid response with high hopes. You are a beautiful woman, and I am honored you are ready to allow us to follow our dreams.* Hmph. Gerald sounds like a beaut." She smirked.

I started to laugh. "Wow. Can you believe this guy? He sounds so unbelievable phony and smarmy, but after looking at his photo, Merle said to answer him and set up a date. She said, even with all the facial hair, he has a familiarity about him. Around the eyes. I'll tell him I can meet up tomorrow." I quickly typed in a reply and waited for an answer.

Oscar entered my office and sat in front of me. It was a stare-down look. I could read him like a book and knew he needed to pee. "Milly, Oscar needs to go out. Let's grab ourselves another coffee. I can check my email on my phone to see if Gerald replies. He may be busy and may not be on email."

While Oscar was outside, Milly dropped K-cups in the coffee maker, and I pulled a chair from the table. I wanted to go over my notes and see if there were any clues I had missed. I had a lot more information now than when I started. My pad was filled with names, dates, places, and impressions of what Merle had told me and from the text exchanges she had sent me. Oscar barked, and I let him back inside and gave him his cookie treat. Milly set my coffee next to me and put hers across from me. She took a sip and glanced at the pad. "So, your notepad is filling. Eventually, we may see a pattern."

"Don't count on it. There are too many moving parts and tons of missing pieces, but I know this is only the beginning." I put my pen down and picked up my mug. I had enough for one day.

"Not to change the subject, but what are you wearing on your date with Gerald, if I may ask," she said, her eyes looking mischievous and her lips curling into a slight smile. "Maybe you should wear something a little sexier. Think Merle."

I cringed at the thought. "I'm wearing the same outfit I wore when I met Omar. I'm not buying new clothes for numerous dates with strange men I'm not out to impress. I'd rather buy a new pair of jeans."

Milly scoffed at that. "I bet if you were dating someone who made your heart sing, you'd be thinking about a new wardrobe and loving every minute of the shopping trip."

That got us both giggling like young schoolgirls.

I told Milly I decided to meet any man Merle thought might be a Krappy match further from our town. "Meeting Omar at the Brown Dog was too close. I'm going to suggest meeting Gerald at the Red Horse Tavern in Farmington."

"Good thinking, and I agree. You're better off meeting at a place at least forty-five minutes away from here, so when you slip out the back door, you don't have to worry about seeing the degenerate again," Milly grinned in a conspiratorial way. "Keep those sex perverts as far away from home as you can. And the Red Horse Tavern is a good choice. They have great desserts. It seems wild that a tavern is known for its specialty desserts and alcoholic beverages. I heard it gets busy there, so best to meet earlier than the luncheon crowd."

"Damn, Milly. I feel like we're partners in crime," I said, laughing. "Except you are having all the fun just watching, and I am trying to be someone I'm not. I think my part is the hardest."

"True, and I'm glad it's you and not me. But then, you let everyone guilt you into everything. You need to work on that, you know." Her eyebrows furrowed, showing her concern.

"I know and don't think I'm not aware of my pattern with Merle. She's ruined the Brown Dog for me. I haven't returned there since meeting Omar. I'm afraid he'll show up and then what would I do?"

"Heard from him since you skipped out the back?"

"Yes. Forgot to tell you, got an email from him last night. With any luck, it's his last. Hope he's not a stalker. He said he was upset I didn't return. Thinking we were getting along famously, he looked forward to setting up a "real date.""

"A real date?" Milly almost spit out her coffee. "I hate to think what a real date means to him."

"I know. Me, too. Omar said he had gone looking for me when I didn't return, and after talking to the bartender, he realized I had scooted out the back door. "Is it something I said?" he asked. "Yeesh! I wanted to type a resounding YES, but I didn't want back-and-forth emailing dragging on any longer. I'm glad he couldn't see my face as I read his emails."

Milly picked up her coffee mug and took a slow drink from it. "Go on. Tell me more," she said, grinning from ear-to-ear. "What else did his email say?"

I tried to keep a straight face. "I replied that I didn't believe we were a proper fit and didn't have the heart to say that to his face. He replied he thought we would *fit* perfectly. Yikes! After listening to his continual sexual innuendos, I know exactly what *fit* means to him."

We broke into hysterical laughter. After wiping our eyes, we discussed Omar and his talent for inserting sexual overtones into every subject. "I never felt so flustered and at a loss for words. I couldn't wait to get out of there and never want to talk to or see that man again."

"Well, 1, Merle; 0, you," Milly chuckled.

"You're actually keeping count?" I asked.

"Yup. Lesson learned. Be careful what you promise and who you promise it to."

I knew precisely what she meant and wondered how much more I could take of being off-kilter and out of my realm.

"Gotta go, Izzy," Milly said, pulling on her jacket. "I've had enough fun for the day, and I have a life, you know." She smiled as she hugged me and said goodbye to Oscar.

"I know. Thanks for being my friend and support." After Milly left, I headed back to my office. I had finished the last two chapters of my book. I placed the draft in a large envelope to drop off at the post office on my way to meet Foxy.

Foxy was already seated when I arrived at the Carriage House Restaurant. She waved when I entered. Dale was waiting on a couple at the bar and gestured to me as I walked by.

Foxy rose from her seat and gave me a quick hug. "Hey, Izzy. It's been too long. I was here a little early and ordered a martini while I perused the menu." There was no missing that she was a reporter. She looked the part and spoke like one, making her a force to be reckoned with. She hadn't changed one iota since we last met, and I was happy I'd decided to run this thing by her. Her advice would be helpful and wise. Everyone in town knew her. She was a celebrity, known for her unbiased truth, making politicians stay in line and the bad guys run for cover.

I was glad to see Dale coming over with his friendly smile.

"Hey, Izzy. What can I get for you?"

"I'll take what Foxy's drinking. That looks delightful."

"You got it," Dale said with a wink. "By the way, there's a new special this week, if you're interested. A small plate of pasta with a creamy mushroom sauce and a side salad."

Foxy looked at me. "I'm fine, having my old standby. Half a sandwich and cup of soup."

"You know, Dale, that does sound good to me. *I'll* have the special. Think that does it for us. Can you bring bread and dipping sauce, along with my martini?"

"For sure."

Foxy nodded her approval. "And, Dale, can you bring me another martini with Izzy's? I'm almost finished with this one." She motioned to her half-empty glass.

"Sure thing, ladies. I'm on it." He smiled.

"Honestly, Foxy, I skipped lunch to finish my last draft of the final chapter in my book, and I'm starving."

"Totally understand. I was up early writing a column for the paper, so I had a large breakfast."

Dale returned with our cocktails and warm bread.

We toasted to good health and a beautiful spring. After clinking glasses and draining her first martini, Foxy set her glass down and looked across at me. "So, Izzy. What is so urgent that you need my advice? It's not a new lover is it?" she teased.

"Wish it were that easy," I stifled a laugh. "This is much more complex. Since you have the skills as an investigative reporter that *I* don't, I really need your help in decoding a huge con my friend fell for. You know me; can't say *no* when someone needs my assistance, so I jumped in, way outside of my comfort zone and experience. I'm trying to figure out if it's worth my effort, and *if so*, my next step."

Foxy sat back and took a deep sip of her second martini. "Well, now you've got my antenna up. Go on."

"I know this is asking a great deal from you, but before I tell you the whole story, can you promise me you won't print anything until I see it through and take it as far as I can. After you hear me out, you can judge if it's worth your time. And one more thing, can you promise that if you run with it, you won't disclose my name or my friends' name? I know this is asking a lot, but something tells me this is worth your time and energy."

Foxy's eyes never left mine. Her face turned serious, her lips pursed, and I heard her take a breath. She smells a story, and I have her intrigued. She knows I am not a loose-lipped woman and asking her to keep what I tell her confidential must be important. Foxy is everything I admire. She's an attractive woman in her seventies, and her eyes are always curious. She leaned back against the booth, deep in thought, pondering what I had told her. I studied her as she contemplated my ask. Her tousled, curly gray hair was cut short and softly framed her face. Foxy is about my height but smaller boned. She's wearing over-sized tortoiseshell glasses that almost cover her face, but they look chic and stylish on her. Foxy has the most piercing dark eyes, and they can see right through a person, which makes her an excellent investigative reporter. She is daring and bold, all that I want to be. She is a no-nonsense woman who lives by her word and fact-checks everything before printing a story. Foxy's a investigative reporter, and I could see why she was still in demand. "Really," she said, leaning forward, hands crossed, eyes staring into mine. "That's a lot to promise, Izzy, but if you're asking me to agree to keep this conversation confidential it must be as urgent as your call. Do I sense a wariness in your voice? You're not in any danger are you?"

I gulped. Did I show my fear that easily? Since my nightmare invaded my thoughts daily, I had a heightened awareness of danger lurking in every corner. My logical side pooh-poohed the possibility, but was my nightmare a premonition? I couldn't tell Foxy about it. She would think I was daft. "I wish I could say there wasn't risk in my search for the unscrupulous opportunist who conned my friend out of her money, but I am out of my comfort zone, and I know it." I tried to smile, but my lips felt stuck in a thin line. "No, no. I don't believe I'm in danger. It's that I'm no detective and my friend thinks I am...or could be. And now she has me believing I can solve her problem. Uh, it's more than a problem. It's a rabbit hole."

Foxy raised her glass again. "Here's to new adventures. A collaboration. Izzy, you have captured my interest. And yes, I promise whatever you share with me will be held in my highest confidence. And *if* your dilemma is as intriguing as you allude, and *if* I believe it is worth investigating, and *if* I decide it is newsworthy, I will leave your name and your friends' out of it, unless you give me the go-ahead."

I slowly exhaled. Stress drained from my body like butter off a hot knife. Foxy was indeed a good and reliable friend. I trusted her. I tapped my glass to hers. Let the fun begin.

As I pulled into the parking lot of the Build-Em-Up-Gym for the first time in a week, I noticed I wasn't stressed out. I felt refreshed and ready to begin the day. I tapped my keycard to open the door, prepared to walk my worries away. I've found that belonging to a gym is mind over matter. My mind says, *no*, but my body says, *go*. A core group of members work out every morning at about the same time—primarily retirees or young people on college break. While I'm not making headway finding Krappy, I feel like a winner once in the gym. My new job as a PI is more mind-blowing than I anticipated, and I need a boost to my psyche to conquer something, even if only two miles on the treadmill. Once I entered, a cacophony of sounds filled my senses, and I almost forgot about my meeting with Gerald.

The groans from Joe lifting heavy weights, the low voices of three of the women on the treadmills, the exuberant sports announcer's voice from the mounted TV, and the background music all mingled together, and I was in my comfort zone.

This is a positive, cheerful place, and I didn't realize how much I missed my morning routine until I entered. I spotted my trainer, Jackie, working with one of her clients. She saw me come in and waved a quick hello.

Knowing she'd ask where I'd been when she had a moment, I'd practiced my reply. *"I've been busy with my new career as a Private Investigator."* I could picture her eyes booming in disbelief. Of course, that sounds insane. It's so unbelievable. No one would *ever* think of me as a PI in, not their wildest dreams. I *am* a writer, not a detective. But I would try to remain serious as I told her about the drama I'd been drawn into. *"Jackie, my whole life has been turned upside down and this new case has eaten up all my time."* Would she laugh at the idea or want to hear more? If she believes me, I'll tell her the rest. *"I've been doing a deep dive into a con, whom my friend got mixed up with, and as part of my investigation, I'm meeting with perv matches from online dating sites that I joined."* I was giggling inside and a smile was coming on. How can I ever say that with a straight face? She'd never believe me, laugh, and think I was joking. If only she knew how crazy my life had become. I tossed that explanation aside. If she asks, I'll simply say, I had an emergency out of town and leave it at that.

The gym is a lively place where everyone knows your name, and you feel welcome when you enter. Members don't talk about anything personal 'cause we're all in the same place and working on common goals: health or fitness. Light bantering is the order of the day each morning, and I'm happy to keep it that way.

David Valentine, the gym owner, was in his office and

looked up when he spotted me coming in. "Hey, Queen. Where have you been?"

David and I generally partake in light chitchat. "Drinking too many cocktails," I yelled back. "I can't indulge anymore like *you* still can. Takes me too long to recover." And so goes our back-and-forth teasing and flippant remarks.

He is a friendly, handsome guy in his early sixties and in good physical shape. Everyone here knows him. He's often on the treadmill when I come in, and he runs the gym like a tight ship. His dating is sporadic, and I wish he could find a girlfriend who cares as much for him as we all do. He's looking in all the wrong places for a woman he can see a future with. Although plenty of women were interested, he has yet to meet one who makes his heart sing, and Jackie and I are always kibitzing about different female matches for him. On the other hand, he may be like many, choosing partners who never work out because, subconsciously, they are afraid to commit to a serious relationship.

As I took my jacket off and placed it with my handbag in the cubby, the lyrics from the *Cheers* theme song danced through my head—always knowing your name and being so glad you came. Why do I always feel like I'm in a sitcom here? I am, by nature, a storyteller and have a habit of dreaming up yarns about different members working out. As I strode to the treadmill, I glanced at George, watching his face as he pedaled the stationary bike. He looks torturous, crinkled, and red-faced, but his effort is impressive. George, who usually wears colorful Western shirts, puts one hundred percent effort into his workouts, building strength and endurance, but I've never seen him lifting weights. And even though he does not look the type or body build, I often envision him as a country line dancer who works hard to build his stamina for the ladies at the dance hall. George has a European accent; today, he's a CIA agent traveling incognito. Now that I'm a PI, I quickly recognize another investigator type.

Another loud groan from Hos caught my attention, and I turned my head to see what's up. Hos is a short, well-muscled, balding guy who lifts heavier weights weekly. To me, that seems more like torture rather than bodybuilding, and his groaning proves my point. I bet he works nights as a bouncer at a biker bar, and in the daytime, he's a mild-mannered accountant—so much for daydreaming.

I stepped on the treadmill, tapped in my weight, and began. It was time to clear my head before I meet with Gerald, the guy I already knew was so full of himself.

I walked for forty-five minutes today, and after waving goodbye and saying, "See ya tomorrow," to Jackie and Dave, the Prince, I made my way to my car and headed home to shower and change into my "date" clothes. I was plotting my escape method from Gerald when my cellphone played "A Horse with No Name," Gus's ringtone. "Hi, Gus. You're home from your trip?"

"Hi, Izzy. Yes, I am. I happened to run into Milly at the Donut Ranch. She said you're meeting a guy from one of your dating sites at the Red Horse Tavern. I asked if I could be there to watch your back this time. She agreed, but said I should check with you first. Her description of this Gerald fellow was interesting." I could picture the grin on his face.

"Gus, the Red Horse is at least forty-five minutes away. Are you sure?"

"Yes, I know. I went there with Bob last month. How 'bout I pick you up and we drive together? I can park far enough away from the entrance, and we can walk in separately. I need to talk to you about Merle's case and what I discovered."

"Really? You have information that may help Merle?"

"Yes, but I don't want to discuss it over the phone. I thought we could talk on our way home from your date," he chuckled.

I struck back. "Actually, Gus, this Gerald is a very handsome-looking guy, and I'm kind of excited to meet him. He sounds a ton better than Omar. Of course, any man would be better than Omar."

There was a slight pause before Gus spoke. "So, Izzy. Wanna take me up on that offer?"

Of course, I wanted to hear what he learned, but I also wanted him to know I was a big girl and could handle Gerald. I feel more in control with Milly watching my back, and I'm not sure if I can work Gerald with Gus's eagle eyes on me. "Hmm. I *am* interested in what you dug up, but I don't want you to interfere with my date. Merle said he looked familiar, but this guy has lots of facial hair. She said it was his eyes that got her. But who knows with Merle? You'd think she could identify the man she slept with for quite some time."

I envisioned Gus stifling a laugh. "I promise. I won't interfere. When you're ready to leave, signal me, and I'll meet you out back. I'll park the car behind the Tavern after I leave you off."

Gus was right on time. I told him that I was meeting Gerald at three o'clock and it was two o'clock when he knocked on my door. Oscar did his dog thing and pushed past me to greet Gus. They had a special connection, and Oscar was jumping up at him, which I did not like, but unfortunately, Gus did. "Hey, buddy. Happy to see you too," he said, rubbing Oscar's ears. I've given up scolding Oscar. He and Gus never listened to me anyway. Gus's eyes looked me up and down. "Damn, Izzy. You look very pretty. Your new date will fall all over you, so to speak," he teased. "Good thing I'll be there keeping an eye on the guy. These types can't be trusted around a pretty woman." He smiled.

I could feel heat spreading from my toes to my face. Our friendship wasn't like that. It was easy and casual. The compliment from the attractive man standing before me made me feel warm and fuzzy, and I didn't want him to see me blushing. It'd be too easy to fall for Gus, and we had never said we were ready for anything more than a solid friendship.

"Thank you, Gus," I said, reaching for my sweater coat.

He got it first. "Allow me," he said, standing behind me as I put my arms in the sleeves. He moved in front of me and leaned close. His warm breath tickled my face. He was smiling ear-to-ear. I couldn't tell if he was teasing me or about to kiss me. *Gus wanting to kiss me? Uh, what am I thinking?* His eyes caught mine. It was the first time I saw more than friendship in them. I quickly moved away and grabbed my purse.

The ride to the Red Horse Tavern was uneventful, and although I tried to get Gus to fill me in on his meeting with his friend from the FBI, he said it was better to talk about it on our way home and after my date with Gerald. So, we spent the time talking about family, horses, and life. I asked how Bob was, and he said they'd been at Happy Harry's Sports Bar to watch a game last week. Gus reminded me the Kentucky

Derby was coming soon and asked if Milly and I wanted to join them. It would be fun for us to watch it at Harry's and place a few bets on the horses. I loved the idea and said I would ask Milly when I saw her later.

We arrived at the Tavern in plenty of time to meet Gerald. He had said it was about an hour from his town and had never been there. His email said, "Distance is no issue, Izzy, and I'm thrilled to meet you anywhere and anytime." Just remembering those words made my heart race and my face flush. All I could think of was Omar.

The beautiful, historic building with wide-plank flooring and aged beams was originally a clothing mill built in the 1800s and sat on a side road off Main Street. The extensive parking lot was set back from the Tavern and surrounded by trees where a green expanse rolled gently down to a narrow river. Although only established six years ago by a young couple with a vision for rehabbing old mills, it was earning a reputation for its variety of cocktails but, crazy as it sounds, its decadent desserts. The Tavern has an elegant ambiance and was a destination eatery known for its luncheon specials, Vodka Sauce Cheeseburgers, Blue Cheese BLTs, and Spicy Reubens. The luncheon crowd was thinning out, but it was still busy when I walked in ahead of Gus. He had waited a bit before strolling in and sitting at the long bar against the back wall. There were booths, small tables, and leather chairs across the room, and although it was sunny outside, the light in the Tavern was dim and cozy. It took a moment to catch sight of a slightly built man sitting alone at one of the tables.

As I approached, he stood and held out his hand. *"Bonjour,* Izzy," he said with a slight accent, at which I fakely beamed.

"Hello. From your photo I recognize you as Gerald." I took my sweater coat off but kept it draped over my shoulders.

"Yes, join me, please."

I sat, and his intense eyes swept over me as he reached across the table to kiss me on both cheeks. I didn't take it as flattery but as a close inspection of a racehorse for sale. His beard and mustache were trimmed closer than in the photo, and his piercing green slanted eyes were jarring. His skin was olive-toned, his nose was slightly pronounced, and his lips were thin. Individually, his features made no sense, but they made him appealing and mysterious. I wouldn't say he was handsome, but he had the intensity and self-confidence to draw a woman in. He was definitely a Merle-type man, and my fabricated profile made me his. I was feeling rattled for the first time. Gerald was no Omar. I sighed in relief when the waiter arrived with menus and glasses filled with ice water.

"Would you like something from the bar?" he asked.

Gerald nodded to me. "What is the drink you desire, Izzy?" He said it with an emphasis on desire.

My plans for coffee and dessert took a back seat. This meeting required something to calm my nerves. Forget the coffee. I need a bigger boost. "I'll have a martini," I replied. I felt like I was in a trance. I was in over my head. Omar, although a pervert, was easy to see through. This man was smooth as silk, and his deep-set eyes never left mine. I broke the stare-down by reaching for the menu.

"Please, I'll have the same as the lady," Gerald said, if that's his real name. He reached over and touched my folded hands. "Your hands are cold, Izzy." Omar's voice was low and oozing with sex, and his grin was rakish. "How can I warm you up?"

My mouth opened to say something, but I was lost for words, and I couldn't think of a reply that would sound witty and confident. "Not to worry. It was a little cold outside. I'll be fine in a minute." My mind was on overdrive. *Distract, Izzy!* "So, how long was the drive for you?" How mundane and silly that sounded.

"No bother. It was pleasurable because all I could think of was meeting you, and, Izzy, you are all that I expected. You are a woman of my dreams, and your profile is everything I yearn for. Are you pleased with me?"

Gulp. I was stunned. Thankfully, the waiter placed our martinis on the table, and before he could ask for our order, I took a long sip of mine. Gerald, who I now thought of as Casanova, was charming, with a beguiling way of delivering flattery that would be music to a woman's ears. He was focused on me and my life. I had to stall, with a sip of martini, to remember my lies. Each time I tried to change the subject, he reverted to what he found endearing about my profile and appearance. He slowly repeated each word from my Silver Love profile to remind me how much he was attracted to an independent, free-spirited woman like me. He *memorized* it?

"You are a man's dream, my love. Please tell me your full name. You are too beautiful to be Izzy."

I reached for my martini. *Slow down.* I wanted to down it. "Isadora Rose Franklin." I had to tell the truth. It was on my profile.

"Isadora," he said with an accent I found titillating, as it made me sound exotic. "That becomes you, my love."

Oh, my God. I need to get out of here. My phone kept buzzing. It's good that I'd turned it on silent. At one time, he asked if I should answer, and I said it was my office. I was working on a project. If he only knew the project was him. After the seventh buzz, I glanced at my phone. It was Merle. She was in a frenzy, and I knew she'd keep calling until I answered. I ignored it and took another sip of martini.

The waiter delivered appetizers. I had no appetite for dessert. I picked at mine while Gerald kept talking. When to leave? And how to bow out gracefully? He asked about my travel adventures and which city I loved the best. Our conversation continued to flow. I told him I enjoyed Boston and loved the city's ambiance, restaurants, and theater. He asked what my favorite car was, and luckily, my dream car was a high-end Lexus, which I knew all about because I had gone to a showroom and driven one. So, we talked about cars and Hawaii, where I had vacationed for three weeks with Max.

Time passed quickly, and I almost enjoyed listening to his voice. But my red flag was up, and something about Gerald did not ring true. He was too slick and overly attentive for a first date. I was about to excuse myself for the ladies' room when Gerald leaned across the table, reached for my hands, and cupped his over mine. He whispered, "So, my love, you enjoy Boston? As I said, I travel extensively for business, and one of my businesses is in Boston. I own a condo there." He smiled wickedly. "You said you are spontaneous. Would you like to drive there tonight?" His breath smelled of martini, and his eyes were soft.

I gently pulled my hands away and took another sip of my drink, trying to maneuver my way out of his invitation. "Oh, Gerald," I said, mustering the sexiest voice I could.

"Unfortunately, I have an important meeting this week. You heard my phone continually buzzing. Perhaps next week?"

Gerald sat back and grinned like a Cheshire cat. "Perhaps not Boston. Would you prefer an island instead, where I can massage your body with lotion from head to toe? You said you loved massages while lying on a blanket next to the ocean."

That did it. I drained the last drop of martini.

"Shall I signal the waiter for another?" He motioned to my empty glass.

"No, but thank you, Gerald. I'm driving, and although I'd love another, my rule is *one drink* only. If you'll excuse me, I'll use the lady's room and be right back." I could feel Gerald's eyes ogling me as I draped my sweater coat over my chair then quickly maneuvered around patron-filled tables. As I passed Gus at the bar, he winked and raised his glass in a silly toasting gesture. I wanted to say something snarky, but my cellphone kept buzzing and would not stop. Merle. She was probably checking in on how my date was going and wanted details. "Damn you, Merle. Stop calling me," I whispered. I wasn't going to answer, but once in the lady's room, the phone was still buzzing. I gave up. I was desperate to escape. "Merle. Can you wait till I get home? You've been calling me for the last hour and driving me crazy."

"Why didn't you answer me, Izzy? I looked closer at the profile. It hit me! The guy you're with is *not* some *Gerald.* I knew I recognized those eyes. He is Karl's cousin. I can't believe it! *He's* the man you are meeting! Say something!"

It took a moment to digest what she was even saying. Wait. Krappy Karl's cousin? *The Blur?* My jaw dropped when it sank in. What on earth? "Are you sure?"

"*Yes,* I'm sure, and he might know where Karl is. Could you ask him?

"I'm hanging up. Don't call me again. I need to think about this and how to ask about Krappy without giving away my intentions. We have no idea for sure if he even knows Krappy is a conman. I'll call you when I get home." I left the ladies' room and motioned for Gus to meet me in a nook between the mens' and ladies' room.

"Ready to leave Mr. Wonderful?" He smiled, but it fell when he looked at my shocked face.

"Merle's been calling me since I got here. She is driving me nuts. I had my phone on silent, and I ignored it till now." I relayed what Merle had just told me.

At "cousin" Gus's jaw grew taut and eyes narrowed. "Don't ask me questions right now, Izzy, but you've *got to* see this through. You can't leave without setting a date with him."

"Gus, I can't. And I can't ask him if he knows Karl Hendricks. He'll know I set him up. He wants me to go to Boston where he has a condo or to some island with him. What do I say? What are you not telling me?"

"Can't explain it right now. But, yeah, *do not* mention Karl's name. Listen, Izzy. Just play the part. Think like Merle. Set up a date with him in Boston, say, next week. I'll fill you in on the way home. Just do it. If you want to find out what happened to Karl, do this, Izzy. Stick it out. You came to play the game. Now's the time to finish the act with all you've got. Go back and make nice with Gerald."

I was so annoyed with all of this, and shaking like crazy, but I had no way out. Another martini might help.

I'd been away from the table too long and I was worried Gerald would come looking for me. As soon as I nodded my head in agreement, Gus hustled back to the bar.

"Lucky bastard," I mumbled. *There goes my potty mouth again.* He could sit back and watch my awkward situation from a distance, but I was left panicking and sick to my stomach. I was glad I couldn't see him from where I was sitting with Gerald because if he ever grinned in amusement, I could never continue to play-act as Merle. And I wasn't sure if I could recast myself into an overzealous woman, like Merle, who can't wait to get Casanova Gerald alone.

I had only a moment to pull myself together. My mind was on overdrive, and I had no time to reflect on what Merle told me or what Gus had me going along with. I had to dig deep and muster Merle's voice to move forward. Having known her since we were kids, I'd witnessed plenty of her behavior around boys and now as a woman around men. I trusted Gus and believed him when he said that my search for Krappy had propelled me into more than a simple dating site scam. My heart was racing and hands began to sweat. I had to return to the table before Gerald wondered where I was. Oh, my God! Everything was happening too fast. If not for Gus driving with me, even with Merle's call, I would have snuck out the back door, and Milly would've been waiting for me to make our escape. Why was Gus so adamant I make a date next week to meet Gerald in Boston, and why was he pressing me to do so?

Meeting Gerald had suddenly changed from a simple date to a tangled spider's web that fired a shiver of fear down my spine. Everything had changed, and instead of escaping out the back, I must return to Gerald and turn into a femme fatale and reel him in like a floppy fish on a hook. Does he know his cousin Krappy is a conman? Is Krappy still in Boston? And why did Gerald answer my profile? What is the common denominator between my profile and Merle's? All these thoughts ran through my head, and I felt like I was on top of a high diving board with no place to go, praying I'd survive the jump and make it out of the pool of the unknown.

Time stood still, and my lungs were about to explode. I struggled to exhale, almost choking. I pulled my shoulders back and strode confidently to the table. Gerald smiled and stood when he saw me. Gentleman, it seemed, he tugged my chair out for me to sit. He paused, then leaned over and kissed my head. Holy hell! I'm glad he didn't see my face. I tried not to cringe. He had ordered us another martini. *Geez Louise!* I needed it more than ever, and against my better judgment, I took a quick gulp. How can I make this meeting a honey trap and become irresistible bait? If I were younger, I'd feel more confident in my sexuality, but can I pull this off at my age?

Doubts seeped into my brain as I took another swallow of my drink, with Gerald's eyes never leaving mine. The pause helped, and my logical self took over my doubting brain. *Stop it, Izzy. He's likely here to trap you, just like Krappy. You must appear vulnerable and bedazzled. Play his game.*

Gerald lowered his voice to almost a whisper. "I thought something was wrong, my love. I was going to go looking for you, but then, there you were, walking toward me like a ray of sunshine. And to tell the truth, I gave a huge sigh of relief. I was worried you were not returning."

I willed my voice to be soft and flirtatious, my eyes smoldering and seductive as I transformed into Merle. I reached for his hand. "My apologies, Gerald. It took me a few minutes. My phone would not stop buzzing, and I had to answer the call. It was my office, and I knew we'd have no peace until I answered. They couldn't move on with the new project without my okay."

Gerald nodded, his eyes understanding.

"You know how I told you I developed a small startup after I retired. Well, it's growing faster than I anticipated. Now, I'm wondering if it's worth it, as it's interfering with my free time and travel plans. I forced a timid smile. It was the most I could muster. I saw Gerald's body language change as I slowly roped him in. "Gerald, darling, now that I've met you, it's plain to see that if all goes well, we'll be spending lots of time together."

He brushed a strand of hair from my face, our eyes locking. Could he see right through me? His eyes narrowed, and his face grew serious as he listened intently to my words. I'd never played this game before, tricking a person, and I'm not a very good actor, but Gus's words kept ringing in my ears. *"If you want to find out what happened to Karl, do this, Izzy. Stick it out. You came to play the game. Now's the time to finish the act with all you've got."*

Gerald nodded, and his face softened. "I understand, my love. My people are always after me with one question or another. Even though I hire the best, the final decisions on a project come from me. I admire your business savvy, Isadora." His hands covered mine, and one of his fingers moved caressingly, like a slimy snake, making me want to yank it away. He leaned closer. His voice was husky and low. "Isadora. I love the sound of your name and believe we are a perfect match. Can't wait to see you again and spend time, enjoying new ventures. I promise you good times and lovely beaches. This is only the beginning, my love."

I gently pulled my hands away from his. "Darling," I gushed, "as much as I hate to tear myself away from you and end our first date, I need to be on my way after we finish our drinks. As I said, my manager needs to speak with me personally. It's confidential. Issues have arisen that I must take care of. I'm sure you understand. But, I *am* thinking that Boston sounds like a fun place to spend more time with you, getting to know you better," I struggled to tack on the word, "*darling*," but I poured it on, thick, hoping to show how much he fascinated me.

He reached for my hands again, and I didn't pull away. His dark eyes revealed nothing. They were impenetrable mirrors. It seemed time stood still. His lips curled into a smile, and his breath was like fire. "Now that we've met to only discover sizzling sparks between us, and realize we share much in common, I hesitate to be away from you. So, my Isadora, we *will meet* in Boston next week? I would be delighted. Can you stay for a few days? You and I have so much to explore."

A slight shudder ran through my body. His definition of exploring was definitely not mine. He released my hands, and his fingers slowly trailed up my arm. I longed to pull away, but I was all in, thanks to Merle and Gus, and stayed still. I smiled, taking a moment to consider my reply. I didn't want to appear overeager. Glancing over at the couple sitting near us, I was immediately self-conscious. Were they listening? Between Gerald's charming European accent, his heady sexual body language, and his overwhelming attentiveness, I was uncomfortable and wondered if the entire room was staring.

"What are you thinking, my love?" Gerald inquired, having noticed my uneasiness.

I flushed a guilty shade of red but answered quickly. "Oh, I forgot I didn't even say anything." I giggled, but the cracks in it kept it from being as flirtatious as I'd intended to feign. "Yes, I would *love* to, *darling*, and I am looking forward to it. I was already daydreaming of Boston, spending time with you, dining at cafes, seeing the sites, and perhaps, even visiting your condo."

Gerald's smile was seductive and irresistible. His intense, narrowed eyes were like magnets, and his voice dripped with animalistic need, but I could easily ignore the unexpected buzz and warmth in my body with my mind fixed on the vital task at hand.

"Yes, of course, we will go to my condo. That is a promise. Isadora, my love, I cannot wait to be alone with you, and we can take the day, *and night*, to learn more about each other."

I swept my fingers across my mouth to hold back a cringe, and also, the start of a belly laugh 'cause it was just too much.

"Let's exchange cell numbers so we can set the day and time. I will be sure to adjust my schedule so we will not be interrupted. And you will do likewise, my love?"

I had to look away. I was out of my league with this man, and the sooner I left, the better. I could barely speak, and my mouth was suddenly dry. "Yes, darling. I will rearrange my schedule so we can spend *uninterrupted* time together." Gerald gave me his number, and I tapped it into the contact list on my burner phone. Gus had me buy one to only use for my online dates. Hope he didn't notice that my hands were shaking. *Exhale, Izzy. Pretend you're Merle.*

Gerald added me to his contacts. After draining our martinis, he signaled for the check, and the waiter stopped on his way to another table. Gerald briefly scanned it and pulled cash from his wallet. From the waiter's look, he must've left a generous tip. "Isadora," he had taken to calling me that when not using, "my love", "allow me to go to the men's room, and when I return, I will walk you to your car."

Oh no. Disaster. Gus had moved the car to the back, and I didn't have the keys. Now what? "Of course, darling," was all I could mumble. As soon as Gerald left his chair, my phone buzzed. I quickly read a text from Gus. *I pulled my car in front of the tavern. Walking out now. Spill your handbag as I go by, and I'll stop to help you and pass you the key. Then, wait for him to leave the lot and pick me up around back.*

Whew. Crisis avoided. When I saw Gus approaching my table, I slid my sweater coat on and knocked my handbag off the chair. A few of its contents fell on the floor. He stopped to assist me, and I picked up the key just in time to see Gerald walking briskly toward me. "Thank you," I whispered.

Gus gave me a quick wink.

I was standing when Gerald got back to the table. He grinned at me like a wolf then linked his arm with mine. We maneuvered out of the busy tavern and headed to Gus's car. Thank goodness we'd driven to the bar in Gus's luxury sedan, not my ten-year-old SUV. We stopped beside it, and Gerald pulled me close. "I look forward to seeing you soon, my Isadora Rose. I cannot wait." Before I had time to answer, he cupped the back of my head and leaned in to kiss me. His lips were warm and lingering. It was my first romantic kiss since Max had passed. And a stranger at that. I kissed him back, not wanting to blow my cover as a Merle-type. When he released me, I was breathless. I was surprised by Gerald's prowess and kissing expertise, and I enjoyed it more than I'd anticipated. Now I understand the art of persuasion that men like Gerald hold over women. And it wasn't his words or looks; it was his kiss. His dark eyes studied me.

My throat tightened. The song "Slow Hands" ran through my head. *"Darling, don't say a word, I've already heard what your body's sayin' to mine. You're tired of fast moves. You've got a slow groove on your mind."* For a moment, I was lost in memories of Max, the man I had loved for many years. I felt tears merging at the corners of my eyes. I squinted to hold them back. If he noticed, he made no mention.

Gerald stepped back and took a quick breath. There was a spark of mischief in his eyes. "Goodbye, for now, my love. We will speak soon."

Without breaking eye contact, I gave him a slow nod.

"Goodbye, for now, my darling." The words flowed from my lips like I'd been saying them forever. "I will see you in Boston." What in the hell is happening to me? The floodgates have opened. I was, as Milly said, morphing into a new me.

Gerald turned and strolled to his BMW, which was parked two rows away.

I slid into the driver's seat of Gus's car, adjusted the seat, and hit the button to start. I watched as Gerald pulled out onto the road before I maneuvered the Lexus to the back of the tavern to pick up Gus. I avoided his eyes as he approached the driver's side. "I'll drive. You talk," I said.

His eyebrows raised, surprised by my authoritative words. But then, he smiled, opened the passenger door, and got in. I sat for a minute, regaining my composure. Thank goodness he didn't see me kissing Gerald. Not that it was any of his business. My mind was spinning, and it was all his fault. He put me in this position, and now, I was shaken. My adrenaline had peaked to the max, and I was suddenly falling in a downward spiral, leaving me as a blubbering bowl of Jello.

As we sat in frozen silence, each waiting for the other to speak. I could feel the heat of his gaze, and I let him simmer a moment longer. I edged the car onto the road, my hands still trembling from my exchange at the table and that kiss. I didn't know if I was feeling anger toward Gus or anger at myself. So many emotions were hitting me at once. Before Gus began to speak, I wanted to make sense of what had just happened and pull myself together. If I am going to be a PI and solve this case, I need to think outside the box and not let my feelings cloud my judgment. It's *my* case. I'm taking all the risks and want to call the shots. With my nerves settled enough, I was able to pull myself together. I attempted to smile. Why was I taking this out on Gus? Didn't I ask for his help? I cursed under my breath. "Okay, I'm ready to listen now. I needed a moment to pull myself together. After spending time with Gerald, or whoever he is, I was a little frazzled at the thought of seeing him again in Boston. It's tougher than I thought it would be to become a Merle type and to meet strange men who are unlike any I have ever known. I didn't know men like this existed, but my eyes are now wide open, and I can see how women put in that position can easily be conned."

Gus was surprised by what I said. He reached over and touched my hand. "I'm so sorry, Izzy, that you had to be put in this spot. I bet if you knew then what you know now, you would've told Merle to take a hike. Your loyalty to friends, especially Merle, has led you down a rabbit hole." His voice was soft, and I knew he meant everything he said. "Believe me, Izzy, I wouldn't have asked you to meet the bastard in Boston if I could have thought of another way to do this. But, you are braver than you think you are. I have faith in you. Of course, you're frightened. Any woman in your position would be, but know that I have your back. I promise I will never let anything happen to you. I care too much for you, Izzy."

Gus's words, especially his hand on mine, helped relieve my anxiety. I could feel his strength, and I trusted him. He was solid and a breath of fresh air after being in the presence of Gerald, that exotic book cover god who knows all the right things to say. Gus was so...real, genuine, steady. A wonder flashed through my mind. Was *Gus* a good kisser? I tamped down a smile and concentrated on driving. "So, what did your friend tell you that's so urgent that I had to make a date with

Gerald in Boston? I can't be left alone with him, Gus. I can't. He has things in mind that give me goose pimples."

"Please don't tell me what he has in mind. I can only imagine." I could hear the concern in his voice. "And, I promise, you will never be alone with him. I don't know how he fits in the picture, but the FBI is all over this case. Come to find out, Merle isn't the first woman to be taken advantage of from this state. The few reported cons match."

"Yeah, we kind of figured. That's why I decided to do this, to save others."

"Yes. She's lucky she's only be out fifty grand. Other women gave up more than that and some lost it all. And they're not sure if it's one man or a ring of men working together because of different physical descriptions. And you are right. This scam is bigger than they thought because many women never report being defrauded. Either too embarrassed or frightened to call the authorities. The Bureau thinks blackmail or threats of bodily harm are also the reason some of the women haven't reported the scam. Gerald is our first solid lead, thanks in part to Merle. I took a photo of him, while he was staring into your baby blues, and forwarded it to the Bureau. They have a much clearer look of him now."

I couldn't look at him because I might stop the car and ask him to get out if he was smirking. I knew he was watching me, so I doubted he was being funny, just trying to lighten the conversation. "But, Izzy, once Merle said she recognized him as Karl's cousin, we couldn't just let him walk away. The feds will follow up on this, and with your help, maybe we can break this case. Who is Gerald and is he a part of this ring along with Karl? And how do they pick their marks is the puzzle that we need your help with. The one piece of information I *can* share with you is that all eyes are on the dating site, Silver Love."

"Woah. Woah. Say that again? A *conspiracy* to defraud women and threats of *harm?* What the hell, Gus. Merle is lucky to get away from Krappy with only losing money. But honestly, she never said she was afraid of Krappy. She really cared for him, and she said he treated her like a precious jewel. This doesn't sound like the same case. Are you sure?"

His voice took on a serious tone. "I'm *sure,* Izzy. The photo Merle took matched what the Bureau has already compiled."

"It was junk, though, and of no good use, being all blurry like that. Couldn't see squat."

"It was good enough for the feds to confirm. My own that I sent in tonight further substantiated it. I know this is difficult to believe, but it's all true. I hate to use you as a lure, but, Izzy, you may very well lead us to a ring of men whose only purpose is to commit grand larceny and defraud women. And who knows what else. The feds thinks this is only the tip of the iceberg. I was hoping my suspicions were wrong, but after seeing Gerald and your phone call from Merle, I believe he is part of something bigger than a dating conspiracy. This is more than a small-scale grift. It runs deeper than that."

I was stunned. I gripped the wheel tighter. Should I be frightened or angry? It was still hard to take in that what I thought was a simple ask from Merle was a case the FBI was looking into. I pulled myself together. *Be brave, Izzy,* I told myself. *Gus needs you. And so do all the women this mob of madmen has harmed.* "Okay. So where do we go from here?"

"I'll run it by the Bureau, and we'll have you set up a day

and time to meet up with him. Seems like you have conned the conman."

I glanced at Gus. He was smiling. And now, I was too.

For the rest of the drive home, we discussed my role as a Mata Hari, a name Gus bestowed on me, and tossed ideas around about how I could entrap Gerald. I was no longer a PI but a genuine spy working for the FBI. But, whatever my title, foremost on my mind was *Boston* and what would come next.

I asked Gus if I could take Milly into my confidence, but promised not to divulge anything to Merle. I knew she'd barrage me with phone calls about my date and ask if Gerald had told me anything about Krappy. I had to come up with a story I knew she'd believe. Gus walked me through answers that would satisfy her curiosity and led me through responses to put her off. I had to admit he surprised me with his knowledge of spying since his job at the Bureau was as an accountant. It was a lot to process and plan, but Gus said he'd be with me to the finish.

We pulled into my driveway and exited the car. Gus walked me to my door, stopped, and hugged me. "You're the best, Izzy. And don't forget it." Then he leaned forward, looked into my eyes, and gently brushed his lips over mine. He stepped back, his irresistible blue eyes still staring into mine, then hesitated like he was going to say something important. I waited to hear him say something—*anything,* but he didn't. Instead, he turned, headed to his car, stopped, and looked back at me. "How 'bout we take the horses out for a ride tomorrow? It'll do us both good."

"Uh, sounds good to me." I nodded with a soft smile intended to conceal my dancing brain, buzzing nerves, and flushed cheeks. *Oh, my Lordy loo! What just happened? Is this what male friends do?*

I had no time to figure anything out or mull over Gus's out-of-the-blue overture because, just then, my cellphone played "Mack the Knife," Foxy's ringtone.

I tugged off my sweater coat and let Oscar run past me and out the door all in one move, then caught my breath and answered my cell in the next. "Hi, Foxy. Just got in the door and was gonna call you. Something important has come up that I wanna run by you."

"Great minds run in the same direction," she chuckled. "I wanted to know if you have time to meet. I have information on the case you're working." Foxy's voice was husky and low. It had a sexy sound, and for a moment, I wondered if my voice was pitchy and high. I'd have to control that.

"As a matter of fact, later is fine to meet. I had a day filled with more than I can wrap my head around and need to bounce my crazy adventure off you. Wanna meet *here* or somewhere else?"

"How 'bout I come to your home? I have a few interviews I need to write up so I'm busy until around three. Is five o'clock a good time for you?"

"Perfect. It'll give me time to take care of barn chores."

"Okay. I'll see you then. I'll bring dessert and you can serve the coffee."

"Sounds good. And I have chicken salad and rolls. We can have a light dinner and your dessert. Coffee is my drink of choice for the rest of the day. I had too many martinis today, and between the stress of my luncheon date and the drinks, I am ready for a nap."

I could hear Foxy chuckling. "Now you have my feelers up. And wait till you hear what I found about your dating website. I bet when I tell you what I've dug up, you'll perk right up."

"And I'll tell you all about my harrowing date with one of the guys who emailed me. I am still on an adrenaline rush. I think the pieces may be falling together. We have a lot to talk about. Maybe you should think about staying here for the night." I ran my fingers through my hair and shook my head. "Everything is moving quickly in the Merle disaster, and I'm in a real dilemma. Your advice and experience are desperately needed."

"I'm driving right now, but don't worry. We'll figure it out together."

My body felt drained and shaky, and I realized I hadn't sat down since I walked through the door. I wanted to blame it on the martinis, but it was more than that. Oscar was sitting on the stoop waiting to be let back in, and I opened the door for him to run through, then collapsed on a chair. "Foxy, I think a perfect storm has sucked me in." I pulled the phone away from my ear as Foxy cursed at another driver, then continued on like I hadn't heard her tirade.

"After what I learned, you need more than my advice, but

not to worry, Izzy. We'll figure this out. I'll see you around five, and a chicken salad sandwich is perfect."

I rubbed my forehead and ran my fingers through my hair, trying to decipher the catastrophe that had tossed me into a web of conspiracy and danger. It had seemed so simple. Join a few dating websites and lure Krappy into dating me using a profile like Merle's. It began as a search to find the scammer who duped her, and then she would handle the rest. And in what I believed would entail meeting men who would never appeal to me but to Merle, I had unwittingly placed myself in grave jeopardy. To my disbelief, the two men I agreed to date were slick with words and grossly overattentive. But what did I expect? These are the types of men Merle's attracted to. Worse yet, according to Gus, Gerald may be dangerous and in cahoots with Krappy Karl. I had been forced to leave the safety of the bubble I had created for myself, was not up to the job, and was scared out of my wits. I had become brave and daring, but at what cost? What had seemed like a game of fun and stealth, using my new PI persona, had gone wrong. Although I had done what Gus had asked and was now going to meet Gerald in Boston, it suddenly hit me, and I was frightened at the thought of the unknown. I am not trained for this, nor do I know how to keep up the charade of a Mata Hari. My head was spinning with too much to digest. I grabbed my cellphone and called Milly.

Milly, thank the Lord, answered on the third ring. "Hi, Izzy. How'd the date go?"

"Oh my God, Milly. The mess Merle has thrust on me is out of control. I just finished talking to Foxy. She's coming at five, and can you please...*please*, join us?" I was almost in tears, and it wasn't like me to beg someone, even Milly, to rescue me. "I need you to be here with Foxy and me. I can't talk about it on the phone. It's too involved and stressful. Milly, I am in over my head." I'm sure Milly heard the stress in my voice as it cracked, and I struggled to breathe.

"What? Oh no! Say no more. I'll be there at five on the dot. I have a doctor's appointment but will make it to your house on time. Don't panic. I'm sure between the three of us, we can work things out. I won't press you for details cause It sounds like only a sit-down will help. In the meantime, catch your breath and know that I am here for you, and we will figure it out. Don't worry, Izzy. We're in this together."

I took three deep breaths. *No, Milly, I am in this alone.* "Okay. See you at five. Thank you, Milly. You're the best."

We clicked off, and Oscar, sensing my distress, came and put his head on my lap.

His soulful, wise eyes asked, "What's wrong, Mom?"

I suddenly felt alone and vulnerable. The waterworks began, and I couldn't hold back. The dam opened, and I fell into a blubbering mess of pent-up emotions. Salty water poured down my face, and I didn't try to stop the deluge. I sat there weeping for so many losses. After all these years, I still missed the love of my life, Max. It's funny how small things bring the loss of a loved one slamming into your body, invading the space filled with busyness that has kept you sane. Tears leak out at unexpected times and flashbacks of fond memories flood to mind. Sometimes, it's a song or the time of year, but there's no stopping overwhelming weeping caused by an unintended trigger. Gus and Gerald had done just that. They'd kicked the door wide open. My heightened senses from being thrown into a situation I had no experience with had caused my protective shield to crumble. Because of Merle and Gus, I had spun an outrageous tale and was starting to believe it. I felt betrayed by my friends and not valued. Were they using me because they thought of me as weak and unable to say no? So many thoughts ran through my mind, and I felt inadequate and sad. I couldn't stop the cascade of tears and wondered if I ever could. My mother always said that the release of tears empties your body of toxins that adrenaline left behind, so I'm going with that for now and making no move to control myself. It is better to happen when I am alone than in front of anyone. My nose was running, and Oscar began pacing. "Enough," I shouted and finally regained control of myself. I was emptied. I got up and went for tissues to blow my nose and wipe my face. *Breathe, Izzy. Just breathe.* I splashed water on my face and dried my eyes. I had to clear my head, and a walk outside should help. I threw on my jacket and called for Oscar.

Once out the door, without thinking, my feet led me to the barn, my place of solace. I needed to ditch the all-consuming dread of the unknown that had sent me into a torrent of tears, which, for a moment, I was helpless to turn off.

Oscar stayed by my side. He had not left me since he heard me sobbing. Dogs sometimes understand more than humans. They don't interrupt, ask questions, give advice, or judge. Dogs listen, love, and provide comfort. Oscar has that canine ability to sense my emotions, and he had picked up on my fragility when he heard me sobbing.

Hearing me enter the barn, Chip, the soon-to-be momma cat, dropped down from her perch on the stall rail and began rubbing against my legs. I bent down to pet her. Her belly had grown two sizes, and she looked like she could have her kittens any day. I poured kibbles into her bowl, and she immediately ate. I began talking to her. The mind can't concentrate on two things simultaneously; this was the diversion I needed. I fussed around in the barn, putting a few things I had left out from cleaning up yesterday back in the tack room. I found that keeping busy in the barn was helpful when I was in a funk. I finally pulled myself together and headed back to the house. A long hot shower should help me relax and recover.

Milly arrived before Foxy, taking note of my bloodshot eyes. "That bad, huh?" She wrapped her arms around me in a big hug, and it was just what I needed. She patted my back as her comforting arms held me close. "I think you've had enough meetings with these evil men whose only thought is how fast they can get you into bed. This Gerald must have been a doozy."

"Damn, Milly! You don't know half of it. I was so rattled when I got home that my mind raced to Max and how much I miss him. I felt totally alone, and once the waterworks started, I couldn't stop. I haven't had a melt-down like that in a very long time. Milly, honestly. I'm at my wits end and into something I am not qualified to handle. These men are oversexed, reprobates. Gerald really turned it on. He's a slick smooth talker and I experienced firsthand how his charm and passion can con a woman out of her money. But worse Milly, I would never tell this to anyone but you, I honestly enjoyed his passionate kiss. I let my guard down by pretending to be Merle, and now I wonder who I am. It has been a long time since a man kissed me like that, and all the while I knew it was a smokescreen, and he was full of danger, but in the moment, I didn't care. I'm questioning who I am and what's wrong with me?" Milly could see I was struggling and hugged me again.

She sat me down on a chair and pulled hers next to me. "Listen here, Izzy. You are the kindest, most giving woman I know, that's why I chose you as my friend, and you chose me. We've been through a ton together, the good and the bad. I know who you are. Never doubt yourself. You've been tossed into a mess that would rattle anyone. Why are you questioning who you are? I have found from experience that breaking down walls built for survival is never easy. And, like it or not, you have been forced to do just that, which has shaken you to your core. Think of your tears as water to grow new beginnings. Take more chances, walk barefoot more often, do things spontaneously, and write books with adventures and risks. You can do it, Izzy, and your family and friends are here for you."

I was choked up and ready to sob again, and I didn't hear the knock on the door. All I could think of was how fortunate I was to have best friends. I thought back to my mother's words of wisdom, *"To have a friend, you must be a friend."* She was a wise woman, and when my children were young and complained about friends, my mother's mantra carried them into adulthood. I try my best to do the same, and I cannot think of a better friend than Milly. I blew my nose while Milly answered the door. Oscar stayed beside me, and I leaned down and kissed his furry head. I heard Milly greeting Foxy. I was ready to tell my two besties about my crazy, stressful day and listen to their guidance to help ease my anxiety and self-doubt.

Milly and Foxy entered the kitchen.

I yelled over my shoulder and asked who wanted coffee. They both said yes, giving me a moment to pull myself together. I set mugs on the table, asked Milly to remove the chicken rolls from the fridge, and placed the dessert box Foxy had handed me on the counter.

Foxy looked as trendy as ever. Her loose gray curls framed her face; today, she wore large dark blue framed glasses that almost covered her face, the same style as her others. She looked chic and fashionable—a woman on a mission. She flung her knee-length red plaid jacket over the back of the chair and pulled a large notepad and pen from her bag. I saw her glance at my red eyes and nose, but she said nothing. After all, she was geared to be observant. Being Foxy, she made no mention of my bedraggled look. "Okay, ladies, shall *I* begin or will you, Izzy?"

I sniffled again. "I think you need to go *first,* Foxy. What I have to say will take some time and I know you both will be floored. This is bigger than big."

Milly's eyes darted to me and back to Foxy, her eyebrows raised with concern. Since I hadn't had time to tell her about my date with Gerald and how Gus pushed me to be a spy, I knew she would be speechless.

For a flicker of a moment, Foxy's piercing dark eyes met mine. "Okay, then. I'll begin. First, Izzy, I want to tell you that although your story about Merle and the con she had you working on amused me, I never thought I'd dig up what I did once I began poking around. I used some of my inside contacts and discovered an open investigation about a group of ruthless men using a dating website to lure women, take their money, and then either leave them high and dry or threatening to blackmail them. Also, a few women reported threats of bodily harm. These men are slick and crafty, and they work in concert with one another. My source said they think there are three of them, but there may be more. They change their appearance and names and play different roles. Sometimes one is the pursuer, a friend of the pursuer, or a family member. It's all a game plan. Create credibility by introducing a family or friend to the mark. Makes the big lie believable and deceives the woman. And, best of all, it lends credence to the con. But the question that still needs to be answered is how they disappear and, foremost, how they find their marks. They have no photos of the men, only loose descriptions. From what I understand, most women are scammed via the phone or computer. They never even meet, and yet, he sweetens them up through talking a good game. But the scam Merle got caught up in is much more dangerous and well-planned. The Merle Con is more cunning and serious, because the man meets the woman and grooms her over time. The feds do know that this ring has been operating for a long time. From what my informant said, they don't know how many women have been bilked, because most are too embarrassed to report."

Milly and I sat frozen in place, awe-struck, as we listened to Foxy. Milly looked at me, studying my face for a reaction. I said nothing, too stunned to speak. Gus had told me some of what Foxy was reporting, but Foxy's insight was more thorough, giving a deeper and more frightening look into the dark side of this dating scheme I had reluctantly jumped into solving.

Foxy sipped her black coffee and reviewed her notes. I waited for her to finish with what she had written down. She closed her notepad, pushed her glasses up on her nose, and looked directly at me. Her eyebrows furrowed and her voice was grave. "Oh, one last thing, but most important. After listening to my contact, I'm very concerned about your safety. This criminal organization is far too dangerous for you to get dragged into, and you might stumble into something that takes a lot more experience than you, or even *I*, have. You need to get out now and let the authorities handle the rest and wrap it up. They think this ring works out of Boston, but they aren't sure where these men even live or if they reside together. So that's what I have. What about you?"

My eyes itched and hands shook.

Foxy studied me, waiting for a reply, while Milly gawked at me with deep concern bellowing in her eyes.

I cleared my throat. Well, where do I begin? "We're going to need some more coffee. And let's open the dessert box you brought. I need something sweet to pull myself together. My saga will take some time to explain. And Foxy, Milly doesn't even know the whole story about my luncheon date with Gerald at the Red Horse Tavern in Farmington yet." I got up and headed to the coffee maker.

Foxy and Milly followed.

The silence was palpable as I cut the string on the container of goodies that Foxy had picked up from the Portuguese Bakery. The box was filled with my favorite custard cups, and I stacked them on a plate while Milly and

Foxy were still talking quietly, giving me time to think. Where do I even start?

After we devoured the delicious custard cups, we settled in the living room. I sat back and shook my shoulders to release my built-up tension and began telling the whole crazy story that started with Gus driving me to the Red Horse Tavern, meeting the salacious Gerald, and ending with Merle's phone call. Neither Milly nor Foxy interrupted me as I spilled the details.

Although she had her pen and pad ready, Foxy didn't attempt to write down anything either.

The words fell from my lips like a waterfall over a cliff. I only paused to take a breath. I felt much lighter to be able to unload the burden.

Milly sat spellbound, her eyes wide and her arms folded while Foxy leaned forward, hands on her knees, listening carefully to my description of Gerald, who Merle believed was Krappy's cousin, and the urgent plea from Gus to meet Gerald in Boston. When I paused, Foxy nodded for me to go on, never breaking in with an opinion or question. It seemed like I talked for an hour, although, I know it wasn't *that* long, but I sighed in relief when I finished.

They sat quietly, reflecting on what I'd just told them.

I ran my fingers through my hair and scratched Oscar's head. He was lying at my feet, head cocked, waiting for my next move.

Milly was the first to speak. "Oh my God. No wonder you have been so upset." She came over and gave me a huge hug. "This is too crazy to believe. And Gerald is a depraved, horny bastard. And, what the hell! Gus wants to use you as bait? I am *shocked* that he asked you to put yourself in danger to solve some case. He doesn't even work there anymore, and he was *only* an accountant. I am so disappointed in him. He said he would help. He didn't say he'd risk your life and guilt you into volunteering for the flipping FBI."

Foxy broke in. "Hold on, Milly. Let's try and make sense of this." She got up and started pacing the room. "By the way, I don't think Gus was a mere accountant. I think he was *a lot* more than that, but that's his story to tell. Damn, Izzy. You got caught up in a horror show, and, as I see it, you only have two choices. Move ahead and trust Gus and whoever's working with him to have your back or tell him you're out, and you don't believe you can playact anymore. I know this is way over your head, but if you can lead them to this group of racketeers, you will be a hero and save other women from the victimization. My money's on you. This Gerald gigolo believes you're so infatuated with him that you're willing to zip off to meet him in Boston for some wild tryst after one dinner? Perfect. Sounds like you have him hooked instead of the other way around."

Milly threw her hands up. "No! No way. I disagree with this scheme, *entirely.* Izzy, you should get out now while you can and run as far and fast as you can from this plan of Gus's and the dumb FBI. You are risking your life here." When Foxy shook her head, Milly bellowed, "How can Izzy pull this off without sacrificing herself? She has a family, and I'll bet, they'd *never* agree to let her take on this risk if it was their own mother. Plus, she's my friend. Nope. Nope. What if Gerald becomes suspicious of her? Then what? There are too many variables. She's no spy. She's Izzy."

Listening to my friends hash out the pros and cons of me continuing on in this treacherous, tangled web of deceit, I felt like a mouse on a wheel while at the same time caught in a tug-o-war. Running and running like mad, with no end in sight, and then, getting yanked, this way and that. *Just stop! For five seconds. Please. So I can think for myself.*

Who was I even? Mata Hari Izzy, or Phoebe, writer of children's books? For safety and privacy's sake, I'd chosen the pseudonym Phoebe, while, as Mata Hari Izzy, all caution had been thrown to wind. This life of danger and intrigue was all new to me. Was there any other choice for me but *forward?* No. This maniacal, predatory group *had* to meet its end, and it was up to me. Regardless of the hesitation and unease I felt, I had to see it through before anyone else got scammed...or *worse*. The walls I'd built up over the course of my life had to come tumbling down.

Yes. It was time to let Mata Hari Izzy on stage.

It was only 10:30 in the morning, and I was already wiped out. I had pushed myself out the door an hour earlier to go to the gym. I didn't want to work out, but I had an appointment with my trainer Jackie, and I was obligated to go. And as much as I didn't want to get dressed and get going, it had distracted me from my intense late-night conversation with Milly and Foxy. My overworked brain felt like it was on computer overload, and I had to delete unnecessary data and clear my mind. Working out had helped some, but now that I was home, I was forced to think about my schedule for the following week. It was already Thursday, and Gus was supposed to tell me when to make a date for Boston with Charlatan Gerald. I shuddered to think about it.

I opened the door, carrying my iced coffee, to be greeted by Oscar. Sensing I was exhausted, he wagged his tail and returned to his doggy bed. Unlike the pressing asks from Gus and the FBI, Oscar demanded nothing from me. I hung my jacket on the hook in the mud room and settled at the kitchen table. I took out my notes written the night before with Milly and Foxy. We spent hours reviewing each possibility of what I might encounter when meeting Gerald in Boston. Against her better judgment, Milly had barely agreed with Foxy to see the debacle through. Foxy had faith in the FBI and said they would never let anything happen to me, and as much as Milly was disappointed with Gus for persuading me to go along with the scheme, she believed he would never put me in danger. Milly was still unconvinced that I was safe and voiced her strong concerns against the sting, as I now referred to the plan to nail Krappy and his band of hooligans. She left the house, reminding me of all the possible pitfalls.

Immediately after she hugged me goodnight, she said with a worried frown, "Izzy, you have not been trained to be a spy. How will you handle Gerald, and where is a safe place to meet him? You do *not* want to go to his condo. God knows what would happen if you were left alone with him."

Milly and I agreed on one thing. If I *were* going to Boston to date Gerald, it required a new wardrobe. I'd never planned to change attire for any of the men I met from online, but I should wear something more appropriate for Boston. I would stay overnight in a hotel but pack different options and several days' clothes in case there was some kind of glitch and I needed to extend my stay. My purchases needed to have flexibility and range to adapt to wherever Gerald wanted to meet or where Gus and the FBI planned for me to lure him.

I slurped coffee while I scanned my To-do List. Gus was coming by later to take the horses out for a ride, and he would have an update from his contacts for the day and time to set the meeting with Gerald. Something told me that Boston and the sting would occur on Monday. Gus said this was the first solid lead the FBI had in tracking these suspects, and they wanted to move in fast. I had to chuckle. It all began with Merle and her tenacious drive to find Krappy. Would *she* have pursued the search herself if she knew a *dangerous man* had scammed her and that Krappy Karl was *not* working alone but with a not-cousin cousin who was only a part of the ruse and not any relative at all? No. I knew for a *fact* Merle would *never* put her neck out for *me* like I was for her. She would've bowed out at the first hint of discomfort and then thrown herself a pity party with a room full of guests to tell it all to.

I had named the scoundrel well, calling him Krappy. He was nothing less. Merle had yet to learn that the single blurry photo she'd slyly taken without Krappy's knowledge was the seal on the deal for the FBI's investigation. Before that, they'd had no clue who these men were. Merle may be a hero when this is finished. No. I can't call her a hero, even if she did sneak a photo of Gerald, too, thinking he was Krappy's cousin. It was uncanny, but, just then, "Who Let the Dogs Out?" sang from my phone. I hesitated to answer, but there'd be no relief from the constant singing until I did. "Hi, Merle."

"Hello, Izzy," she said in her same rat-a-tat-tat style. "Did Gerald give you any clue where Karl is and how *you* can find him?"

I noticed she emphasized "you." It wasn't as hard as I thought to lie and say Gerald hadn't spoken to any relatives *that recently* when I'd prodded him for not-so-nosy tidbits about his family, but he'd get back to me to let me know if I could meet any of them when I head out to Boston for a day trip, maybe next week. In a hurry to end the chat with her, I said I'd talk later, since I was driving—another barefaced lie. For the moment, she was content with that, but I knew she'd soon be pestering me to find out if Gerald mentioned any specifics about Krappy Karl. I crossed Merle off my list and stretched. I still had tasks on it, waiting to be completed. Too many. Maybe I can get at least one done. Maybe. Without further distractions, that is.

I tossed my leftover, watery, iced coffee into the sink, replacing it with hot, freshly brewed instead. Yum. I grinned as I drank in the rich aroma and let the steam bead on my lip.

A puff of air, that sounded a lot like disappointment, came out of Oscar's nostrils as he lifted his head and padded to the counter. His dog cookies were there. Was he judging me?

"Damn, Oscar. I waste more coffee 'cause I only enjoy it either ice cold or steaming hot. You know that."

Oscar cocked his head in response.

"I *know* I can be wasteful, but *only* with old coffee. You wouldn't drink it gross either. Don't look at me like that."

His tail wag and nose bop on my hand showed me he understood.

"Here ya go." I removed a cookie from his jar, and he quickly crunched it. "Oscar, you are the most handsome dog in the world, and my sweetest buddy." I petted his soft head.

His round, dark eyes stared at me, waiting for another, and against my best intentions to limit his daily calories, I tossed him one more cookie for being so good. I sat down with my piping hot coffee, just the way I like it, and reviewed my list again.

Oscar's nails gently clicked on the floor as he followed to

be close to wherever I ended up parking myself. At my desk. He curled up by my feet but jerked up, matching my surprise, when a phone somewhere actually *rang* rang instead of sang.

I tilted my head in befuddlement, then zoomed my gaze around. *Oh! Burner phone! Forgot. Oops. That's right.* Only one person had the number. *Gerald.* I'd left it on the table in the living room. Oscar stayed where he was already comfortable when I shot up and rushed to get it. Before I picked up, though, I took a second or two to find the right words to put him off until I received further instruction. *Gus had better have a plan when he comes over!* I gulped and tried to make my voice low and throaty like Foxy's. "Hello, *darling.*"

"*Bonjour,* my Isadora Rose. How is my jewel today? I couldn't wait to talk to you again. I miss you and can still feel the heat from your body and your soft lips on mine." His European accent was flirtatious, and the timber of his voice reminded me of a sexual animal prowling for a mate. Knowing he was a part of this wretched scheme, I found him more revolting by the second and blanched.

My eyes popped wide open, and I quickly picked up the mug of steaming coffee and took a gulp, nearly spitting it out. I'd forgotten how hot it was, and it burned my tongue. I stopped myself from running to the sink for a glass of cold water. *Pull it together, Izzy. You are Merle. No, you are not Merle. You are Izzy Femme Fatale. I* forgot my burned tongue and answered in the sexiest voice I could muster. "And, I couldn't wait to hear from you either." I prayed my tone was soft, husky, and seductive enough for him to buy my interest. "I miss you already. I even dreamt about you last night. You were holding me in your arms and kissing me passionately in a way no one has ever kissed me before. I am so excited to see you again." I covered my mouth with my hand and held the phone away, as I felt a nervous laugh bubbling up.

"My Isadora Rose. You have filled a place in my heart that's been waiting for a woman like you. I never believed in love at first sight but, you, my love, have changed my mind." His voice purred with sexuality. "Can't wait to travel to Europe with you and spend time learning more about each other. Boston will be only *one* among many cities we will travel to."

"Oh, Gerald. You make my heart melt. I'd love that. You're all I've been waiting for and more." *Oh my God, did I just say that?* "I'm heading into my office to tie up loose ends on the project I told you I was working on. I'll have it completed by tomorrow." I could picture Gerald with that rascally Cheshire cat grin of his, believing he'd snared me, which gave me courage. "I promise I will call you this evening with the date, time, and place where we can best meet up. I love Boston and cannot wait to see the city with you."

There was a pause at his end. Did he have me on speaker with his criminal cronies listening in, winking, smirking, and encouraging him to indulge in more sexual talk? I can imagine their leers as he promised me kisses and long nights filled with lustful lovemaking. Desire oozed from his lips. "Yes, my love. Call me as soon as you free up your schedule for next week. I must make plans at my end too. My body aches to touch you again, my precious jewel."

And my body *aches to kick you right in your down below.* When I was young, to protect my innocent ears maybe, that was what my mother called unmentionable body parts.

I stifled a laugh. "Oh, my darling. My body is aching for you, too, right this minute. Can't wait to feel your strong arms around me and your hands caressing my body. The thought of your touch is causing me to shiver with anticipation from the tip of my toes to the top of my head." I sighed into the phone so he could hear my longing. *Does he believe me? Did I pour it on too thick? Need to get a move on. Gus'll be here soon.*

His voice turned eager. "These are words to my ears, my love. You have me spellbound. I look forward to hearing from you again this evening. Goodbye for now, my precious jewel."

"Goodbye, darling. Kiss, kiss. I will talk to you again this evening, and see you very soon." I tapped off and bent down to expel all my pent-up laughter, put on my jean jacket, then briskly strode outside to clip the horses in at the crossties. I'd finished brushing Speed and was working with Maverick when Gus's pickup pulled in and his door clicked shut. I bent to pick out Mav's hooves as Gus strode my way.

Chip was on the rail of the stall, watching me finish up.

"Hey, Izzy," he called, sauntering in. "Looks like you've got everything under control."

"Huh, I wish," I said as I patted Maverick on the rump.

"It's a beautiful afternoon for a ride. I feel spring in the air," Gus remarked as he walked past me to the tack room. He returned, carrying Maverick's saddle, pad, and bridle, then handed me the saddle pad. After I placed it on Maverick's back, Gus lifted my saddle onto it.

"Thank you, Gus. I'm glad you suggested we take the horses out. I really need it."

"It's the least I can do for you Izzy," he smiled wanly.

We worked without speaking, each focusing on our horse.

I unclipped the halter, draped the reins over Maverick's neck, and slipped the bit into his mouth. I tightened the girth and led Maverick out of the barn. Gus was almost finished tacking Speed, and I mounted my horse to wait for him.

I took a long look at Gus as he led Speed out of the barn. Although handsome and kind, I had always considered him a riding buddy and never allowed myself to consider us more than good friends. And even though now and then I sensed interest in more than friendship, he had never acted on it. But then, the kiss happened. My lips curled into a knowing smile.

He caught my look and grinned. "You're looking good, Izzy. It's time to ride. You lead the way."

I headed Maverick to the side of the barn where a trail led behind the small field where the horses got turned out.

The four-acre pasture ended with an old logging road that meandered through ten acres of wooded land, crossed a dirt road, and sloped down to a stream. I had ridden this trail with Gus or Milly many times, and each season offered a unique, beautiful landscape. April, with the extended daylight hours, after the short, dark, cold days of winter, was one of my favorite months to ride, like a fresh start. Although we were both wearing jean jackets, the sun was warm, and I knew we'd soon toss them aside. I couldn't wait. I love spring, and I'd be celebrating another trip around the sun in May.

Milly and I have already talked about enjoying a weekend in the city to celebrate, and I was ready to kick up my heels. It was time for a fun getaway, and the latest chain of events made leaving town more appealing than ever.

Gus and I rode without speaking. Our mounts blew through their noses as they relaxed their heads and settled into the ride. My body swayed gently to the rocking movement of Maverick, and I eased into the mindscape of my imagination. My horse, dog, and lifestyle had comforted me, and I wondered why I had dared to upset my quiet, secure life. For an instant, I longed for those peaceful days, one rolling into another without change or upheaval. Those days were over, and Merle, Krappy, and even Gus, had pulled me into the unknown and knocked my socks off. I know it's not too late to back out, as Milly urged me, but I was determined to see this through. My mind ran through several scenarios, but none seemed solid, each with its downside. I had to trust Gus and place my life in his hands and those of his buddies from the FBI.

Maverick walked at a steady pace with Gus, riding Speed, following. I leaned forward and ran my hand down the side of his neck. "Good boy, Maverick. You are just what I need today." My old saddle creaked as it gave way to Maverick's rocking movement, and the aroma of leather and horse mingled into a soothing medley of relaxing fragrance. I pulled my shoulders back and forth, inhaled a deep cleansing breath, and exhaled my built-up stress. I wondered if Gus was feeling the same way.

Flocks of birds were migrating from the south and finding nesting spots in the tall trees that lined the dirt road, and the sound of their chirps was music to my ears. The trail ended, and we descended a slight slope that brought us to a slow-flowing brook. I had packed a few snacks and bottles of water in my saddlebag, and this was an excellent place to stop for a moment and talk.

Gus and I had ridden the horses to the brook dozens

of times. But back then, when we stopped to talk, it was about our lives, children, and spouses who had died too early. Gus and I had looked forward to retirement and having the freedom to travel, see our kids more, or take up a new hobby. Although he had become an accomplished artist and I was writing children's books, it wasn't the life we had planned, but it was better than most.

We tied our horses to low branches and walked to our favorite spot. Two trees had fallen and left stumps just the right height to sit on. Neither of us spoke. I handed him a package of peanut butter crackers and a bottle of water and took one for myself. The sun was directly overhead, spilling over me like a warm blanket. With the promise of spring helping to brighten my mood, I was happy for the first time in a week. I had been in a funk all morning, and it was good to be outside and riding my horse. I stared at the brook, lost in its rippling sound, as a million thoughts ran through my mind.

After the stressful time with Gerald, the ride home with Gus, and the long evening with Milly and Foxy, I was not eager to begin a conversation. My last chat was with Gerald, and that had done me in. I found it challenging to playact and become the Femme Fatale I never was, nor planned ever to be. It was all so draining. I left the silence lingering in the air, and it was up to Gus to break it. He placed the cap back on the bottle and the cracker wrap in his pocket. I took another sip of water and set the bottle on the ground beside me.

"Izzy," he said.

I turned to look at him.

He smiled slightly. "I am so sorry you've been dragged into this. First, by Merle, and now, by *me*. I know the toll this has

taken and how this has totally turned your life upside down."
He waited for me to reply, but I said nothing. He turned away,
then peered at me again, and I sensed he had more on his
mind than my meetup with Gerald in Boston. "My friends
want you to set the date for Monday at noon. You will tell
Gerald you'll meet him at Boston Commons. Then say you are
famished and want to go to lunch at The Dangling Bait, which
is walkable and near the Commons."

"The Dangling Bait? Seriously? A little on-the-nose, huh?"
I smiled but tension seeped down my face and stiffened my
jaw, and I ground my teeth together.

"I didn't pick it. You need to buy us some time. Someone'll
be following you, every step of the way. Once you are seated,
they will, from a concealed vantage point, take photos. We're
arranging where you will sit, and there'll be no wait time, but
Gerald will have no idea. You'll be at a booth near a window.
Another couple, both agents, will be seated nearby. You will
be wearing a broach with a hidden microphone."

A mic? Panic doused me at others hearing any discussion
with Gerald. If it goes like our morning call, it'll be sexual in
nature, and I could never, ever continue acting like a femme
fatale, knowing others are listening in, among them, and most
especially, *Gus.* Oh, heck no. "Oh, no, Gus. No mic. Nope. I'm
not that good of an actress, and if I know I'm being heard and
recorded, I couldn't keep up the farce, and Gerald will realize
right away that I'm faking it."

Gus saw the fear in my face. "Okay, no problem. I will tell
them to skip the broach then."

I gawked in astonishment. "Really? That's it? The Bureau
will actually accommodate that?"

"Sure. If I say. It's *your* neck on the line, with our safety net, of course. You need to be comfortable with it."

"Wow. Okay. Thanks. I appreciate that."

"I think they'll have enough evidence with the new photos, but we *need* a location—the base of their operation. So, after lunch, tell him you'd *love* to see his condo. If you do *not* want to wear a bug, ask him where it is—the exact address, and then excuse yourself to the ladies room. A female agent will meet you in there to get it. As I said, we will, of course, be tailing, but knowing the location ahead of time will give agents time to stage and get a speedy warrant for the raid. Sound better to you?" At my nod, he asked, "Hear from Lover Boy this morning?" He grinned.

I rolled my eyes. "Does a bee stay far from a hive?" A ripple of nervous laughter began building. Monday was looming, and my body began to quiver at the thought of the danger I was putting myself in. I detected a trace of concern on Gus's face, and his eyes showed apprehension, but my analogy of Gerald as a bee and me, as honey, caused him to crack a smile.

"Honestly, Izzy. Rest assured, you will be thoroughly watched over, and the agents will die to protect you. You are our main asset, and the agents will never leave you out of their sight. And I'll be close by. Your job is to get Gerald to take you to his condo. And then, you will be finished with your life as a spy."

My body racked as I took a deep breath. "I kinda *have to* do it, don't I?"

He brushed my arm and pressed his lips together in concern. "I'm so sorry about the stress this is causing. You are the key, the best shot we've got really, to the whole takedown of this ruthless bunch of men. I believe you can do it. But, I'll ask you again. Are you ready and confident you can do this?"

I pushed my hair behind my ears, trying to make sense of the deep hole sucking me down, dragging me deeper and deeper in. I could only slowly nod. My head felt dizzy and numb. Although Gus was sitting right beside me, I seemed to be drifting away on a gazillion balloons, but they were zooming me off too fast. I clutched my throat and gasped for air as my heart sped. A crackling fuzz filled my brain. It felt like a dream, no, a nightmare, where I could wake any minute, or maybe, not at all, ever. Who am I? I am...Isadora Franklin, a spy? Isadora Rose, a Femme Fatale? Izzy the Mata Hari? Isadora Franklin, mother, grandmother, friend? Isadora Rose Franklin, the woman who'd tasted a lustful, deep kiss from a shark on an FBI list? I am...Izzy, and I'm promised. At that thought, everything scary and soul-crushing zipped away, leaving just the needle focus of victory. Mine.

Gus's voice crashed me out of my haze, prodding, "To take charge on Monday?"

I jumped back to reality. "Yes, Gus. I'm ready. I intend to lure Gerald with the oldest trick in the book, the promise of sex." I didn't look at Gus, but I knew that without a doubt, I had shocked him with those words. And I'd blurted them out with a chunk of anger and a ton of resolve.

We mounted our horses, the stillness wrapping us tightly in a dark cloak of conspiracy. But there were unspoken words that had nothing to do with Gerald and Monday. I needed to ask Gus something personal. Since his lips had brushed mine last night, there was more I needed to understand. I mustered all the bravado I could. "Gus, about yesterday. Have you and I reached another chapter in our lives where we can be more than friends?"

A startled look came over his face. I was not the same Izzy he'd known for so long. This Izzy was fearless and mighty. Me being so forthright had caught him off-guard, but I didn't care if his mind was absorbed with this case. I had something to say, and unlike before, I was no longer too timid to say it. He'd asked for my trust, and now, I was asking for his honesty. Where were we? I had to know.

"Um, Izzy."

I peered into the windows to his soul, eager for his reply.

Gus drew in a slow breath. His brow crimped and eyes became hot and piercing, making me blink furiously and flutter my lashes. After he swallowed hard, his long pause told me he was trying to choose his words carefully. But, no matter. I already knew. "Although you are the prettiest, smartest, most enjoyable woman in my life, and I've been plenty tempted to ask you out on a real date, I just don't think I'm ready to dive into a romantic relationship right now."

A flush took hold of my face as my spirit sank along with the corners of my lips. "Oh. Okay," I dryly said, ripping my stinging eyes away, fixing them to the grass.

"But, rest assured, Izzy, it'd totally be you if I were." He clucked to Speed. And, just like that, Gus rode off, leaving me so utterly embarrassed and sorry I had even asked.

*T*he weekend bustled with activity—some fun, some, not so much. After our horseback ride on Friday, Gus and I had little to say. I didn't attempt to apologize for my boldness, and the meeting with Gerald in Boston filled our conversation. Gus left the farm immediately after we untacked the horses and turned them out. He seemed flustered and said he had calls to make. Usually, we had coffee or a cold drink when we finished riding, but he couldn't leave fast enough. I wondered if our easy-going friendship would ever be the same. Besides being humiliated, I was sad that he led me to believe his kiss suggested more than it did. And to know that he had second thoughts about dating and was now uncomfortable around me hurt. Damn! I wished he had never leaned in and brushed my lips with his. Since we were both embarrassed, it was best he left when he did. There was nothing more to talk about. I told him I would call him after talking to Gerald and getting him to agree to the time and place, although knowing how anxious

Gerald was to consummate his hold on me, I didn't think any questions would be asked. I dreaded talking to Creepy Gerald. Worse yet, it wouldn't be the last time. I never wanted to see the lout again, but I was caught up in a sting, and the way I looked at the plan, I was the queen bee, and Gus and the agents, the drones. Everything hinged on how convincing I could be with Gerald.

After Gus left, I poured a fresh mug of coffee and braced myself for my call to Gerald. I would need to switch into my role as a femme fatale and hope to pull it off. I had done some acting in college but discovered I needed a better career choice. Hollywood was never going to call me. Who would have thought I could use that experience to help me act as the lead character in the best performance of my life? If my drama coach could see me now. I took two deep breaths, opened my burner phone, and tapped Gerald's number. Gerald answered on the third ring. I squeezed my eyes tight, shook my shoulders, and transformed myself into the role of Isadora Rose, Femme Fatale.

"Hello, my love. I have been anxiously awaiting your call." His voice was low and dripped with sexuality and innuendo. "What are you wearing?" When we met at the Red Horse Tavern, Gerald revealed he was into phone sex.

I almost burst out laughing. I was in sweats and smelled like a horse. I swallowed hard and rolled my eyes, forcing my voice to sound silky sexy. "Oh, my darling Gerald. You are a naughty boy. I just came from showering and I'm wearing my white sheer robe. And you are all I could think of when I was soaping up. My heart is bursting with longing for you, and my body feels like it's on fire from my toes to the top of my head."

And then it began. I had to endure Gerald's descriptive romantic plans for my overnight with him. He bragged about his sexual prowess and ability to pleasure a woman in ways I never dreamed. His words flowed like sweet maple syrup over a warm waffle. He droned on and on about never-ending sex waiting for me and that we would spend the whole night making love.

Ugh! I said I'd booked a hotel room, and thankfully, as Gus and his band of merry men intended, he said I could spend the evening with him at his condo. Check off number one on my list. I told him I wanted lunch at The Dangling Bait and hadn't been there for some time. Gerald said any restaurant I chose was fine with him. Check off number two on my list.

After we said our goodbyes, I did take a long, hot shower to wash off his sickening words of desire and his lustful description of slowly running his hands over my body. He gave me the creeps. My only hope of seeing this through was the knowledge that Gus and his G-men would not let any of that happen and would always have eyes on me.

After dressing, I phoned Gus and told him Gerald would meet me in front of the State Capitol, and if I wished for lunch at The Dangling Bait, he was my slave for the day. To be annoying, I added that Gerald also said, *"And you will be my lover all night."* Gus's phone was dead silent, but I could hear him clearing his throat. My hurt feelings had disappeared, and now, I was seething with humiliation over his kiss and my rejection. I smiled, knowing I had hit a nerve. Gus said I had reservations at the Ritz Carlton, and a driver would pick me up at my house. My transportation was a black Lincoln SUV, and if Gerald asked, I would say I always have a driver when going into Boston or New York. I told Gus that Foxy would be joining me, and after they snagged Gerald, we would stay a night or two at the hotel to unwind. Although he tried to talk me out of bringing Foxy with me, I said that subject was off the table. I knew he had no choice but to give me anything I asked. I was his asset, and he and his agents would agree to anything, even if he disapproved. He ran over the plan again to be sure I didn't forget even the tiniest details, but I was still so upset with him that I only half paid attention.

Gus ended our conversation with, "So, Milly's staying at the farm to care for the animals, and Foxy's driving with you for support. I'm glad you have good friends. Remember, Izzy, I am your friend, too. Agents will always have eyes on you, and I will be there as a backup. Just play your part and you will be a hero to all the woman these men have conned and save future women from falling for their love trap. I am proud of you for being brave enough to move forward with this plan to catch these lowlife thugs, and we will never forget that you are the one who, thrown into a viper pit, reluctantly led us to them. I have the utmost faith in you and care too much for you, Izzy, to let anything happen to you."

I was still angry with him, so his words did not ring true. "You know, Gus, since the day we first met at that fundraiser, you told me you were a retired accountant and that you had worked for the Bureau. But now, I find it interesting that you've gotten so deeply involved in this case. Someday, you and I will need to chat about it." *There. Let that set in.* Must think he's talking to the *former* Izzy. "I'll see you in Boston, Gus. Hope you and the Bureau can pull this off. You'd better not let me down and leave me alone with this predator."

There was an obvious pause at his end. "I promise, Izzy, I won't." He clicked off without another word.

Since I hadn't been able to sleep much, planning to drop into the belly of the beast, I'd been up since dawn. Chores done. Check. Packed and ready to go. Yep. Dressed. Done. I was in my new fitted black pants and purple cashmere sweater that Milly and I bought on Saturday. I'd also purchased black boots and a black leather handbag. And, I'd found a gray plaid short coat like the one I admired on Foxy. It fit perfectly, so I bought that, too, along with a black dress for evening that looked good with the boots in case I needed to spend more time with him or anything fell through. Milly also prodded me to buy new makeup and body lotion, infused with the light scent of peonies. I also packed another outfit for the next day and my new nightgown, robe, and underwear, in case. I even bought a pair of over-sized reading glasses like the smart ones Foxy wore. I was feeling very modern. If all goes as planned by the end of the day, Foxy and I will be toasting each other at the best restaurant in Boston, and when I get to the hotel, I may even call for a massage. I deserve it.

I raced to the bathroom to check out my makeup and was pleased with what I saw. Staring back at me was Izzy, the Mata Hari. "Yes, Izzy. You can do this. And if you succeed, you may be up for an Oscar and have a new profession, actor, or spy. Your choice," I chuckled. I was liking the new Izzy.

Milly and Foxy were on their way, and I was on my second cup of coffee when my cellphone played "Bennie and The Jets." It was my daughter Sarah, and I quickly answered. "Hi, darlin'. Home from vacation?" Sarah and her husband had been in Hawaii, and I knew she was due home any moment.

"Hello, Mother. Yes, we arrived late last night and are exhausted from the long flight. How have you been, and did you finish your book?"

"Yes, I sent the last draft to my editor. Check."

"So, what have you been doing for fun?"

Oh, boy. If Sarah only knew I was leaving for Boston in a Lincoln SUV, chauffeured by an FBI agent. More shocking was that her retired mother was now a spy and involved in a dangerous ploy, pretending to be a femme fatale. I choked back a laugh. "Oh, nothing much. Same ole. Same ole."

There was a pause at her end. "Really? Nothing *new* you care to share with your only daughter?"

I could hear the questioning lawyer in her tone. What was she talking about? "Aw, mmm, *no*. Nothin' new here. Milly and I have spent time grooming the horses, and Gus and I took them out for a ride. Oh, and she and I are planning a weekend away to celebrate my birthday. But, other than that, yeah, nothing new, nothing much. As I told you, you came home in time to enjoy warmer days. Luckily, you and Geoff missed the last blast of winter while you were in Hawaii. I bet you have a lot of work to catch up on."

"Yes, I have a case I'm looking into right now. A woman was swindled out of money by a man she met on a dating site. Are you familiar with dating sites, mother?" Her voice was accusatory and one I am not accustomed to.

I squinted in shock. *Sarah's* working on a case for a woman duped out of money like Merle was. Which dating site? Her client's case sounded like Merle's con, and was it only a coincidence? The tone of Sarah's voice when she asked if I knew anything about dating websites jarred me. Like she knew something about what I was up to, but how could she know? "Yes, Sarah. I'm not ancient. I know all about online dating."

I wanted to spill the beans and ask her for advice, but I would not draw her into the unbelievable world I was thrust into. The first thing she'd do would be to call her brothers for help. Next, she'd call Gus and use her lawyer threats to warn him to stay away from me, and then, my kids would surround me with advice and warnings. They'd never believe their standard fair mother would become a Mata Hari for the FBI.

I sat back, trying to answer without saying too much. "Merle meets men all the time on elite dating sites. She tells me it's the thing to do now if you want to meet someone. Says she's met some nice men, and some duds, on elite dating sites, the only ones she has joined. All the book club ladies know about online dating, thanks to her. You just must be careful because, as with every place on the web, there are scammers lurking. Just curious, which dating site did your client use?"

Did she just tsk, tsk, me? "I can't say. Client privilege, but these cases are tough to prove. Tell your friend *Merle* to just be careful. You are right. Scammers galore." She hesitated and dropped the subject, but I knew she had something more pressing to ask. Sarah was a laser-sharp attorney when questioning someone for information, even me. She has been this way since she could speak. "Mother, you didn't happen to be at the Red Horse Tavern in Farmington, a few days ago, did you? My friend Margie said she saw you there and she was going to stop and say hello, but you appeared occupied with a man who seemed very captivated by you."

I was annoyed by the description of Gerald and me that

Margie had relayed to Sarah. What else did she tell Sarah? I could feel my cheeks burning.

Hearing silence at my end, Sarah continued. "I told Margie that I was surprised to find out that you were dating someone, and I asked her if she was mistaken. You have not dated anyone since dad died and I would be the first to know if you were interested in doing so. I know you have had plenty of opportunities because we share everything. We are not only mother and daughter, but each other's confidants. So, *are you* dating someone, or did she see an Izzy lookalike?"

My mind was racing. Of course, Sarah knew it was me, and what were the odds that a friend of hers would be at the same tavern Gerald and I were at? I had purposely picked a restaurant to meet Gerald where I didn't think I would bump into anyone I knew, and I was trying to keep my online dates away from home. Should I come clean with my daughter? Forget that. I couldn't tell the truth, so I gave a half-truth. "Margie should've stopped and said hello. My friend's brother was in town and asked me to join him for lunch at the Red Horse Tavern. He lives in Pennsylvania and was here for a short visit. Thought it would be fun, but he was a little too overzealous with his affections. I gently turned him down."

Sarah started laughing. "For God's sake, mother. I can't picture you on a date, never mind, with a man who was as attentive as Margie said this one was. *Thank God* you're not on those sketchy online sites like Merle, and he was just some one-off luncheon date. She did say you looked very pretty and well put together. You usually wear casual clothes unless you're attending a function of some sort."

I was stunned. Is that how my daughter views me? A mother who lives a mediocre, dull life? Does she only see me as a retired older woman who's just interested in working out, reading, writing, riding horses, and hanging out with friends? Worse still, one with zero interest in men or dating? She doesn't see me as Izzy, the fearless, or Izzy, the adventurous woman. Well, to be fair, neither did I until now. I had to get her off the phone—and *now*, before she peppered me with more questions. I knew she'd want more details. Time to deflect with a change of subject. "Oh, by the way, I'm going to Boston overnight with my friend Foxy. You've met her before. She works for one of the newspapers. So, I'll be out of touch for two days. I'll text when I'm back. Oops, I gotta go. She's at the door. We're leaving now. If you have time, we can have dinner next week at the farm."

"Which hotel are you staying at?

"The Ritz Carlton. I'll call you later tonight or first thing in the morning."

"My, my. *The Ritz,* is it? Now, aren't we getting hoity-toity?" she laughed. "Yes, dinner for sure next week. I'd love that. We don't get together enough. I miss you, and as soon as you get back, we'll plan on it. Love you. Stay safe, Mom."

"Love you too, darlin'. Talk to you soon." I set the phone on the table and ran my fingers through my hair. Now, I'm lying to my daughter? What next?

I had no sooner rinsed my coffee mug and placed it on the rack than Oscar began barking. I went to the window and looked out. Milly and Foxy were pulling into the driveway. We had an hour to chat till our driver picked us up. Now, it was real. I was so glad to have two friends to help me through this caper. I opened the door before they even came up the sidewalk.

Milly gave me a huge hug. "All set for the day?" she asked.

Hearing the worry in her voice, I hugged her tightly like it was the last I'd ever give her. "Yup. All packed and ready to go since early this morning. I couldn't sleep. I tossed and turned all night, so I finally gave up, got out of bed, and got going. If we weren't heading to Boston, I'd be ready for a nap right now. Damn, I'm so wired and ready to get going, my hands are shaking."

Foxy stood behind Milly. She stared at me with knowing eyes. I'm sure she's been in tricky situations like this before, so she knew exactly how I was feeling. I held out my hands, and they were both quivering. Foxy gave me a quick hug. "Don't worry, Izzy. Jitters are good for you, believe it or not. You wouldn't be normal if they weren't, and they will keep you on your toes. By the way, you are looking quite attractive this morning, and Gerald," she grinned, "will be very eager to have lunch with you."

"Thanks for your words of assurance. Maybe I've had too much coffee, which is making me jittery. And thanks for the compliment. I think women dress more for other women than their partners. Women have an eye for style and notice new hairdos or a change in makeup. Like this sweater. Milly talked me into buying it and I love it." Foxy nodded. "I agree. My last boyfriend never noticed anything different about me, even when I lightened my hair."

Milly set her mug, filled with tea, on the table. "You know, Izzy, I kind of agree with that. Which is why I like to shop with a friend. I appreciate their input."

My hands had stopped shaking. A change in subject helped. "Milly and I shopped for two outfits to fit my new identity. I need to play the part of the femme fatale Gerald believes I am, so I even bought new sexy underwear."

Foxy raised her eyebrows, and she began laughing.

Milly placed her hand over her mouth in mock surprise. "Crap," she said. "Haven't had a man for so long, I only wear white cotton undies, but after shopping with you, I'm thinking of buying expensive, pretty ones again. I think I'm learning that if I don't make myself happy, what's the sense of it all? It's time to change it up a bit."

"There you go, Milly. We all get stuck in a rut but don't realize it. Not that Gerald will ever get a chance to see my new lacy bra and skimpy bikinis, but I can't be who he thinks I am without being in costume. I'm calling it a dress rehearsal right now, and soon, I will be on stage in the biggest performance of my life."

Foxy chuckled. "A star is born! By the way, Gus wasn't too happy about me tagging along, but he caved. You need me with you. Hope you send the FBI a bill for all your expenses."

"Damn, Gus! I knew he didn't like it when I said I wanted you to go with me. But I didn't know he'd call you. I'm glad you stood your ground. I'm not lying when I tell you I am scared that I can't pull this off, and, Foxy, you give me the confidence that I can do this, and I'm relying on your firsthand experience with tricky spots you've been in. I so appreciate you agreeing to go with me."

"That's the only thing that makes me feel better." Milly's face was wrinkled with worry. "Izzy needs you, Foxy. Even though Gus insists she'll be safe, Izzy is out of her realm here.

We all are. But she is the one who is in the middle of this elaborate fraud. I know I could never do what she has done and has to do today."

I hugged Milly again. "Thanks for those words, Milly. They mean a lot coming from you."

Foxy's eyes narrowed, and she adjusted her large green swirly glasses that had slipped a smidgen from her nose. I swear she must have the same frame in every color. "I can't agree more, Milly. Izzy, if someone told me you would get pulled into a sting like this, I wouldn't have believed them. You have a ton of guts that I never saw in you. It's funny how we're all capable of doing things we never dreamed of. Heroes aren't born heroes. They're thrown into a situation, and then, in a split second, they rush in and save the day. And that's what happened to you. What you thought was a ruse that Merle snagged you into, turned out to be a ton more, and now you have been pushed into unknown territory. Another woman may not have been able to pull it off, but, Izzy, you have more fortitude and guts than you dreamed. I promise you will be okay. You are the right hero at the right time. Everything in life is timing, Izzy, and this is your time."

My head almost spun in place. Did I hear Foxy say "promise?" My mother's words came blasting through my brain. Although I've often heard the word, it had lost its luster years ago, until that brief flash the other day, but I still had no clue what it meant or what it would be. Like a lightning bolt, my mother's voice whispered, *"You are the promise, Izzy. You'll know when you know."* Suddenly, without a doubt, I understood. I *would* be okay, and I am fearless. Maybe, the promise is something I already possess. Or must do. A promise

I *make* not get. So, I, Izzy, *promise* to fulfill my destiny and save women from these dangerous, ruthless men. Yes! I stood taller and felt a tad braver.

Milly noticed the spaced-out look on my face and snapped her fingers to get my attention.

"Sorry, my mind went elsewhere for a minute, and I know what I must do. There's a lot to consider, but Foxy and I can discuss it on the way to Boston."

Foxy filled a mug with coffee. "Well, Izzy, although I'm geared up and ready, I'll be honest, it's for selfish reasons. Not that you aren't first on my list, but I smell a huge story brewing, and I want to get the scoop before the Bureau hands it off to their insiders for publication. Thank you, Izzy, for trusting me," she said, taking a sip of coffee and placing the mug on the table. "Plus, staying overnight at the Ritz Carlton on the government's dime is like frosting on the cake, and if all goes according to plan, you'll have this finished and over in no time, and we'll be celebrating in Boston *in style* for *free.*"

Even Milly couldn't help but laugh.

We sat at the table, still talking, when we heard our drive to Boston pull in. We grabbed our coats and bags. Oscar walked beside Milly, knowing that she was staying with him. I had a long talk with him in the morning. I explained everything, my doubts, fears, and determination to see this case through. After a wet doggy kiss, I knew he understood what I said and would be waiting for me to return home, which was a comforting thought for my terrifying day.

A driver dressed like an agent in a spy thriller got out to meet us. By the time we reached the black SUV, he was holding the doors open for us. I gave him a quick look over.

He was a younger, fit guy, who I guessed to be in his fifties. From going to the Build-Em-Up-Gym, I could tell that under the suit jacket were well-muscled arms. His neck was thick, his jaw square, and his dark brown eyes narrow and deeply set. He looked like a typical G-man. He was clean-shaven, a rugged-looking type, with brown crew-cut hair and shoes that were so spit-shined they looked brand new.

He cracked a slight smile. "Good morning, ladies. I'm Brad, your driver for today." His voice was assertive and to the point. "Let me take your bags, and you can settle in."

I smiled back. "Thank you, Brad. I'm Izzy, and this is my friend, Foxy."

"Oh, I know who you both are. And I want to reassure you that you're in good hands. I'll be your driver to Boston and back. Also, I'll be listening and watching. I will drop Foxy off at the hotel, and then you, Izzy, in front of the State House."

Foxy spoke right up. "Oh, no you won't. You will drop me off, close by, and I will wait for you to pick me up after you drop Izzy off. Then, you're stuck to me like Gorilla Glue. And, you can double check with Gus. He agreed to this plan."

Brad looked directly into Foxy's eyes, and when she didn't blink, he shrugged in surrender. He knew he had no choice. I think he was testing her resolve. After we settled in the back seat, Brad closed our doors, and we quickly hooked our seat belts. He got in up front and started up the Lincoln.

Foxy and I waved goodbye to Milly and Oscar.

As the SUV began down the driveway, the agent beside Brad turned in his seat and said, "Hello, ladies."

We both gasped.

The passenger riding shotgun was Bob Earley.

I did a double take. Bob? Gus's best buddy? Why was he here? Am I dreaming, and will I suddenly wake up from this nightmare I've been thrust into? I was dumbstruck.

Foxy was quick on her feet, without hesitation or a loss for words. "Bob, what the hell are you doing here?"

Bob gave his most charming smile to combat my utter surprise. "Sorry to surprise you ladies like this, but I'm here for the ride. I know you have lots of questions, but, Izzy, when you and Milly confided in Gus and me at the Brown Dog, we decided to take a team approach and work together to elicit information from our former contacts at the FBI."

I was still at a loss for words, and I could hear Brad, the driver, chuckling under his breath. Everyone was in on the joke but me. Not funny! I felt duped, and a red-hot fire began bubbling in my stomach and slowly crept toward my head. "Stop this car immediately," I shouted.

Foxy grabbed my arm to quiet me but then nodded in her agreement.

"Pull over right now," I demanded. "I am out of this altogether unless you can convince me otherwise. Do you take me for a fool?"

Bob nodded to the driver, who maneuvered the SUV to the side of the road and stopped next to a large, tilled field ready for planting. I unhooked my seat belt, opened the door, and climbed out. I was seething mad that Gus hadn't told me Bob was also involved with the Bureau. It was all too much. Gus, the retired accountant, and Bob, his buddy, retired from a law firm in cahoots. I couldn't wrap my head around it. My hands shook, and my heart almost jumped out of my chest. Everything about Gus was a lie, and now, Bob, too? Were they laughing behind my back and using me to their end? I felt betrayed. And was the Bureau's need to break the Krappy case stronger than their trust in me? I had too many questions. And smacking me in the face was the question: was Gus's kiss another lure to keep me close to him and ready to do his bidding? Is that why Gus said he wasn't prepared to pursue a romantic relationship with me? I was done with it all.

I walked away from the SUV. I needed to breathe. I heard Bob moving up beside me. He said nothing, sensing I was prepared to blow up or cry. He was right. The straw that had broken the camel's back was *him* showing up out of nowhere. I took a moment to clear my head and gazed at the sky, trying to get my bearings.

Thin wisps of clouds drifted slowly over the sea of blue, and the day promised to be beautiful. I could smell the pungent aroma of tilled soil, and the air was crisp and cool. I, however, was ablaze with rage. Finally, I pulled myself together and turned to face him. His face looked as kind as ever but more thoughtful, and his eyes stared straight into mine. He stood quietly, waiting for me to gain my composure.

I squeezed my eyes shut to stop unwanted tears from leaking. *Pull it together, Izzy. Keep him from getting the upper hand. Ask the right questions. Wait to leap before you hear the correct answers.* I took a deep breath and let Izzy, the quivering bowl of Jello, shape shift into Isadora Rose, the Mata Hari. "So, Bob, is there anything you need to explain right now before I ask Brad to turn around and drive me home?" Foxy had lowered her car window, watching, and waiting for my next move.

"Ah, Izzy. I apologize for startling you so. What I thought would be a good idea turned out to be a bad one, and I don't blame you for doubting me and Gus. I would feel snookered, too, if I were you. But trust me. You are our friend, and I am here as a support, not a hindrance. I know what you endured in your search for Karl Hendricks, aka, Karl Maldurano, but I couldn't disclose how much I knew until now. Gus and I didn't want to muddy the water in your search for Karl with too much information, so we chose to tell you as little as possible. We wanted you to concentrate on Gerald and his game, not us. If we'd told you everything, you might not have been able to continue with your action of seduction, feigning interest. But, I *insisted* to Gus that *I* ride in to Boston with you and Foxy, go over details, and fill you in. I didn't realize it would knock your socks off like it did." He stepped closer, and I could tell he was sincere, but I still didn't completely trust him. "If you agree to see this through and not turn around and head home, I will explain everything on the drive to Boston, which was my plan all along."

I pulled my coat tighter. A sudden chill ran through me. "Listen, Bob, when I decided to hear Gus out and move forward with his plan, I knew I had crossed the Rubicon, and I also knew I was up to my neck in a swamp of intrigue and lies, but I didn't see any way out. Thanks to Milly and Foxy, I knew I had to stay true to my new identity and see this tangled web of deceit to the finish line. But I have one question, before I get back in that car."

Bob nodded, his gaze fixed on mine. "I get it, Izzy. You're angry. I promise to answer all your questions as honestly as I can."

"Well, aren't you perceptive." I was irritable and on edge. I folded my arms, stepped back, and looked directly into his eyes. "Just so we're clear, Bob. Who *are* you?"

Bob's face turned serious. "Okay," he says. "I'll make it short. The clock is ticking. I think you have an idea who Gus and I are. You are a bright, savvy woman, and I'm not blowing smoke at you, Izzy, but you have the making of a skilled detective. Before we retired, Gus was a special agent for the FBI, and I was his boss." He rubbed his chin, a habit I had seen him do when he was thinking. "Gus was genuinely concerned about your safety after he phoned his former contacts at the Bureau, and they told him they were working on a case with the same MO. He had a gut feeling you were unsafe, so he wanted to drive you to the Red Horse. Your profile on the dating sites matched the other women these men had preyed on. After speaking with his contacts, Gus knew it was only a matter of time before one of these guys swooped in on you. He also knew one crucial fact that you didn't. All the marks came from the same site, Silver Love. This ring of predators is judicious in selecting their targets, and from what we learned, they have been in business for at least three years. The pandemic offered ripe pickings of vulnerable wealthy women who were isolated and lonely. These reprobates zoomed in, and when women searching for companionship signed up for Silver Love, they were there to fill the need. Lots of people were finding friendship online, and the scammers were ready. So, they charmed and groomed them via email and phone calls, and when the Covid ban was lifted, they met up in person and set the trap with the promise of long-term love."

My eyes blinked then opened wide at that phrase. *The promise.* "Yes, a promise can be good or bad, and the promise of love is the most enticing."

"Now you're gettin' the picture. It was simple. After promising a forever love, and whatever else was used to ensnare, they'd move on to the money con. They needed cash, only temporarily, to keep their fronted business afloat. This scam was fairly fruitful, slipping under the radar, 'cause many businesses needed money after the pandemic. As their Covid funds depleted, and it got more complicated, they moved to the properties' scam. To seal the deal and make themselves appear legit, they'd introduce a woman like Merle to a cousin or business friend. These guys are clever and cunning. When Merle guilted you into finding Karl, your profile matched their typical target. You were trying to hook Karl, but *Gerald,* aka, Gerome Maskavona, took the bait and emailed you. And it was all because you were clever enough to tweak the bio and make it your own. These guys switch it up, sometimes playing some sexy, sharp co-worker, and other times, a friend or cousin, but they work together as a tag-team. You had no idea how dangerous the game you were playing was, nor that the Bureau was deep into finding the criminal ring. They believed it was only a matter of time, when something bad would happen to one of the women they were scamming."

"I know Merle never thought Karl capable of harming her, but she was hellbent on finding him. God only knows what she would have done if she did, but I bet she had a plan." I smiled at the picture of frenzied Merle beating Krappy Karl with a shoe. I nodded for Bob to tell me more. I watched as his eyes narrowed, and his brow knitted as he unloaded the background story of intrigue and deception that was now mine. But I knew Bob was also picturing Merle's wrath if she found Krappy Karl when the corners of his mouth lifted slightly, holding back a grin.

He cleared his throat and continued. "But your friend Merle possessed something to break the case that the Bureau didn't. Merle had a photo of one of the men, Gerald, Karl's supposed cousin, who you met at the Tavern. When she phoned to tell you this significant piece of information, it was to ask Gerald if he knew where his cousin, Karl, was. After you told Gus, he was immediately on the phone with our agents. That photo gave them their first huge lead and blew open the case. You, Izzy, had one of the players in this gang of thugs sitting across from you, drinking martinis."

Feeling a smile coaxing my lips upward, I placed my hand over my mouth to hide it. The martini description loosened the tight knot of anxiety that stopped me from exhaling. My body relaxed, and my mind focused more on Bob's words.

"So, after you told Gus that the photo Merle secretly took was Karl's cousin, he stopped you from running out the back

door and told you why in as few words as possible. Gus told
you it was imperative for you to go back to the table and
persuade Gerald to meet you in Boston. There was no time to
relieve your concerns, but enough to convince you to help the
Bureau apprehend Karl and his band of criminals. We needed
you to work on Gerald, using all your grit and charm, to help
us take down the den of thieves." This time, he did smile.
"You, Izzy, are the key to the Bureau bringing down this mob
of gangsters, and Gus and I, although retired, believe you can
lead us to his cohorts, and we can keep you safe. Gus didn't
want to leave your safety to the Bureau and insisted we be in
on the sting. And, Izzy, even though you were frightened, you
came through for us and became our reluctant spy." He
rechecked his watch. I knew I had to decide whether to stay
or go. Time was running out.

Did he just say I was *a reluctant spy?* Me, Izzy? Adrenaline
coursed through my body, and I was kick-assed, ready to see
the sting to the end. Izzy the Mata Hari was on stage. "So, I
guess I'm the bait, Bob?" I turned and walked to the spy
mobile, determined to entrap Gerald, and bring him to justice.

As I buckled my seat belt, Foxy leaned over and whispered,
"I don't like this one bit, but are you good-to-go?"

"Yes," I smiled knowingly, feeling relieved and revived. I
reached forward and tapped Bob on the shoulder. "Bob, can
you fill Foxy in while I take time to digest all we talked about.
And then, we can go over the plan, step by step."

Brad put the pedal to the metal with no fear of being
stopped for speeding. Foxy and I were Queens of the Road as
we sped toward Boston. We were on a mission, and the
Bureau had all hands-on deck. Brad said the Staties and other

law enforcement agencies were in the loop. Foxy and I finally grasped what Bob had told us. This case was huge and high on the FBI's list to crack. There were abundant state police on the Pike, and when we passed, they saluted Brad as we sped by.

We arrived in Boston with plenty of time to drop Foxy and Gus off at a small café, and then Brad drove straight to the front of the State House, where Gerald would be waiting. Before I retired from the Department of Public Health, I attended monthly meetings in Boston. I loved the city and vowed to visit more often. I didn't realize how much I missed it. The Boston Common and the State House looked as charmingly beautiful as ever, and people of all ages were milling around—some on the sidewalk and others exploring the Common. The trees on the Common were budding and the intense sun had increased the daytime temperature to sixty degrees.

Brad slowed when we drove by the State House.

Gerald was standing at the far corner, waiting for me and right on time. He wore an open white shirt under a black knee-length coat that covered his black pants. Gerald's eyes, which missed nothing, were covered with aviator sunglasses, and I knew the man with the con was eagerly watching for me. I had to admit Gerald was strikingly handsome and easy on the eyes. I could see why he could seduce and cheat women out of their money. I wondered if Gerald ever felt guilty hurting women and stealing from them, but that was my moral compass talking. Of course, he didn't. A woman walked past him with a small dog on a leash. I saw him nod to her, and as he turned his head, I took a quick photo with my iPhone to send to Merle for further confirmation.

"Okay," Brad said as he pulled up in front of the State House. "You know the plan, and we'll be watching you. Just play the role, like you have done so well. I will see you at the end of the day. Keep your head down and your mind alert." His half-smile told me nothing, and his sunglasses shaded his eyes. He was all business. He opened my door and gave me his hand as any chauffeur would. I closed my eyes briefly, shook my head, and left behind Izzy, the mother, grandmother, horsewoman, and writer. Isadora Rose, the vamp, actress, and spy for the FBI, pulled me onto center stage.

When Brad drove away, Gerald saw me leave the SUV and was at my side. "My, my. My Isadora Rose. You travel in style," he said, pulling me close for a kiss.

"I know, darling," I said in the most sexy, low voice I could muster. I've been practicing a Foxy voice, aware it was more appealing than my own. "It's a gift I give myself when visiting Boston or New York. I hate driving into the city and parking and all that. And what's the sense in acquiring wealth if I don't treat myself the best. I have more money than I can ever spend." There. That should sweeten the pot. "Brad is my employee for two days, and he'll pick me up tomorrow and drive me home. But, my love, although I have reservations at the Ritz, I'm looking forward to seeing your condo."

His lips met mine, and I could feel the heat, but it was a quick brush. After all, we were standing on the sidewalk before the Capitol, with a crush of people walking by. He stepped back and looked me up and down. I held back a shudder. "Ahhh, my precious jewel. I'm so pleased to see you, Isadora Rose, and to spend the rest of the day and night discovering more about you. I've been longing to touch you again and to look into your beautiful eyes. You look stunning today. Even more lovely than the first time we met."

I slowly batted my eyelashes and whispered, "Thank you."

Gerald linked his arm to mine to begin our leisurely walk to The Dangling Bait. All else melted around me and into the background as I fell deeper into my role as Izzy Franklin, femme fatale. I immersed myself in my new acting gig and leaned in closer. Gerald lowered his face to touch mine.

I looked up and smiled. I was stunned to find myself actually enjoying his adoring attention, and I realized how much I missed having a man desire me again. Since my loving Max died, I had filled my life with my writing and friends and vowed to live the rest of my life single and content. I had convinced myself that no one would, or could, ever replace the love of my life. Was I wrong? Gerald kissed my head, causing tiny shivers to run up my arm. I switched off my desire for more and reminded myself that we are both actors in a play, performing the scene of seduction. An ad lib was required. "It feels so good to be walking after the long drive in the car. I'm glad you agreed to have a late lunch at The Dangling Bait. They have the best lobster bisque, and it was one of my favorite places for lunch or dinner when I had meetings in Boston."

Gerald's voice was almost a whisper, and his European accent made his words melodic. "Anything you want or need, my love. I am at your bidding for now and as long as you'll have me."

Damn, he's good. Sweet nothings most women would love to hear. He has his seductive persona down perfectly. Let me do the same. "Gerald, my darling, I am blushing. You are saying the words I've been longing to hear. And I will be yours, for as long as you want me to be. I believe we've found something special, something that comes around, only once in a lifetime. We have a physical and emotional attraction for each other, and you are the man I've been waiting for all my life."

He pulled me closer. I did it! He believes he has me gaga over him. Just what Gus and Bob persuaded me to do. The fish is hooked, now to reel him in. I'm no fisherwoman, but if I were, I bet this would be the largest fish I'd ever caught.

The sidewalks were crowded with people, and we passed several men and women, either standing by a post looking at a map or talking and laughing, enjoying the day. I wondered if any were agents or just ordinary folks visiting Boston. For a moment, I envied them. Students, visitors, and workers enjoying the fabulous spring weather, not fearing for their lives, and not walking with a man the Bureau believed used and abused women. I am playing with fire and hoping I don't get burned by coming too close. One day, I'm Izzy, a typical retired woman hoping to celebrate my big seventy trips around the sun in May, and my life suddenly changes like a bolt out of the blue, and I am tossed into hell's fire.

The walk to The Dangling Bait was refreshing, and we talked about the city, our travels, and our food choices on the way. It was strange. We were both acting, and I was so immersed in my character that walking and talking with my soon-to-be lover and future partner seemed so normal and relaxed.

I was enjoying my new Izzy identity.

The bloom of spring and its promises of new beginnings

opened the door to change, and I hadn't experienced this feeling since I was a young woman. It was revitalizing for my soul. Something deep inside told me I could never return to the same Izzy, content with the life I'd made since Max died. The rigid structure and fluffy pillows that I'd placed all around me no longer seemed to fit. I was fortunate beyond my wildest expectations, but I can see I wasn't making the most of the years I had left on this earth. Change is good, and now I understood why.

As Gus had planned, Gerald and I entered the restaurant and were immediately escorted to a booth near the window.

Gerald reached across and grasped my hand. "I don't know if my appetite is ready for food when all I want is to devour you, my Isadora Rose."

I smiled, set a palm over our vile fusion, and coquettishly said, "We will have *worlds* of time for that later. Your words of anticipation are giving me goose bumps and tingles." The waiter saved me before Gerald could say more.

Gerald immediately ordered two martinis, and as soon as the waiter left, he said, "We must toast to an exciting adventure of two days of love and exploration." He smiled, knowingly. His dark, deep-set eyes were lit with desire.

I attempted to change the subject by pointing outside to an older woman, donned in a bright green colored jacket, baggy gray pants, chunky black shoes, and blue curly hair. I remembered Gus saying agents would photograph Gerald, so this was the perfect opening to have him turn his head toward the camera. "Oh my gosh, Gerald. Look at the way that woman is dressed. Maybe that's my next do-over," I laughed.

He stared out the window momentarily, then turned to

look at me again. "My jewel, you'd be beautiful in my eyes however you dress, but I like the style you show now. Don't change a thing. You are perfect the way you are."

I gave the most beguiling smile I could conjure.

The waiter brought our drinks, and we ordered.

I selected the lobster bisque I raved about and a mixed green salad. And although Gerald said he wasn't that hungry, he ordered the baked flounder.

Fortunately, his cell, although muted, buzzed. When he looked at the caller's identity, he excused himself to take it outside. "Sorry, my love. It's my cousin. I must take this call." He leaned down, lightly kissed my lips, and left the booth.

I sighed in relief and scanned the room. Gus said agents, acting as a couple, would be close by, but there were so many couples seated I couldn't identify them even with my spy superpowers. My eyes snapped wide open. Wait. Did he say his cousin? I shuddered as my gut told me this was a red flag. What does this mean? I was on high alert. My brain ran wild with scenarios of guns and violence. *Stop it, Izzy. Agents are protecting you.* I took a deep sip of my martini to quiet my nerves. As I worked to gain composure, I understood the temptation to eat the gummy bears kids talk about. But I was here and stuck in my old ways of sipping a libation to calm myself down. I took another gulp of my almost empty glass of martini.

Gerald returned to the booth and apologized again for the interruption. Fortunately, the food had arrived, and we could concentrate on eating. Our conversation dwindled.

Whenever there was a pause in our discussion, Gerald filled it with talk about the spice to come and his attraction to me. It was all I could do not to yell, "*Enough* already! I get the point." I was tired of it all and couldn't wait for lunch and everything else to be over and done with. Acting was so exhausting. After we finished our lunch, or *linner*, as Milly and I called it, Gerald was ready to order another martini, but I wisely said, "But, darling, I am so anxious to be alone with you. Perhaps you have wine at your condo?"

His smile was a sealed envelope, so I couldn't tell if it was a smile of passion, jest, or if I was now in his kill sight. His eyes turned steely and all-knowing.

My gut clenched at the red-flag warning. I excused myself for the ladies' room and attempted a slow, sauntering walk. I could feel his eyes plastered on my back, and it was enough to cause the hair on my neck to rise.

The ladies' room was spacious with a long counter top and five sinks. A young blonde-haired woman dressed in jeans was washing her hands. She turned to me and smiled sweetly. "Here, take this paper towel. They're almost out."

I looked at the paper towel container and was about to say, "No, they're not," when I realized this was my contact. "Thank you," I said. The agent quickly exited the ladies' room, and I looked in my hand. Wrapped in the paper towel was an earring identical to the one I was wearing. It occurred to me that Gus had said to wear the large white earrings he had given me as a gift for my last birthday. He said they would identify me to the agents.

On the paper towel, it read, *'Sorry, we're going to need audio. Remove your earring and replace it with this one. If you need help ASAP, say* , **"RULE."** *As soon as we hear it, we will be there.'*

After rubbing my hot face, knowing everyone would be getting the nitty gritty from here on out, I took a deep breath, straightened my shoulders, and pulled out my right earring and tucked it into my pocket. I inserted the new earring and leaned forward to check myself in the mirror. Looking back was a woman I hardly recognized. Sharp, slick, and attractive. *Yup, this'll work. Just keep your cool. You're almost done with this charade. Last leg. You can do it, Izzy.*

When I returned to the booth, Gerald was on his second martini. He stood when he saw me and kissed me on both cheeks before I sat down. I noticed that he had paid for lunch and the drinks with cash, as he had done at the Red Dog Tavern. I recalled Gus telling me groups of these swindlers never used credit cards. It made it too easy to track the owners, but Karl had used one with Merle. I thought he'd down his drink so we could zip to his condo, but he seemed in no hurry. His eyes studied me in a way they hadn't before, and there was no intentional sexual conversation. Something had changed, but I didn't know what. I broke the silence with a question. "How did you enjoy your fish today?"

"Ah, my Isadora Rose. It was as perfect as you are." His eyes still held mine but were deep, dark, and mysterious. He gulped down the rest of his martini and said, "Are you ready to leave for our escapades, my love? My condo is a twenty-minute drive from here. We will catch a taxi. Then, we will truly begin to enjoy the day."

My chest grew tighter, and my breathing was subtly increasing. Something about the tone of his voice had shifted, but I assumed my jitters were occurring because I was going to his condo. Was I imagining his change in demeanor?

Gerald helped me with my coat, and we headed toward the exit. The restaurant was filling with early dinner arrivals, and as we weaved our way to the door, my eyes scanned each person we passed, but I didn't catch anyone watching me. I trusted the agents had heard Gerald say we were leaving the restaurant through the mike in my earring, but he didn't say the address, which concerned me. Maybe they would hear it when he gave it to the taxi driver.

We strolled out of The Dangling Bait arm-in-arm, and Gerald hailed a taxi that was parked close by. He gave the address to the driver. *Yes. Finally!* I hoped that was caught by Gus and Bob and that he and the feds would be there by the time we arrived.

"Which floor do you live on, darling," I asked as the driver pulled into traffic.

"The top floor, my love." He set a wiggling hand on my leg, and my instinct was jerk away and smack it, but Izzy, the femme fatale, just smiled. "Can't wait to hold you in my arms and feel the warmth of your body." The old, sleazy Gerald was back in true form.

I leaned my head against his shoulder and beamed. "Oh, Gerald, you make me feel like a young schoolgirl on her first date." I sighed. My face flushed when I caught the eye of the driver in the mirror. Did he think I was a hooker? No, hookers are young women, but still, there was a hint of knowing in his eyes. I looked away and snuggled up closer against Gerald.

As the driver maneuvered the cab expertly in and out of traffic, Gerald placed his lips close to my ear and whispered a string of sexually explicit words. I cringed at his salacious verbiage, growing so hot in the face, knowing people could now listen in. I hoped to God, Gus wasn't one of those ears.

We pulled up to the condos, and Gerald got out, paid the driver, and held his hand for me to exit. His place looked to be located on one of the older streets near the Charles River and was extravagantly stunning. The beautiful gray stone building screamed old money and millionaire lifestyles. Gerald tapped his iPhone, and *walla!* The magnificent doors clicked open. The entryway was large and ornately decorated, and the carpet had a plush, deep red pattern. We walked hand-in-hand down a long corridor to a bank of highly polished brass elevator doors that screamed luxury. Although we passed doors on each side with brass number plates and peepholes, I wondered if anyone else lived in the building. It was so quiet.

Once inside the brass-trimmed box, Gerald used a key to access the button of the 10th floor, the highest in the building, and pressed it. While we waited for it to lift, he pulled me in close, tight, too tight, and a little too frisky as well, and gave me a lingering kiss.

I pulled back, set a palm on his chest, and smiled. "I'd like a *little* privacy as we indulge in the things we've discussed. So, I assume you live in the Penthouse?" I fluttered my lashes to show him that I longed to see and do more. "Is there a parking garage underneath the building to park your Bentley?"

Gerald leaned over, took my hand, brought it to his lips, and kissed it. "I live in style, my love, and the penthouse is my domain. Can't wait to indulge in *everything* we talked about."

The old, seedy Gerald was laying it on so thick. Real or fake? "Yes, my love, there's a garage beneath the building. Most of the time, I take a taxi or Uber, but when I leave the city, I drive my Bentley. I enjoy driving my car whenever possible."

"Must be appreciated when it rains heavy or snows. Is your office nearby? I *love* this street. It's gorgeous, and with the tall old trees lining the road, it's hard to believe the bustling center of Boston is only a few minutes away. This is a fabulous building, and I can see why you love it here."

The elevator stopped. Stunned, I gaped when the elevator doors opened to direct access. The condo's magnificent living area was breathtaking, wide open, and beautifully decorated in deep red colors, dark grays, and touches of gold. Through long, tall windows, I could see the city's skyline, and if I hadn't felt in grave danger, I would have been more wowed.

Gerald paused, waiting for my reaction, but I said nothing. I was at a loss for words, and it wasn't from the beauty of his living space; it was my raised antenna, screaming, *Danger! Danger!* A chill ran through my body. Was I in a lion's den, and Gerald's prey, left out in the cold by the two men I had trusted? Damn! Where were Gus and Bob, or the other agents? This was not going according to plan. What was going on? Was my bug working? Gerald gave the address to the taxi driver, and they *should have* heard it. OMG! My nerves were unwinding faster than a zip line, flying a hundred miles an hour through a canopy of trees. *Control yourself, Izzy. Be brave. Play the part for as long as possible.* I tilted my head to Gerald while giving my most adoring smile. *Hang in there. Stick to the act, Izzy. You're still on stage.*

As I strode into the room, my eyes took in the aged, highly

polished, wide-plank floorboards, covered with antique oriental rugs. Rich, dark red wallpaper with thin, swirly gold lines complemented the room, filled with gorgeous furniture that trumpeted the luxury of the rich and famous. But these criminals were not notable in a good way; they were infamous, living in style off the money they had stolen. My eyes moved from one side of the vast living space to the other, trying to capture the beauty of ornate gold-framed oil paintings and several tall ivory statues of Roman figures. At the far end of the room, a magnificent fireplace with white tiles completed the scene of what millions had bought for the criminal I was with. The room was decorated in a fashion comparable to a picture from Forbes magazine. Then, I got angry, really—*outraged.* These men were living high off the hog with money, fleeced from innocent women who were duped into believing them. I could only hope my face didn't reveal my deep loathing for this gangster with whom I was breathing the same air. Gerald stepped behind me to remove my jacket and began kissing my neck. His heated breath caused shivers to trickle down my arms, and I wanted to run, screaming away, but I stood frozen in place.

"Let me pour you a glass of wine, my love." He led me to a long gold tapestry-covered sofa with a glass coffee table held up by heavy, dark, ornate legs.

So, what's my next move? Alone with a man who thinks I'll be his sex toy? No. I *had* led him to believe my attraction and intentions were real, but due to heightened nerves, I, *Isadora Rose*, was running out of lines. Now what? How do I hold him off, waiting for the feds to bust in? Should I hot-foot it out of here while he's distracted pouring the wine?

The massive living space opened to an enormous white kitchen with white granite counters and built-in appliances. I watched as Gerald retrieved a chilled bottle of wine from a built-in cooler. He set the bottle on the counter and used a silver automatic cork opener to pop it open. While the wine breathed, he reached into a cabinet and took out two glasses. I rested my head against the back of the sofa and briefly closed my eyes. I drifted to another time and place. It was the Gilded Age, and I was an actress in a spy movie, and co-starring with me was a handsome leading man. The drop-dead-gorgeous secret agent leaned over, and his soft lips touched mine. The kiss startled me, and the movie abruptly ended when Gerald called my name. I blinked my eyes open and slipped back into the role of Isadora Rose, a stealthy, sexy spy.

Gerald handed me a glass of wine and lifted his for a toast. "To the woman who was one step ahead of me." Gerald's lips pulled into a tight smile and his eyes drilled into mine. I gulped. My lips did not touch the rim of the glass.

"What do you mean, Gerald, darling?"

Gerald set his glass on the table. "Come on, Izzy, you know what I mean," he snarled. Where was his accent and his low, come-hither voice? I was in trouble, and it was big trouble.

Before I could speak, another man entered the room. "So, Izzy. You have met Gerald, and here you are. What do you think of my friend?"

Oh. My. God! From the description Merle gave, without a doubt, I knew this man was Krappy Karl. I didn't have to act shocked. I was. All I could think of was *please save me*. And I had yet to learn if reinforcements were coming. Now what? I forced myself to smile. "I think Gerald is a dashing man. And may I ask who you are?" Krappy wasn't even close to the gorgeous man Merle had continually talked about at the ladies' book club. He didn't even look hot. He was short and probably twenty pounds overweight. Krappy's arms, which she described as solid muscle, looked like beef sausages. His face was narrow, and one eyebrow needed a lift. The adorable dimple on his chin, she raved about, appeared like a dark, deep hole, and his voice was high and crackly. However, no doubt, he was Krappy Karl. His rolled-up white shirt sleeves exposed a large red heart with the word mother tattooed on his forearm, and that was a major giveaway. Merle said a man who adored his mother so much that he had a heart tattoo on his arm was a keeper. I stared at it. On closer look, it spelled the word mutha, not mother. I had heard that expression before and it didn't mean mother.

Krappy's beady eyes gave me the once-over. Was he hoping his eyes were intimidating? I gulped. They were.

Gerald watched the act play out. He took another sip of wine. His eyes were locked on me as he waited for Krappy's next move. In comparing them, I did notice subtle similarities.

Krappy moved to the tufted green patterned chair across from Gerald and me. His icy eyes bore into mine. "So, Izzy. How is Merle? She was a fascinating woman and more than I expected. I was almost sorry to have broken her heart." His wide mouth curled down when he spoke. I was riveted by his appearance, trying to discover what Merle found so attractive about him, and of course, I knew it could have been only one thing, and I shuddered to think about it. Those sausage arms, that sleazy body, and his wretched garlic breath invaded my space. I took a sip of wine to hold myself together. Did he know I was a spy and I was working for the FBI? If he had any inkling, I was in grave danger.

Not ready to give up, I decided to play dumb. "Why'd you break Merle's heart?" I made no mention of the scum bucket stealing her money. The less I said, the better. I glared at him.

"Come now, Izzy," Krappy said with a smirk. "You know all about me and Merle. Did she send you on a quest to find me? Merle spoke a lot about you. We shared our lives over pillow talk, well, I should say, *Merle* shared hers. Silly Merle fell head over heels for me and talked openly about her friends. She showed me a photo of you and her on Facebook. She said she wished you could be more like her—*a free spirit*, and that you were too up tight. Is that so, Gerald?"

"She wasn't uptight when she was with me." Gerald's tone was terse. It was the first time he had spoken since Karl entered the room. I could see who had the upper hand. "Izzy, my Isadora Rose, was into kinky sex talk, but I see *now* that she's all talk, no action."

I couldn't help but smile. I had played my role well, and my fear, although still there, diminished incrementally each moment. I was a hero running through fire to save Merle, hoping to knock the bad guys off their feet. A light bulb went off, and I realized Krappy believed I was working for Merle and knew nothing about the FBI closing in on him and his den of thieves. I prayed Gus was listening, and I moved quickly to use my finely tuned PI skills to entrap them into my web of feigned innocence. "So, *K-Karl*," I faltered, almost calling him Krappy. "How did you know I was Merle's friend, and when did you give that information to Gerald? Was it when we were at The Dangling Bait? I bet it was when you called Gerald that you told him who I was." I turned my words to flattery. These boneheads were so full of themselves, I knew it would work to buy attention and praise. Krappy's only redeeming quality was his straight white teeth, which showed when he slowly cracked a thin smile. "Honestly, Karl. I admire your craft and seductive skills. From what Merle told me about you, you are every woman's dream for a man."

He was puffing up like a peacock in the Best of Bird Show. Karl leaned forward, his breath too close for comfort. "When Gerald said he was bringing you here for the night, he asked the waiter to snap a picture of you and sent it to me while you were in the ladies' room. He was bragging about you and wanted me to see what you looked like. I recognized you as Merle's friend, and you instantly became a liability, not a mark."

"So, Karl, let me get this straight. Merle was *not* the first woman you led into believing you were crazy about? And then, you absconded with her money, like the others'? And Gerald, *you're* in on this, too? I am so disappointed. I thought you really liked me." I smirked.

Karl placed his glass on the table. He wiped his mouth with the back of his hand. "Well, let me say this. Our job is not easy, even if you think so. It takes finesse and saying all the right things to make a woman believe in you, and willing to part with her money. And Gerald and I possess the special skills and mannerisms to seduce any woman. It's a game of seduction, and we always come out on top." He laughed at his joke, but I found it disgusting and shallow. "After spending tons of hours, maybe weeks, wining and dining, not counting endless romantic adventures, the women we latch on to are more than willing to help us when we are in financial need. We fulfill their needs, and it is only right they fulfill ours. We offer sexual gratification and companionship, and we are well worth it. But getting back to Merle, your friend, she was an easy sell, and she was one among many. Once I bed a woman, she is mine for as long as I need her. I am what a woman might describe as enormously endowed." His eyes glistened with amusement as he watched my face pink up.

Ugh! How disgusting, but I couldn't stop my eyes from dropping from his wicked smile to his skin-tight, stretched gray pants. Yes, I could see, for once, he was telling the truth. I remembered Merle describing Karl's sexual attributes to the book club ladies and how they encouraged her racy descriptions of her overnight forays. But one thing didn't add up. How did they pick their marks on Silver Love? Karl said the women gave money willingly, but he didn't say that after he and his group of grifters disappeared, a woman who threatened to report the fraud was terrorized with fear of blackmail or, worse, bodily harm. I bet they took secret photos of all their marks in lewd poses. A woman of means and status would rather take the loss than have intimate images show up on social media. Living high off the hog, this gang had it all figured out. Another light bulb went off. After Krappy told Gerald who I was, why didn't he fly out the back door and leave me there? Why bring me to his condo? I needed answers. I gingerly stepped into the black waters of deception and asked Krappy the question I wasn't sure I was ready to have answered. "I don't understand why you brought me here if you knew who I was. You could have just let it go."

"Ah, Izzy," Karl said. "I was waiting for that question. After we realized you were a friend of Merle's, I wondered how much more you had found out. For your information, we have been very discreet, and I wasn't sure who else you told about Gerald. Of course, you must have told Merle, because it is she who had you searching for me. I'm telling you now, she is not getting her money back, and I have a few photos that may convince her to stop trying. So, the question is, what do we do with you, Ms. Isadora Rose? Gerome. Take her phone."

Gerome? Oh, right, that's Gerald's real name. I opened my bag and handed my phone to Gerald. He took it, then turned my bag upside down, dumping the contents onto the table, looking for who knows what. I hoped he didn't think to rip my earrings out of my ears, but I knew by now that the gang of bumbling fools wasn't as sharp as they thought.

Gerome tossed my phone to Karl. "What's your password," he asked threateningly. Since it was my burner phone, I quickly gave it to him. He was about to open it when his cell rang. He raised his hand to Gerome and walked to the kitchen. I could hear him talking. "Yeah, Boss. Okay. Whatever you say. Sure, we'll take her there. Leaving now."

Krappy threw my jacket at me. "Put it on. We're heading out of here. The boss wants to talk to you."

A flash of fear sent my heart racing. I almost forgot the code word for help if I found myself in danger and in need of assistance. "Who the hell is the boss and does he *rule* the both of you?" '*RULE*,' was the code for 'HELP!'

Gerome rolled his eyes and said nothing. He retrieved his jacket, and they both linked their arms in mine and pressed the button for the elevator. The doors opened, and Krappy hit the button for the garage. My mind was racing. What the hell!

Where is Gus? Where is Bob? Something is wrong with the damn earring. I was not getting in the Bentley, and I booted my brain into overdrive to devise a plan of escape.

I would fight to my last breath. The elevator stopped at the ground floor, and I went limp. I had to buy time. Krappy and Gerald dragged my dead-weight body from the elevator. The garage was filled with luxury cars, but empty of drivers. There was no one to hear me or to save me. I kept my legs flaccid. My knees scraped the hard cement floor, and my boots felt like they would be torn off my feet as Krappy and Gerome grunted and groaned, pulling me by my arms so hard I thought they would be ripped out of their sockets. There was no sign of FBI agents or Gus and Bob. I had a dreadful feeling that my microphone was not working, and even though I said the word for help, I was on my own. I took a self-defense class at the Build-Em-Up Gym and wasn't going down without a fight. I remembered the words from the police instructor. *"Never get into a car with the bad guy. Fight like your life depends on it because it does."*

Gerome snarled, "What the hell's wrong with you? Pull it together and walk."

I pretended to cry. "I'm feeling weak. Why are you doing this to me? I was only trying to find you for Merle. She loves you," I sobbed.

Krappy barked, "Stop your whining. Merle doesn't give a freakin shit about me. She just wants her money back, and I told you, she's not getting it."

Luxury vehicles filled the garage, but like Gerald had said, most of the owners Ubered or taxied into the city. And there was not a single person around to help me. *Empty.*

As I sniffled and sobbed and asked them to stop dragging me, my eyes darted to the far end of the garage, where I saw the exit. I faced the hard truth. There was no one to rescue me. I was on my own.

Gerald and Krappy dragged me, cursing for me to stand, but I stayed limp, like a used-up ragdoll. *Let them work for it.*

Krappy struggled to hold me up, and I let my body fall deeper into dead weight. "Why do you always park so far away?" he growled to Gerald. "No one is going to touch your precious Bentley. I'm going to pull my arm out, hauling her this way. I'm carrying all the weight."

"Pick her up and carry her then," Gerome, aka Gerald, barked at Krappy Karl as he yanked me harder to try and make me stand.

I tried another stall. "I feel sick." I began fake dry heaving.

"Drop her!" Krappy yelled. "She's gonna puke on me."

I slumped to the ground, hurling, and spitting, trying to buy myself some time. As I lay face down, Krappy and Jerky Gerome stepped aside and began talking in low tones. I heard them say something about the boss was going to be crazed it was taking so much time to get me there.

Krappy stood over me. I got up on my knees but still pretended to retch. "Ya through yet, Isadora?" He tried to wrench me to my feet, but I begged for more time and started gagging again.

Gerald's eyes darted from one end of the garage to the other. "Let's get the hell out of here. Someone may show up, and we can't waste any more time."

Krappy snarled. "Grab her by her arm and pull her up. I'll take the other. We're almost at your car."

As much as I had always wanted to ride in a Bentley, this wasn't my day for a test drive. I was glad I wore boots cause shoes would have been shredded from my feet as they struggled to pull me across the cement floor. My beautiful black pants were scuffed and torn when we reached the Bentley. Krappy clutched my arm while Gerome went in the driver's side and started the car.

Krappy grunted and huffed. He was as exhausted as I was.

I slumped to the floor, and he gripped my arms, half carrying, half dragging me, to the rear door. He had zip ties in his back pocket. For me, no doubt. Going to the Build-Em-Up-Gym, training with Jackie and walking the treadmill three days a week just had to pay off. I felt the adrenaline flooding my body. This was my *one chance* to run before they tossed me in the car and tied my hands and feet together. I flopped to the ground, pretending to faint.

"What the frick? She fainted!" Krappy yelled. He bent to pick me up, and I saw my opportunity.

In a flash, I kicked up, smashing the heel of my boot into his jaw. I heard a crack. Bet I broke it. Yeah!

He flew back, not expecting fragile, little me to explode on him with such strength.

As Krappy fell to the ground, groaning, Gerome jumped out of the car to help him, but with the rush still running strong in my veins, I jumped to my feet and hot-tailed to the exit, leaving them both in my dust. I ran like the devil was chasing me, weaving in and out of parked cars, hoping to elude Gerome, who was close behind. I sprinted as fast as my legs could go, and he was breathing down my neck.

Not having run that fast in years, I didn't even know I had

it in me. Finish line was the exit! Go, go! When I heard him yelling for me to stop, I kicked it up a notch. I wasn't sure I'd make it. I was prepared for Gerome to, any minute, reach out and tackle me when I ran smack into Gus's safe, strong arms.

"Get down Izzy!" he ordered.

I dropped to the ground and lay there shaking and sobbing. My breath was coming out in short gasps, and my lungs felt like they would burst. They and my calves were on fire.

The next thing I heard was, "FBI. Drop your weapons and get down on the ground! We have you surrounded."

Everything around me blurred, and I felt like I was in shock. Somehow, I made it to my feet, and with the help of Gus and Bob, we rushed out of the garage and into the sunlight. I was still dazed emotionally and bruised physically. They must have called for the spy mobile because Brad pulled the Lincoln to the curb just as we got there, and without hesitation, Gus, Bob, and I got in and buckled up. No one spoke. We were wiped out. I was still shaking, sandwiched between Gus and Bob. Still stunned, I had barely made note of them escorting me from the garage to the car.

"You're okay, Izzy," Gus said as he held my hand. "We had your back. I was never going to let anything happen to you. I promised you that, and I always keep my word."

I was in a daze. Although I believed him, his words didn't help ease my mind. I needed to depressurize before I could listen to anyone. Well, my acting days were over. Count me out! I'm a retired actor now, and this was my last movie.

Brad dropped us off at the Ritz and spoke to Gus.

I paid no attention.

Foxy opened the door, and I numbly shed my jacket and

headed to the shower. I needed a long, hot one. My body was aching, and I knew I would have tons of bruises the next day. My knees were scraped, and my arms were in raging pain. After about twenty minutes, I got out, wrapped a thick white hotel robe around me, and went to the bedroom. It was the first time I relished and appreciated the fact that we were staying in a high-end, luxury suite. I lay on the bed for a few minutes, then dressed. Foxy was waiting for me with a steaming cup of coffee and a bottle of ibuprofen.

"You okay? Gus and Bob filled me in. What a debacle *that* was. You came through fine, Ms. Femme Fatale, star of the Build-Em-Up-Gym. You could be their poster ad queen after this. Gus said you broke Krappy's jaw." As pathetic as I must have looked, Foxy couldn't hold back any longer, and she doubled over with belly-aching laughter, tears streaming down her cheeks. That broke my trance. I joined in.

I laughed so hard I cried. Relief washed over me as tears ran down my face.

Foxy handed me a tissue to wipe my eyes and runny nose.

The dam broke, and I emptied all the toxins from my surge of adrenaline that gave my mind and body the will and power to escape. I wiped my nose and face.

We finally caught our breath and gained control, still on the cusp of more laughter.

Foxy handed me two ibuprofen, and I took them with my coffee. "Thanks for being here and helping me come to life. I can finally exhale. And knowing Krappy Karl, Jerky Gerome and their other conspirator are sitting in jail is what I call a happy ending in my books."

She leaned forward and looked straight at me. Her eyes,

behind her giant purple glasses, were earnest and knowing. "I've been there and know what you are going through. It's over, and you will be okay. I'm glad you're feeling better, and I told Gus not to worry. I know who you are Izzy. You are just like me. You have gone through the fire and come out the other end, forged and steel hardened, stronger than ever."

Did Foxy say I was like *her?* That was the most meaningful compliment anyone has ever given me, and coming from Foxy was music to my ears. She was right. I, Izzy, did it. "Where are Gus and Bob?"

"They're getting debriefed. I told them I would call if you wanted to meet them for dinner and close the case. So, how about it? Dinner on the Bureau?"

Foxy and I stayed at the Ritz for a couple of days. While I was decompressing, she was busy writing her article. We took full advantage of a mini vacation on the government's dime. I deserved it for having done work! *Dangerous work* at that. We ate at waterfront restaurants, surrendered to soothing massages, indulged in mani-pedis, swam in the hotel pool, sipped martinis, and ordered room service. And talked, and talked, and then talked some more.

*T*wo days after returning home, I was still trying to find the missing puzzle pieces that tied together what I'd endured in Boston. Gus informed me that Krappy, Gerome, and their buddy had all been arrested. I couldn't stop reliving the hell. It was unnerving, like an old CD stuck on one track, playing the same scratchy, patchy music, repeatedly. I needed to clear my head and ask for help from someone not involved in the case to help review all the facts Gus had briefed me on.

I'd mulled over every detail, and something about the whole scam still did not sit right with me. A nagging question still loomed. How did three hapless jerks weed out thousands of profiles to find their marks? Gus said they perused Silver Love and picked the wealthy, lonely women whose needs matched a very specific mark profile. But after meeting Krappy and Gerome, I found it hard to believe that these two inept, absurd men could have pulled it off to such success. Neither were skilled or savvy enough to do it without help.

Bet their buddy, the third guy, was as dumb as them but maybe too ugly to be a face of the operation. The old saying, *'Friends of a feather stick together,'* told me all I needed to know about those degenerates. Another thing, when Krappy's cell rang, he referred to the caller as "Boss." Something told me he was not the boss. When the FBI interrogated the three criminals, they bragged about their con and showed no remorse. One thing is for sure: the Bureau had them on attempted kidnapping and causing bodily harm, and I would testify to that. After the three criminals lawyered up, the Bureau had more work to do, but right now, a cell would be their home, a far cry from their penthouse lifestyle.

By mid-afternoon, I still could not let go of the nagging thought that something was missing, and I was exhausted from reliving my ordeal. My brain was tired, and I needed a change of scenery. I left the house and drove to the Carriage House Restaurant. As I made my way to the entrance, I counted only three cars in the parking lot. The moment I opened the lounge door, I could feel my distress from overthinking, shedding like a dog's furry coat at the end of winter. Dale waved to me as I passed the long bar to the quiet booth I liked to sit in. The day was sunny and warm enough to wear a sweater jacket. I dropped my new blue jacket onto the seat and waited for Dale.

Dale walked quickly to my booth. "Hey, Izzy. How ya doing? So, how about the big news in town. I read Foxy's front-page exposé about three con artists who were bilking women out of millions of dollars on a dating website, and the FBI's sting that led to their capture. The article talked about a woman who had worked as an undercover spy and was now a hero, but no name was provided." Dale grinned ear-to-ear. "I knew *right away* it was *you*, since you and Foxy are such close friends. You don't need to say anything, but for my own curiosity, nod if you were the undercover spy." He suppressed a wry smile, waiting for my answer.

I grinned, drew in a deep sigh, and nodded. I could never lie to Dale.

"I knew it," he said, lifting his arms to applaud, then thought better of it and dropped them back down to his sides. Dale's grin grew. "Damn. Good for you, Izzy, and this time, the drinks are on me. I'll be right back."

I settled in and scanned the bar. Life seemed dull now. I wondered about the couples at the bar with beers and pretzels in front of them. How did they meet? On a dating site? It was trendy, and many had met forever mates, unlike Merle, who only searched for wealthy men whose needs met hers.

Dale returned and set my martini on the table. "Dale, I have a question. It would help me sort out something nagging me about the, uh, article that Foxy published."

"Ask away." He said. "It's payback time for all the helpful advice you've given me."

I took a sip of my martini. Sitting and talking to Dale for the first time since coming home made me feel normal. "Aww. Thank you Dale, but you only needed a little push to help you focus. Now you're ready to graduate and you've earned your Engineering degree in IT. I'm impressed with you, young man." I was beaming like a proud mother. I'll miss seeing Dale once he finds a real job and moves on. "Now, for my conundrum. There's still something about the three grifters that I don't understand. How could they find their prey on a website that hosts thousands of women and zero in on the same type of profiles for their cons? The idea those three were technically competent is ludicrous."

"That answer's very simple, Izzy. They had expert help."

After listening to Dale walk me through his thought process, I immediately called Gus and told him what Dale had clearly explained.

"On it, Izzy," Gus replied. "Hey, would you like to take the horses out later?"

"Would love to." I was ready to ride and soak in *freedom.*

It was the day after Gus and I had gone for a ride. It had been all I had hoped for, and I was finally able to unwind.

My cellphone rang for the hundredth time. *Oh, crud!* The jig was up. Someone had caught wind that *I* was the reluctant spy working undercover for the FBI. Hearing it on the news, all three of my kids phoned, and when I explained everything to them, they congratulated me for my bravery and then proceeded to scold me for doing something so dangerous.

I almost didn't answer the next caller, but reluctantly did so. It wasn't regrettable, though, learning it was the producer for the cable show, Women of Worth. She asked if Foxy and I would come on to share our experience with their audience and if we were available on Thursday. And after hanging up, I ran it by Foxy, who immediately agreed.

Foxy and I drove together to the station. She was smartly

dressed in gray pants, a red blouse, and a dark gray jacket. Her glasses of choice were dark orange and almost covered her small face like all she wore. She had helped me pick out my outfit for the show, and I hoped I looked as fashionable as she.

Women of Worth, hosted by Michelle and Kelly, was a highly rated and prized cable show, and we were excited to be invited for the interview.

Michelle and Kelly ushered us into the room where a cameraman was preparing to film our interview. He said hello and went about his work. The set was designed for cozy, easy conversation. Four chairs and a coffee table were placed before a yellow-painted She-Shed backdrop, which helped set the stage. The show always began with Michelle and Kelly discussing life in their community, and current happenings around town. I could see why they were so popular. Their sense of humor and timing was professional and inviting. They were noted for introducing women to viewers from all walks of life and professions, who made a difference in the community and were worthy models for other women. I was honored to be one of them. Michelle and Kelly each had a newspaper copy of Foxy's story in front of them. Her investigative article was now front-page news in many of the syndicated newspapers across the country.

The show producer raised her hand and signaled Michelle to introduce us.

Michelle looked into the camera and turned serious. "Today, Kelly and I would like to introduce two women who are heroes in our eyes." She lifted the newspaper with Gerome and Karl's picture. The camera zoomed in to take a close shot. "Izzy Franklin, the woman who risked her life to take these men down, and well-known investigative journalist, Carol Foxy, better known to her followers and friends as Foxy, are here to tell their story. Izzy will share her harrowing experience with an online dating site programmed to exploit female targets. Online dating sites are popular and gaining more subscribers every day. So, this is a subject all women should be aware of and take note of. Many women are finding love and companionship with online dating apps, and most are legitimate and successful. But, for women who do so, listen to your gut, and if the man seems too good to be true and asks for money, whether to invest or borrow, run."

Michelle began talking. "Capturing the criminals, who have scammed women out of money and threatened them if they went public, was high on the Bureau's list of crimes against women, and I wonder, Izzy, how did you get involved with the FBI in a situation where you willingly made yourself a target for dangerous men by joining a dating website to entrap them? Were you employed by the FBI before you retired?"

Her question made me chuckle. "Oh, my goodness, no. The FBI never employed me. I was merely trying to help a friend find a man she met on a dating site, who wined and dined her, and then conned her out of a great deal of money. I did it for her, never dreaming the FBI was also searching for the same ring of dangerous men."

Michelle's eyebrows raised, and her face showed surprise. "Are you saying you were able to help the FBI capture these lowlifes, but your only intention was to help your friend who was conned out of money?"

I knew many people were asking the same question. "Yes, I

unintentionally became an undercover spy for the FBI, when I found one of the men who my friend had met."

Kelly leaned in with her question for Foxy. "Oh, my goodness, Izzy. That was so dangerous and brave. So, Foxy, how did you get involved?"

Foxy's eyes narrowed. She was wrapped in reporter mode. Her steepled hands rested on her knees. "I'm a friend of Izzy's, and when she told me about the scam her friend had fallen for, I believed it was something I needed to investigate and write about. It's a warning for all women who may find themselves in a situation like hers. Dating websites are prevalent, and evil men always seek new scams. With Artificial Intelligence, a woman may believe she is talking to someone in England or California when she may be taken in by a man living in Africa, Russia, or Brazil. Even voices can be changed, as can live videos. It's a new world out there. And nothing can legally be done once a woman willingly gives the man money. It's gone."

Kelly turned to me and asked a follow-up. "So, Izzy. Although three men were initially captured, the FBI arrested another man. Who was *he* in all this?"

"Perry Tucker, an IT coder for Silver Love, who wrote an algorithm to identify the ideal marks. After the three grifters were apprehended, the FBI zeroed in on their boss. That was him, the brains of the scam. The wealthiest ladies looking for love and a little sizzle became easy prey. Who would've suspected an inside job? Tucker lived in the basement of his grandmother's house and worked his magic, choosing exactly who to scam. I never believed those amateurish idiots were clever enough to run the caper on their own." I tried to control the smile breaking out on my lips. "And, to think, this nerdy kid, barely out of high school, was the boss of the other three losers? It's crazy." I glanced at Foxy, who had her head lowered, trying to keep herself from cracking up..

Michelle and Kelly asked more questions, and Foxy and I answered as best we could. We were careful how much we revealed. The FBI had warned us there might be other like-minded predators out there, and we didn't need to help them in any way.

The time on the show passed quickly, and before we knew it, Michelle and Kelly were thanking us for providing information that all women needed to know. Michelle ended my part in the interview with her last question. "Well, Izzy, I understand you write young adult fiction with the pseudonym name, Phoebe S. Malave. Are you planning a new book and perhaps a new career?"

"Thank you for that question, Michelle. I am writing adult mysteries now, using my own name, Izzy Franklin. And I have a new passion working as a private investigator. I never thought I'd begin a new career, but I want to help women who have been hoodwinked by men, whether on a computer, a phone, or in person. Some men use women for their own selfish reasons. They take advantage of lonely women and once they get what they want, they toss them aside and home in on the next target who they can lie to, cheat on, and exploit. We woman must stick together. As of today, I have two clients in need for my services, and I'm excited to begin."

Michelle and Kelly nodded their approval.

Kelly finished with a question for Foxy. "And you, Foxy. Have any final words on the piece that has gone viral?"

She looked directly into the camera to say, "Izzy is the real hero here. I was along for the ride, but I had a passionate interest in these sorts of scams. It can happen to any woman, and we need to be alert. I'm not saying dating sites are something you shouldn't try. I know many women and men who have found friendship, companionship and even love. The internet has changed everything. But every good thing has a possible negative outcome. So, women out there. I want to give you some advice. The first time someone you meet on social media asks for money, for anything, delete. Be careful. The world is full of frauds. Listen to your gut and be aware of the red flags. There are good, decent men out there and they would never ask for money. Find someone who values you, respects you, and will love you unconditionally."

Michelle and Kelly smiled. Michelle took the lead. "Thank you, Izzy and Foxy. You are truly *Women of Worth*. And that does it, for our show today. You ladies have provided all women a service, and it has been our pleasure to have you with us today. Congratulations to you both."

I was so happy to have shared my experience. Sometimes, music and the words from a song dance through my head. It happened the moment Foxy and I left the building, and I began humming. The memory of Gus and I, riding Speed and Maverick on a beautiful spring morning, came to mind.

We rode to a large meadow, dismounted, tied the horses to saplings, and sat on an old rock wall. The day was filled with promise and life was good. The warm sun, the smell of horses, and the company of a friend I enjoyed riding with were seared forever in my memory box. The dormant grass of winter was growing tall, and soon, a hay field would be ready for cutting.

Gus and Milly would help me stack the fragrant bales into my barn loft. During those times of riding horses, Gus and I got to know each other better. We talked about life, family, our spouses who died too young, and our favorite songs. On that day, we talked about music and our favorite songs. I said mine was "Turn! Turn! Turn!" by the Byrds.

Foxy and I had almost reached the car.

Hearing me, she began humming along with me.

Undoubtedly, it *was* a new season, a time to build up, a time to dance, and I was ready.

EPILOGUE

*M*y seventy trips around the sun came and went. As with each birthday, I took the time to reflect on the ups and downs of the past year and set my sights to new beginnings. I have a new title, Izzy Franklin, Private Investigator, and I have earned it. I've begun writing my first sizzling adult mystery novel using my name, Isadora Rose Franklin.

Milly said that change is inevitable and can work for or against you. The new Izzy was making *change* work for her. I was unsure how I felt about leaving my sixtieth decade and entering my seventieth, but it was as my grandmother said, *"Izzy, live fully in each moment and make happy memories."*

On the morning of my birthday, Gus called to say he was stopping by with my favorite bagel and cream cheese.

When I opened the door, he was grinning ear-to-ear. "Happy Birthday, Izzy." In his arms, he was carrying a wiggly bundle of sweetness, a chocolate lab puppy. It was my best birthday gift, and I decided Gus was a keeper, right then and there. I just needed *him* to figure it out, hopefully, soon.

I named the puppy Olive, and my farm was filled with new life. Olive and Oscar were inseparable. When I asked Oscar if he was happy to have Olive live with us, he wagged his tail and tapped my leg with his paw. I think I saw him smile.

Chip, the stray cat, gifted me five adorable kittens. My morning routine in the barn now begins with snuggling kittens and playing with the bundle of energy, Olive.

My family and friends threw me a surprise Birthday party at the Carriage House Restaurant. They hired a band with lead singer Mike Mellen, and the room was filled with laughter and music. Merle and the book club ladies all came, and my good buddy, Dale, sat at the table with my family.

The cake was beautifully decorated, and a large 70 candle sat on top. It was an unforgettable affair, and after surviving Boston, I was in the mood to kick up my heels. I sat at a table near the band with my extraordinary friends: Gus, Bob, Milly, and Foxy. After everyone sang Happy Birthday, I made a wish and blew out the candle.

Milly asked what I wished for, a mischievous look in her eyes, and I replied, "You know I can't tell you that, Milly. Birthday wishes are secret. But, I promise, I'll tell you on my next birthday, and we'll see if it came true."

I blushed as a certain gentleman asked me to dance with a simple, romantic outstretch of his hand. He didn't even need words. His eyes said so much.

I smiled as I drifted into his welcoming hold.

Gus and I took the floor as Tony Bennet's song "Because of You" began to play. I gasped, and he winked. He knows how much I love that song. I could tell that a new memory was being seared into my brain as we began to dance. The lovely melody of a matched pulse quickly found us beyond the score, and everyone around us seemed to dissolve. This felt so...nice and right. What was happening here? Was I imagining a tug that wasn't there? Or these zesty sparks? My face flushed and goose bumps sprouted on my skin. Please don't let this be a trick. I haven't felt like this in a long, *long* time.

Gus pulled me in closer.

Mmm, that's more like it. This was clearly not "just friends" but on the far side of it into something new. I tucked my nose into his neck, drinking in the scent of sweet leather and spice.

His voice sounded richer and more decadent than usual as he softly said, "This song's for you, Izzy. I asked Mike to sing it special. Your boldness and risk-taking has truly inspired me, and I am done running. I am ready now. So, what do ya say? How 'bout we start that next chapter?"

His words and gaze cast a spell over me, and for a moment, I was Lauren Bacall, and he, Humphrey Bogart. I beamed as I nodded. "About time, Mister."

Gus grinned and a puff of amusement flew out of his nose. He kissed my cheek then drifted the delicious pecks of his affection over. His soft lips and warm breath grazed my ear, making me shiver, but the whispered words that only *I* could hear sent a raging hot flash rolling through my body. I certainly won't be writing about that!

Looks like I got my birthday wish *and* my promise.

And in this glorious moment, all I could do was breathe.

Acknowledgments

Thank you to the women who shared their online dating experiences with me. There were times I laughed so hard, I cried. On the other hand, stories of women who met grifters on dating sites, social media, or via the phone made me angry. Izzy and her friend Merle share a story screaming to be told in an entertaining, fun-filled read, and I was happy to shine light on this serious danger that people need to be made aware of.

Thank you to my manuscript readers, who spurred me on to finish this book and rooted for Izzy's success. Izzy has reached a milestone in life, celebrating seventy trips around the sun, and she has proven that good friends can make life's journey fun, rich, and fulfilling.

Thank you, Sarah Loos, my granddaughter, and first editor and reader.

Thank you, Marge DellaValle, my longtime friend who kept me writing Izzy's story and asking for more.

Thank you, Carol Fox, who made Foxy come to life—a great editor and friend.

Thank you, Michelle LaChapelle, my daughter, and reader, for your encouragement to keep writing Izzy's story.

Thank you, Aline Earley, my cousin, who read the first three chapters and loved it so much, she urged me to finish.

Thank you, Courtney Vail, co-author of our multi-award-winning *Angels Club Series*, for formatting the paperback and eBook and finalizing the cover.

And, thank you, Nan Hurlburt, a fabulous artist and friend, for creating the inspiration for my book cover.

About the Author

Photography by Diane Darin

Sandra J. Howell is a retired college professor. She lives on a farm in Massachusetts. Her Curly horses have been showcased in area shows, newspapers, and Equine magazines. A foundation breeding program was established in Sweden with one of her Curly mares.

Check out her other equine novels: *Spirit of a Rare Breed*, *Saving GiGi, Golden Horse, Lost Legacy* and the heart-warming and award-winning, *Angels Club Series* that is not just for kids.

WEST RIDGE FARM

PUBLISHING

WestRidgeFarmPublishing.com

facebook.com/horsenovels

Made in United States
Orlando, FL
10 November 2023

38809447R00168